Tunnel *and* Once Over Lightly

TWO CLASSIC ADVENTURES OF

DOC SAVAGE

by William G. Bogart
and Lester Dent writing
as Kenneth Robeson

plus THE EYE OF THE COBRA by Charles S. Verral
writing as George Eaton

BILL BARNES VS. THE YELLOW JACKETS
illustrated by Frank Tinsley

and new historical essays by
Will Murray and Anthony Tollin

SANCTUM BOOKS

This Sanctum Books edition is an unabridged republication of the text and illustrations of three stories from *Doc Savage Magazine,* as originally published by Street & Smith Publications, Inc., N.Y.: *Tunnel Terror* from the August 1940 issue, "The Eye of the Cobra" from the January 1942 issue and *Once Over Lightly* from the November-December 1947 issue, plus "Bill Barnes vs. The Yellow-Jackets" from *Shadow Comics* #1 These stories are works of their time. Consequently, the text is reprinted intact in its original historical form, including occasional out-of-date ethnic and cultural stereotyping. Typographical errors have been tacitly corrected in this edition.

ISBN 978-1-60877-171-4

First printing: May 2015

Series editor: Anthony Tollin
anthonytollin@shadowsanctum.com

Consulting editor: Will Murray

Proofreader: Carl Gafford

Cover restoration: Michael Piper

Doc Savage cover circle: Kez Wilson (miscmayhemprods.com)

The editors gratefully acknowledge the contributions of David Saunders (www.pulpartists.com), Nicky Wheeler-Nicholson, Matthew Schoonover and Jack Juka in the preparation of this volume, and Elizabeth Engel of the Missouri State Historical Society for research assistance with the Lester Dent Collection.

Sanctum Books
P.O. Box 761474; San Antonio, TX 78245-1474

Visit Doc Savage at www.shadowsanctum.com.

Thrilling Tales and Features

Front cover art by Emery Clarke

Back cover art by Emery Clarke and Walter Swenson

Interior illustrations by Paul Orban, Edd Cartier and Frank Tinsley

A Complete Book-length Novel by KENNETH ROBESON

Death fog . . . a terrible, new menace . . . mummified corpses... and more—all these can't stop Doc Savage and his pals from throwing their best punches!

Chapter I
STRANGE FOG

HARDROCK HENNESEY had once been called the toughest little mucker who had ever crawled through a river's belly. It was said that if a drill broke while he was on a tunnel job, he could eat his way through rock. He looked as though he had been eating rock now.

He spat on the dusty highway, stared up and down the deserted stretch of dark road, and started swearing. He swore for three minutes. He was just getting warmed up. And then he shrugged disgustedly, spat again.

He murmured, "Ah, nuts!" and started hiking along the dusty road once again. He wished to the blasted devil that he had never left New York City.

But there were no tunnels being constructed at

the moment in New York, and here—in the West—they were calling for miners and muckers on the greatest water tunnel ever built. A tunnel that was going to convey nine hundred million gallons of water a day a hundred miles into a great city.

And Hardrock Hennesey needed a job. He was broke. Like every mucker or miner who had ever helped build a tunnel, he was broke between jobs. Money came fast in this game. And it was spent the same way. It was a wild, reckless—and dangerous—existence.

Thus he was bumming his way through the country. According to estimations, he had only about three more miles to go. But on this out-of-the-way back highway, a car hadn't passed him in the last hour.

It was some time after nine o'clock, and the moon was just coming up when the farmer came rattling along in his old flivver.

Hardrock Hennesey spun around. His leathery, flint-hard features brightened. That is, a few more wrinkles appeared on his scarred, old-looking face. He hitched up his trousers around his skinny waist and got his thumb stuck out in a "how-about-a-ride" gesture.

The farmer rolled his heap right on past Hardrock Hennesey.

Hardrock swore. This time he wasn't very subtle about it. He jumped up and down and kicked at the dust with his worn shoes. He just wished he had his hands on that blankety-blank so-and-so's throat. He wished—

Ahead, beyond a slight dip in the road, there floated back the sound of worn brake shoes chattering. The flivver was stopping! The farmer must have decided, after looking Hardrock over as he passed, that it was all right to give him a lift.

Hardrock went into a sprint, his thin, hard-as-nails legs carrying his tough little body along furiously. He arrived at the dip in the road, started to yell, "Hey—"

He skidded to a stop in the dust and stared.

He gawked at the sight of what might have been ground mist ahead. The night was warm enough, and this part of the road in a hollow cool enough to cause slight ground fog.

And yet what he saw wasn't fog. He could see through it. It was like the kind of mirage effect you see coming off tarred pavements on August days. It wasn't quite white, nor quite gray, and it seemed to float and swirl up from the dust.

Yet it wasn't this that held Hardrock Hennesey spellbound. He rubbed his eyes, deciding that he'd never drink any more of that stuff that he'd bought last night. It must have been distilled from coal. Perhaps he was getting astigmatism.

Because he stared at the fog ahead—the stuff that he was positive he could see through—and he couldn't see what should be parked there. No car. No farmer.

Hardrock Hennesey growled, "Say, who's kiddin' who?" and stalked ahead toward the vague stuff that was like mist. He reached the spot.

And he let out a whoop of pain and leaped backward as though someone had hit him with a ten-foot pole. He jerked up and down, waving his hands and blowing on his fingers. He felt of his face, drew his hands away quickly.

It was just as though he had been burned by live steam!

THE tough little tunnel worker backed off from the spot, squinting out of his intense gray eyes. He got down on his hands and knees in the dust. He stared. He tried to see beneath the peculiar, wispy-gray stuff ahead. In a way, it made him think of a huge spider's web.

He got up again, walked cautiously forward and stuck out a questing finger.

The finger felt as though he'd plunged it into the spout of a hot teakettle.

"What the hell?" Hardrock Hennesey asked himself, and started doing some more enthusiastic swearing.

He knew damned right well he wasn't drunk. He hadn't had a drink all day. And he didn't have a hangover.

He moved to the side of the road, climbed a fence that adjoined a farmer's field, started circling the funny gray stuff that floated in the air in the dip in the road.

Hardrock Hennesey was certain he could see through the stuff. And he knew, absolutely, that he'd heard the old flivver come to a chattering stop. But where was it now? Where was the farmer?

Dammit, something was cockeyed here and he was quite sure it wasn't himself. He edged toward the foggy stuff.

And got burned again. Howling with pain, Hardrock Hennesey once more backed off and sat down on a rock to watch the stuff. He rubbed his eyes. He stared at his raw-red fingertips. He couldn't figure it out.

He sat there for perhaps fifteen minutes, and no other cars came along, and the night was very quiet, with the moon climbing up in the sky like a white, round face.

Hardrock Hennesey had once whipped a dozen muckers in a tunnel riot. For a small-looking man—who, from his weathered features, could have been forty or sixty—he was about the hardest individual on two feet. Nothing much ever scared him.

But there was something uncanny about this strange fog stuff that had stopped him now. He put his head in his gnarled hands and sat there thinking, and he wondered if he was cracking up. Perhaps too many years of working "under pressure" had caught up with him. Maybe.

He looked up, and the fog had dispersed.

Hardrock jumped up, started carefully forward, stretching out his hands in front of him. This time they didn't touch anything hot. There seemed to be nothing ahead.

Nothing, that is, except the farmer's old car. He saw it clearly now, there in the roadway. He gulped. He stood very still and rubbed his eyes and swore. His fists knotted, and he stalked furiously forward. Somebody was damned well going to pay for pulling this gag on him. And that somebody was going to be that gangling farmer, that guy seated behind the wheel.

But there was no gag about the dead man slumped over the steering wheel of the car. Hardrock Hennesey jerked back in horror at sight of the withered features, and skin that was like old, brown leather. He stared at the man.

The corpse that was like a dried-up mummy!

HARDROCK HENNESEY had, at various times in his dangerous career, seen men die. He had observed half a dozen men buried—smothered beneath muck in a tunnel cave-in; he had seen a giant Negro shot through planking and sand and water in a "blow" beneath the East River. He had seen men crushed to death beneath tons of falling rock.

But what he observed now sort of sickened him. He took off his dusty old hat and wiped at his perspiring brow. Then he reached out an inquiring finger and touched the corpse's face.

The browned, dried skin literally cracked beneath his touch. The entire face was shrunken like something out of a tomb thousands of years old.

Hardrock Hennesey shuddered. But he got up nerve enough to reach inside the car and push the mummified thing across the seat. Then he climbed in behind the wheel and started up the engine.

He had to get to the town that he knew was ahead; he had to tell them of what he had seen. He figured he might have to bust a few noses before he got anyone to believe his story.

The car ran forward perhaps a quarter of a mile before it started hammering and bucking. Hardrock Hennesey could even *smell* the engine heat. Then the motor stopped completely, "froze up."

Hardrock climbed out, looked into the radiator. He stuck his finger in the top. Dry! He raised the hood and tried the petcock drain located at the bottom of the radiator. No water ran out.

Puzzled, Hardrock recalled that the car had been running all right when it passed him on the road the first time. Even though it had rattled considerably, there had been no indication of its being without water.

He noted the license number of the old car, went back to take one look at the mummified farmer. He'd have to walk the remainder of the way into town.

He was standing up on the running board, and just as he started to turn away again something that was on the back seat caught his eye.

It was a package, neatly wrapped and apparently addressed for mailing. Hardrock leaned over and looked at the thing. He picked it up.

The package was about six inches square and half an inch thick. It was very light in weight. It was addressed merely:

To:
Clark Savage, Jr.
New York City
New York

Hardrock Hennesey stared.

"Hell's fire!" he exploded, and got down off the car and started running down the road toward town. He had heard of Clark Savage, Jr. In fact, he knew a fellow who worked for him. What connection had this mummy with the remarkable person known as Doc Savage?

A mile down the road Hardrock came to a roadside tavern from which was coming enough racket to tell him a certain fact. The racket from inside indicated either a revival meeting or a riot. Ten chances to one, it was the latter. Also, it was Saturday night.

And that meant—tunnel muckers!

HARDROCK HENNESEY hurried inside and immediately big men lined up at the bar turned and hailed him and started yelling things like:

"Well, you old buzzard!"

"Hardrock! Line up, boy, and drink!"

"Say, boy!" another man yelled. "It's about time Hardrock showed up. Now you'll see some *work* on this new tunnel job!"

A new man among the muckers asked a question of an old-timer. He was told:

"Look, fella, Hardrock Hennesey's the greatest little mucker that ever ate hardrock. He ain't afraid of hell and dynamite. He's worked on every big job from New York to Frisco, the South, everywhere."

Tunnel workers—miners and muckers and hardrock men—probably make up the greatest fraternity of workmen in the world. You'll find the same gangs on jobs from Boston to Alaska. You'll find them working like demons, drinking hard and fighting on their nights off. And you'll find them sticking together. Hardrock Hennesey was perhaps the best hardrock man in the game. He was known everywhere.

Hands now slapped him on the back and drinks were pushed in his face.

But suddenly, and strangely, other muckers realized that their old friend was not accepting the drinks or returning their greetings. He was just standing there staring at them oddly, his intense gray eyes wide and bright.

"Look," Hardrock demanded. "I'm not drunk, am I? And—"

Someone laughed. "Hell, no! Maybe that's what's wrong with you. Come on, fella, catch up!"

"And I don't look crazy, do I?" Hardrock Hennesey managed to get in.

The men quieted somewhat. They grouped around the hard little tunnel worker and looked at him puzzledly.

Someone in the group finally managed to describe the thing that everyone saw—but was afraid to admit.

"I'll be damned!" the man exclaimed. "Look at 'im! Hardrock is... well, he's *scared!"*

Just about that moment someone got a drink into Hardrock's hand. It was a water glass half full of whiskey, a hundred proof. Hardrock Hennesey took the stuff down at a gulp.

He grabbed the one who had called him scared. His right fist traveled in a short arc. The fellow went down without even a grunt.

Then Hardrock rapped, "Now, listen to this."

He started talking. He told about walking along the road a mile or so back. He mentioned the peculiar fog, the misty stuff that you ought to be able to see through—but somehow could not.

He said, "The stuff burned me!"

Someone asked, "You mean... the fog?"

"Whatever was there around the car that I couldn't see," Hardrock said.

Men stared. Someone laughed.

Hardrock grabbed the big man and slapped his face, and the fellow's head jerked around on his neck.

"You ever see a man change into a mummy?" Hardrock demanded.

Apparently no one had ever seen such a phenomenon. Hardrock led the way toward the door.

"You guys come along with me," he ordered, "an' I'll show you something that'll knock your ears down."

He led the men back along the dusty roadway. There were perhaps two dozen tunnel workers in all. Big men. Hard men. Guys who knew Hardrock Hennesey from former jobs. They were now convinced that hard-boiled little Hardrock Hennesey was far from being drunk or crazy.

They were all now anxious to see a farmer who had become a mummy. They pushed past one another as they arrived at the old battered car.

They stared. They turned and looked at tough Hardrock Hennesey and their faces were grim.

A worker said, "This ain't a very funny gag."

"Let's take him apart!" suggested another.

But Hardrock elbowed them aside and himself moved up to the car.

The mummified man had disappeared.

This wasn't the only thing that held him rigid. His gaze had jerked to the rear seat, to the object that he had left there. It was the one thing that might have explained a part of this mystery. Hardrock was thinking of the small package that had been addressed to the man known as Doc Savage.

The package, also, was missing.

Chapter II
CALL FOR HELP

THE free-for-all battle that followed was somewhat of a honey.

It started when the fellow who was new to the gang called Hardrock Hennesey a liar. Hardrock climbed down off the old car's running board and commenced throwing punches in various directions.

Several of the muckers had had enough to drink to get sore about the whole business. They joined the mêlée enthusiastically.

Hardrock Hennesey knocked two men down, swung on a third and growled, *"Now* are you convinced, wise guy? I tell you the fog burned me. It musta burned up that farmer in the car!"

"Crazy as a loon!" said the big tunnel worker, and that got him a bust on the nose. He howled with pain and sailed into tough Hardrock Hennesey. Others helped out. They finally got Hardrock down in the dusty road and tried to pound some sense into his head.

But the more they pounded, the more Hardrock Hennesey swore and kicked and battered away at his opponents.

By the time several State troopers arrived in their white-painted car, the battle was really going great guns. And it was fifteen minutes before Hardrock was finally subdued and carried off toward the local jail.

That was after Hardrock Hennesey had tried to tell some of the troopers his story. For now that they had enjoyed a good fight, few of the tunnel workers wished to see their old friend carted off to the local hoosegow. And so they merely suggested that Hardrock Hennesey repeat what he had told them about the mysterious fog and a farmer who became a mummy.

Hardrock was halfway through his account when one trooper looked at another. Then they grabbed Hardrock and piled him in their car.

"Balmy!" was their opinion.

From conversation that Hardrock Hennesey heard as they rode toward town, he gathered that the troopers had recognized the old flivver. It appeared the farmer's name was Brown—Zeke Brown.

As one officer remarked, "Zeke's so damn' tight he's always running out of gas. He must have run out again and walked to the village."

"That's about it," a second trooper agreed.

Hardrock Hennesey started to put in, "Listen, he didn't walk *nowheres.* He's dead, I tell you! He's as dead as—"

"Shuddup!" a trooper rapped, and slapped him on the mouth.

Hardrock subsided again. And shortly the trooper car drew up before a small building that bordered the town ahead. In the distance, Hardrock Hennesey could see a towering steel framework, some buildings and the reflection of floodlights against the night sky. That would be Shaft 9, where he had been headed. Shaft 9, one of the many units in the tunnel project.

The troopers climbed out, stood aside, motioned Hardrock Hennesey out also.

Hardrock came out of the car in a flying leap, bowled over two of the three officers, clipped the third on the jaw, circled the small jail and took flight in the woods that pressed up close behind the building.

ANGRY bees arrived over his head. The bees were bullets, and they were from the troopers' guns. They thunked into trees, and were too close for comfort. Luckily, Hardrock Hennesey got deep into the woods, and none of the slugs found him.

He kept running. He ran for perhaps a mile before he paused to listen. The moon was overhead now, and it gave enough light to help him find his way. There was no sound behind him save the occasional scurrying of some small animal through the brush.

Hardrock made his way back toward the highway again. A half hour later, cautiously, he emerged on the roadway and stared up and down. He was at a point beyond the town, and in the distance he could see the light of Shaft 9.

The old fellow seated on the rock beside the road watched Hardrock Hennesey's cautious movements. Then he asked:

"Reckon you saw it too, eh?"

Hardrock lumped. He had not seen the old man. He gawked at him now.

The fellow was all of ninety years old. He was bent over and withered. He leaned on a cane that he must have cut out of a gnarled piece of hickory. His withered old skin looked like that of a—

A mummy!

The thought gave Hardrock Hennesey a start.

But then this mummy was alive. What was it he had said?

"See *what?"* Hardrock demanded suspiciously. He looked up and down the road, but he saw no one approaching.

"The thing that follows you in the night," said the old man. He sounded worried.

"What thing?"

Something about the tone of the old fellow's voice made a chill slide down Hardrock Hennesey's spine.

"The thing that is like a ghost. I reckon, mister, I've seen it a dozen times. It almost got me t'other night. Reckon it'll get me anytime now, too. I'm too old to get away from it."

Hardrock swallowed. Maybe this old geezer was nuts. And yet he remembered the strange thing that had happened to himself. Thinking of that, he recalled the package.

The package that had been addressed to Doc Savage, and which had disappeared.

He suddenly grabbed the old fellow's arm and asked, "Maybe you can tell me where I can find a phone." And, as an afterthought, "A phone where maybe there won't be too many people around listening when I make a call?"

The oldster nodded. He almost creaked when he moved, pointing toward town.

"You foller this road a piece until you come to Sam's garage, and in there you'll find a phone, mister. Sam'll probably be across the road at his house. He only comes over when someone honks for gas. But you go right ahead and use the phone, and he won't mind a bit."

"Thanks," said Hardrock quickly, and got away from there. The old fellow had sort of got under his skin, what with all that had happened to him in the past hour.

HE reached the garage without being spotted by any troopers with guns, without being seen by anyone.

A light was turned on above the single gas pump outside the place. As the old man had said, Sam was apparently across the road in his house. There were lights visible in the kitchen of the place.

So much the better, Hardrock Hennesey figured. He preferred that no one know of the phone call he was going to make.

Two minutes later, using the phone he located inside the garage building, he was connected with the New York headquarters of Doc Savage. Hardrock made a single request. He would like to speak to a man named Colonel John Renwick, the engineer in the organization of Doc Savage.

He got a break. Colonel John Renwick happened, at that moment, to be at the headquarters.

A great, booming voice came over the wire. Hardrock yanked the receiver away from his ear. It had been so long since he had seen his old friend that he had forgotten about the giant-sized fellow's bulllike voice.

"Yes?" said the man on the other end.

"This you, Renny?" Hardrock asked.

"Yes. Who's this?" the crashing voice demanded.

Hardrock gave details about himself. He finished with, "Remember that Hudson River tunnel job where they called you in for advice? Remember that fight one day up in the heading?"

The man named Renny suddenly laughed. Hardrock thought the receiver diaphragm would split.

"Hardrock, you old buzzard!" Renny said. "How's everything? Where are you?"

Apparently the fellow named Renny was glad to hear from his old friend.

Hardrock Hennesey said tensely, "You, Renny, you gotta come here."

"Where?"

Hardrock outlined the particular section of mountainous country where he was. He mentioned Yellow River Dam, a mammoth storage shed that was being constructed in conjunction with the one-hundred-mile long tunnel project. Yellow River Dam was only a few miles above Shaft 9, where Hardrock hoped to get a job.

"There's something funny up here," Hardrock continued.

"What do you mean?"

"Well," said Hardrock Hennesey worriedly, "there was a fella with a package for Doc Savage. He died. He died, and he looked like a mummy."

The man named Renny said, "Hardrock, you've been drinking again!"

The hard-boiled little tunnel worker rapped, "Listen, Renny: this isn't any joke. An' I'm cold sober. You just listen to this. There was a peculiar sort of fog. It was sort of transparent stuff, and again it wasn't. Well, this farmer—this fella that died—got into the stuff and I couldn't get near him. He's the one who had the package for Doc Savage."

"Have you the package now?"

"No, it's gone. But about this fog—"

"Yes?"

Hardrock paused, wiping at his brow with the crook of his arm. He realized that it was a warm night, but suddenly he felt unusually hot.

He continued: "This fog stuff was as hot as a furnace. It burned like live steam. Later, I found this farmer and he looked just like a dried-up mummy!"

Renny said nothing for a moment. Then he put in, "And he's the one who had the package for Doc Savage?"

"Yes. And, Renny, there's something else!"

"What?"

"It's—"

This time, Hardrock Hennesey *felt* the heat that seemed to crawl over him like something alive and menacing. He turned slightly away from the phone, staring over his shoulder.

And he let out a yell as the instrument slipped from his stiff fingers.

Because the fog stuff was right there behind him; floating like tendrils of clawing, ghostlike fingers through the open doorway. Hardrock Hennesey could apparently see through the strange stuff, and yet couldn't. It was uncanny.

He leaped out of the chair where he had been seated, stared frantically around the small space. His face already felt as if it was frying in the steamy heat. The stuff was slowly enveloping him with ethereal, opaque fingers.

With a gasp of horror, Hardrock Hennesey jumped toward the rear of the room. He sought a window. But before he could locate one, the floating, peculiar fog was upon him. He sank down in a shuddering heap, and as the strange veil dropped over him he let out a frantic yell.

"Renny! Help! *It's got me!"*

Chapter III
LIVING DEAD MAN

THE fast, streamlined plane came down out of the night sky, circled the field, landed and taxied to a stop not far from the roadside gas station in the mountains.

The first person who stepped out of the plane was indeed a strange-looking individual. He was about as broad as he was wide. All parts of his exposed body contained bristly, red hair that looked like stubby, thin nails. He had incredibly homely features made to hold up traffic at street corners.

In a squeaky, almost childlike voice he piped, "Blazes! We oughta fumigate that plane. Something's been bitin' me all the way from New York."

Without bending forward, the homely one scratched at his leg, in the vicinity of his knee. This was accomplished because the man's arms dangled well below his knees. He was built like an oversized ape.

From the plane had followed a slender, nattily dressed man with a waspish waist. He carried a neat black cane. He frowned in disgust at the apelike individual and said, "Did you ever try soap and water for that?"

Immediately, the hairy one made a roundhouse swing at the dapper-looking man. He glared and said, "That sounded like a dirty remark."

The slender one grinned. "It was suited to the occasion, you hairy baboon!"

Just then, two queer-looking animals scurried from the plane door. One was a pig, a scrawny-looking pig with beanpole legs and a snout made for rummaging inside long tin cans. The other animal was a runt-sized ape that looked suspiciously like the hairy individual who spoke in the childlike voice.

The runt ape moved toward the person who looked not unlike himself, and took a nip out of the man's leg. The spot where the animal took the bite was right where the fellow had been scratching.

Abruptly, understanding leaped into the hairy one's eyes.

"Ye-o-ow!" he squalled. "It's that blasted Chemistry that's been biting me all the way up from New York!"

He made a dive for the chimp. The tall, well-dressed man got in the way and quickly swung the animal up in his arms. Apparently Chemistry was his pet.

He kicked at the scrawny pig, remarked icily, "Take that Habeas away from here before I annihilate him! He must have fleas!"

There threatened to be a riot between the two men until the giant-sized figure stepped out of the plane and said, "We seem to be missing something." He pointed to the gas station building down the field.

The third arrival was the man whom Hardrock Hennesey had phoned—Colonel John Renwick, but better known as Renny to his friends and the other aides in Doc Savage's organization. Renny was six inches over six feet, weighed well over two hundred pounds, and had hands like quart-size pails. He also had a gloomy-looking face which reminded you of an undertaker without clients.

When he spoke, his booming voice shattered the summer night's quietude.

It was the hairy fellow who demanded, "Missing what? Where?" He squinted out of his small eyes toward the spot that Renny had indicated.

"There seems to be some sort of fight in progress," Renny explained. He turned to the well-dressed man who had been ready to clout the apish fellow. "See it, Ham?"

MONK

"Ham," apparently, did. His face brightened. He set down the pet chimp.

"Monk must be slipping," he remarked coolly. "First time he's ever passed up a fight in his life!"

Obviously Monk was the hairy individual with whom he'd been arguing.

Monk let out a howl as he spotted some sort of mix-up taking place over near the gas station. His short legs took him in a wild gallop across the field.

Renny and the one called Ham followed along in time to enter into a shambles that sounded like a dog fight with a stray alley cat cornered in the middle.

BUT it was hairy Monk who was in the center of the fight. Around him fists swung and there were assorted kinds of cursing.

The faces of the fellows behind the swinging fists looked like something made to frighten small children. They were of the thug variety.

A rotund, red-faced man was on the outside of the mêlée, jumping up and down and yelling.

"These men just broke into my gas station!" he screamed. "Help!"

Giant Renny plowed into the group and his fists started swinging. Men were knocked sprawling. The sound the giant engineer's fists made as they hit various individuals was like the noise a chunk of cement makes striking soft leather.

Renny looked unusually gloomy—whereas he was probably enjoying himself immensely.

As was the one named Ham. Instead of using roughhouse tactics, he merely flicked at some of the battling men with what appeared to be a slender sword. He had drawn the sword from the black cane, which was obviously some sort of sheath.

Two men sighed and lay down and seemed to forget all about the fight. They could hardly know that the end of the sword cane contained a mild anaesthetic drug that would hold them unconscious for some time.

Three fellows broke loose of the surging battle and took out for the nearby woods.

It was hairy Monk who howled, "What the blazes! I was doin' fine all by myself. What's the idea of interrupting?"

He glared at well-dressed Ham. Someone cracked Monk in the jaw during this momentary intermission. Monk howled, grabbed the one who had hit him, upended him and started bouncing the fellow's head on the ground.

And all the time the plump gas station owner hopped up and down outside the fighting mass and yelled things like, "Help! Murder! Police!"

The police arrived in the form of a state trooper

car loaded with husky, powerful young men in snappy uniforms. But before they could swing into the battle, three more men had ducked clear and disappeared into the nearby woods.

All those that were left lay sprawled in the dusty roadway. That is, all except hairy Monk, smooth-looking Ham—whose collar was not even disturbed—and giant Renny.

Monk complained, "Blast it! An' we was just gettin' started!"

A trooper rapped, "What goes on?"

HAM

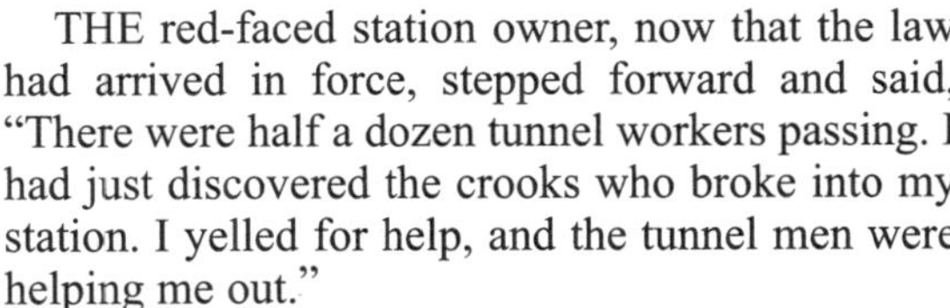

THE red-faced station owner, now that the law had arrived in force, stepped forward and said, "There were half a dozen tunnel workers passing. I had just discovered the crooks who broke into my station. I yelled for help, and the tunnel men were helping me out."

He turned, indicated the three who had arrived from the plane. "I don't know about these three. I don't know whether they were helping these tunnel men or the crooks!"

It appeared that all six men lying on the ground were tunnel workers. One at a time, they started sitting up and rubbing at bruised jaws.

The thugs—the ones who had broken into the station—had disappeared to parts unknown.

It was quick-thinking Ham who asked, "Why did they break into your station, mister?"

The fat owner apparently didn't know.

"The fight," he said, "started before I could investigate."

The troopers were looking at Ham and his partners suspiciously. Ham said, "Perhaps we should explain." He looked at big Renny, and the engineer nodded.

"Explain what?" one trooper asked.

"About Hardrock Hennesey."

There were seven state troopers. All stiffened at Ham's words. Because all knew of the crazy story that had been told by Hardrock Hennesey earlier tonight, a cockeyed yarn about a mummified man and a fog that burned.

"What do you know about Hardrock Hennesey?" one of the troopers demanded.

"This," put in Renny. "He called me in New York. He told us about some sort of mystery taking place up here. Since he's an old friend, we hopped up here to investigate. And we ran into this."

Renny made no mention of Doc Savage. He did not explain that Ham was really Brigadier General Theodore Marley Brooks, a well-known graduate of the Harvard Law School, and the attorney in the organization of Doc Savage.

Or that Monk, the hairy individual, was really Lieutenant Colonel Andrew Blodgett Mayfair, a renowned chemist—regardless of his resemblance to a belligerent gorilla.

The two pets, Habeas and Chemistry, had scurried back to the plane.

The troopers, their forces augmented, were still seeking tough little Hardrock Hennesey. Naturally they were somewhat suspicious of Renny and his partners.

"Where's Hardrock Hennesey now?" one inquired.

Monk stuck out his jaw. "Brother," he piped, "that's what we come up here to find out. Hardrock was talkin' to Renny, an' all of a sudden he cut short his call and started yellin' for help. Something's phony as hell around here."

One trooper stared curiously at Monk's ugly features and commented, "Yes, I guess so."

Monk was ready to take a poke at the fellow when Ham suggested quickly, "It might be a good idea to look around. There must have been a reason for crooks breaking into this man's gas station. We had Hardrock Hennesey's call traced—and it came from here."

Everyone shoved inside the small building, and it was in there that they found the mummified corpse.

THE thing that had once been a man was quite hideous.

The whole body had shrunken, as though drained of every bit of moisture that had ever been in it. Skin hung onto the skeleton that was left like dried-up, dirty, stiff cloth. The features of the face had shrunken so that it was impossible to tell whether the man had been young—or very old.

One of the tunnel men had pushed forward. A little while ago he had been pretty drunk; now he was sober.

He murmured in awe, "It… it's Hardrock!"

Another mucker agreed. "Yep. Look at his clothes. That's what Hardrock Hennesey was wearing when we saw him tonight."

The speaker's voice grew hushed. "And we didn't believe Hardrock when he tried to tell us about that farmer!"

A trooper had been going through the mummified man's clothing. He removed a letter from an inside pocket, opened it, read something.

Then he nodded. "It's Hardrock Hennesey, all right. This is a letter of introduction to the super at Shaft 9."

Everyone started talking at once. During this, Renny stepped up to one of the troopers and requested, "Mind if I just look at him a moment?

He was an old friend." Renny indicated the shrunken corpse on the floor.

The trooper shrugged. "O.K. by me, fella."

Renny stooped down while Monk and Ham were busy questioning the tunnel men. No one could explain the mystery. But for big men who pitted themselves against constant dangers below the Earth's surface, who were in the habit of treating life as something that might be snuffed out at any time, they now looked awed.

One said, "I wonder what Hardrock meant about that fog?"

"What fog?" asked a trooper who, apparently, had not heard Hardrock Hennesey's story earlier.

Before anyone could answer, there was a shout of excitement from outside the small building. Monk and Ham were first outside.

The stout man, Sam, who owned the station, was indicating a large barrel that was on a small platform beside the building.

"Look!" he cried. "It's completely dry!"

Monk squinted inside the barrel, and then at the fat man.

"So what?" he wanted to know.

"Listen," the stout man went on, "that barrel was almost plumb full of water a couple of hours ago. It's a rain barrel."

"Maybe somebody dumped it," Monk said.

But the man shook his head. "How could they?" he demanded. "It's fastened down!"

No one had an answer for that.

It was Monk who ambled inside, took another look at the mummified man, then came outside again and stood staring at the empty rain barrel. But, for once, he kept his mouth shut. Ham gave him a peculiar regard.

While fat Sam was trying to figure what had become of his rain water, Renny drew his two partners aside and murmured. "There's something we ought to investigate." The powerful engineer had a time trying to keep his voice down to a whisper.

"Investigate what?" Ham queried.

"Hardrock Hennesey."

"But he's dead!" the dapper lawyer insisted.

"Come on," suggested Renny, and he led the way as they slipped away from the group. He said nothing until they had returned to their plane. There, Renny locked the cabin door.

The pets, who had been chasing each other wildly around the field, joined them.

Monk, puzzled, demanded, "What are you gonna do, Renny?"

"Find Hardrock Hennesey," the big engineer said.

MONK pointed back toward the gas station. "You mean that—"

Renny nodded.

He said, "You see, Hardrock, for a tough little guy, was always somewhat superstitious. He always carried a miniature rabbit's foot on a chain around his neck. But the rabbit's foot was not being worn by that fellow who became a mummy."

Ham had an answer for that.

"Someone could have removed it," he said.

"Naturally," agreed Renny. "But they couldn't have removed the thing that was on Hardrock's chest. I recall it very well."

"What?"

"Hardrock always figured that some day he might die in a river tunnel. In water. So he once had a mermaid tattooed on his chest. He was a great one for doing crazy things like that."

"And there is no mermaid tattooed on the man's chest back there?" Ham asked.

"Correct."

Monk's small eyes brightened. "Then Hardrock must still be alive!"

Ham gave his homely partner a sour look.

"Sometimes," the lawyer said icily, "you almost show signs of intelligence!"

It looked, for the moment, as if there was going to be a fight. For these two unusual fellows liked nothing better than an argument.

But Renny stopped it with the remark, "The logical place to start would be at Shaft 9, near here. That's where Hardrock was headed in the first place. We'll walk."

They started out, hairy Monk commenting in his squeaky voice, "I'm gonna enjoy meetin' that Hardrock Hennesey. Bet he's a great fighter, from what I've heard."

Ham said, "You've got a one-track mind, you hairy mistake. What we really would like to learn is what was in that package Hardrock mentioned. The package addressed to Doc."

Monk growled something.

"I'm still more interested in that little tunnel mucker," he insisted.

The hairy chemist was due for a surprise when they got to Shaft 9. But before that happened, they ran into something else.

It was the excited, shoving, noisy argument that was taking place near the opening of the shaft.

Chapter IV
THE DISAPPEARING MEN

SHAFT 9 was only one in the series of openings that formed a chain in the great water tunnel project. South of here there were others; just north, a great dam that was nearing completion. The dam would be used as a storage shed for excess water that came down out of the mountains.

Aboveground there were various buildings.

There was a powerhouse. Another smaller building housed the machinery for running the shaft lift that plunged more than fifteen hundred feet into the Earth. Above all was the constant throbbing of a unit that drove fresh air down to the workmen far below. A pipe that carried this air led to the shaft itself and crawled down its sides. It looked like a fat, black snake.

Overhead were bright floodlights. The shaft was using three shifts of miners and muckers. The pile of rock that had been carried up out of the new tunnel looked like a small mountain beyond the shaft buildings.

It was at the shaft opening that the trouble was taking place.

Monk, Ham and Renny moved close. The pets remained at a safe distance.

Monk grinned. His eyes brightened hopefully. "Let's join the fight," he suggested.

"Let Renny handle this, dunce!" Ham rapped coolly.

While they waited, big Renny moved forward and talked to some of the grimy workmen on the edges of the group. He returned shortly.

"There's been some kind of queer accident down in the tunnel," he announced. "Some of these fellows want to quit. Others are trying to keep them on the job. There's liable to be trouble."

"What happened down there?" Monk demanded.

"From what I gathered," Renny said, "a man was found dead. Others are saying they saw a queer fog. They're afraid to go back to work. There seems to be some sort of jinx on the place."

Ham said, "Let's talk to them and explain that Hardrock Hennesey is not dead—as far as we know."

As they moved up to the group of arguing and struggling workmen, Renny and Ham took it for granted that Monk was right behind them.

He wasn't.

Monk saw the thin, quick-moving man in overalls, a fellow who was acting suspiciously. The man had come out of the surrounding darkness and stepped hesitatingly toward the circle of arguing tunnel workers. For just a moment, light from one of the floodlamps illuminated his leathery, oldish features. It revealed the open flannel shirt at the throat.

In that brief instant when Monk turned, the strange-acting man was quite close to him. And so the hairy chemist saw the thing on the man's chest when it was exposed, momentarily, to the light.

A tatooed mermaid, as large as your hat!

Instantly the fellow had swung back and disappeared in the shadows. With Monk taking out behind him!

The trail led wide of the shaft buildings and several huge Mack trucks parked nearby. It led beyond the small mountain that was broken-up rock taken from the tunnel bore.

Monk saw the wiry little guy disappear toward a square, steel building set well apart from any others. A big red sign on the side of the building warned:

DYNAMITE

Monk ducked behind a truck in order to watch. In doing so, he momentarily lost track of the fellow he was trailing. He waited several moments, not certain whether his quarry had gone into the dynamite storage shack or not.

Hairy Monk was not one to wait long on anything. He came out from behind the truck and hurried up to the small building. He saw that the door was ajar.

Damned funny, he thought, that the guy was coming *here.* And that Hardrock Hennesey should be that strange-acting fellow! Hardrock Hennesey, with a mermaid tattooed on his chest!

Monk slammed into the building.

And a small hard fist slammed into his face, while another got hold of his stubby, bristly hair.

The girl's voice snapped out, "Brother, you sure got one hell of a nerve!"

MONK stared.

The girl had been standing to one side of the door, just inside the building. There was a dim light glowing, and now it revealed her quite plainly. Abruptly, the girl was staring with as much open-mouthed amazement as was the homely-faced chemist.

The girl said, "Maybe I should scream!" as she looked at Monk.

Then Monk grinned. He grinned because he liked what he saw, because the chemist had a fondness for the ladies—especially pretty ones—and this girl here had features and a shape that contained just about everything.

Her slender, boyish form was startlingly outlined by the whipcord breeches that she wore. Her flannel shirt, open at the throat, emphasized the lovely curve of her throat.

She had fine, smooth features, and Monk thought that her eyes were aquamarine.

She also had red hair. And a temper.

She took an angry step toward the hairy chemist and rapped, "What are you staring it?"

Monk grinned. Strangely, the chemist always went over big with the ladies. Perhaps it was because of his utterly homely face and nerve.

He said, "Put you in a silk dress and a picture hat, and you'd have Dietrich backed off the boards."

The girl's trim, taut figure relaxed a bit. There was no woman that could hear that kind of flattery without reacting to it.

She asked, "Just who *are* you?"

Monk liked the way she held her chin and the manner in which her hands were clenched at her sides. He was willing to bet she could well handle herself.

"I was lookin' for a fella named Hardrock Hennesey," he said. "Thought I saw him come in here. I was gonna—"

The girl gasped. "Hardrock? You… you've seen *him?"*

"If he's a bird with a tattooed mermaid on his chest—yes," offered Monk.

Suddenly the girl's firm hand was gripping his powerful arm. Her green eyes were bright with worry.

"Then you've got to help me," she blurted. "You've got to help me locate Hardrock. He can help us. I've been trying to find him."

"You know him, lady?"

"Of course. For years. He's the only one that can explain."

"Explain what?"

Caution came into the girl's eyes.

"You haven't yet answered my question," she reminded. "Just who are you?"

"Ever hear of a man named Doc Savage?" the chemist asked.

THE girl's eyes narrowed; she seemed to give a slight start. She said carefully, "Yes, I have. Why?"

"Well," Monk went on, "Hardrock Hennesey found something that was addressed to Doc Savage from a man up here. A guy who got killed strangely. That's why I want to find Hardrock Hennesey."

Monk then went on to explain how he was the chemist in Doc Savage's organization. His chest swelled a little, as he added: "There are a few men in the world who consider themselves greater chemists—but that's only because of professional jealously. I'm broad-minded enough to overlook—"

Beside them, from outside the doorway, Ham's cutting voice said, "Only reason this baboon is broad-minded is because he was dropped out of a tree when he was very young. On his head. You'll note that it is almost flat—"

Monk let out a roar and swung on his nattily attired partner.

"Listen, shyster—" he started.

But Ham was smiling gallantly at the red-haired girl. He introduced himself. He pushed between Monk and the girl, then used his most effective manner.

As a famous Harvard Law School graduate, Ham was an orator when it came to talking. It was also his ambition to take any girl away from hairy Monk.

He was saying now, "Perhaps I can help you, my dear girl. You see, I am an accomplished—"

"—father!" Monk added. "He's got thirteen funny-faced kids, all kept locked up in the Bellevue psychopathic ward!"

Ham swung on the chemist. The two pets, Habeas and the runt ape, appeared behind them. They started glaring at one another like their masters. For Monk's favorite gag was to tell pretty young girls that his partner had thirteen children, whereas Ham was a bachelor.

It was the girl who stopped the argument. She moved between the two, knotted her fists, said coolly, "Are you two going to stop acting like boys, or do I have to slap one of you down?"

She sounded as though she could really do it.

Monk gulped. Ham stared. For such a lovely-faced girl, there was something about her attitude that said she had spent much time around construction workers—and could handle herself.

Both Ham and Monk grinned sheepishly.

"Guess we better start lookin' for Hardrock Hennesey," suggested hairy Monk.

The girl nodded. "That's better. And now, if you say you saw him, there's one place to start."

She had locked the shed door behind them; they were returning toward the spot where tunnel workers had been staging a near riot.

"Where?" Ham wanted to know.

"The shaft. That Hardrock will want to see some of his old pals, if he *is* here. He'll be down there in the tunnel, first chance he gets. Try to keep *him* out!"

The two Doc Savage aides learned that the girl's name was Chick Lancaster. It appeared her brother was one of the chief engineers on this tunnel project. She, herself, was a graduate civil engineer.

Monk and the lawyer immediately had deep respect for Chick Lancaster. She was apparently a very capable young woman.

Through the night, a booming voice crashed out and reached them. Chick asked, "What in the world is that?"

"That's Renny," said Monk.

"Renny!"

Ham explained that Renny, the engineer in Doc's crowd, was making a speech to the tunnel men. He was trying to keep them on the job. He was explaining that he was an old friend of Hardrock Hennesey's, and that he believed the little mucker still alive. He would do all he could to solve the mystery that had killed a tunnel worker and a farmer who was well known to everyone at the shaft.

The big workers were listening quietly, convinced that here was a giant of a fellow who got results.

Suddenly the girl gripped Monk's arm.

"Look!" she cried.

Monk and Ham stared. They followed the girl's pointing finger. All they saw was the platform built at the opening to the deep shaft going below ground.

"Look at what?" Monk queried.

"Hardrock. He just went below in the bucket!"

THE "bucket," the girl explained, was like a giant pail that could accommodate about eight workmen. It was lowered down the fifteen hundred-foot shaft at the end of a steel cable.

As Chick explained, "In a few days, they'll have the regular elevator car installed. But, at first, we always use one of these until the shaft walls are lined with cement and rails for an elevator cage."

Monk stared over the railing into the black pit. Far, far down he saw a vague light glowing, one of the few electric bulbs strung up and down the seemingly endless shaft leading into the Earth.

"Whew!" he murmured.

"There's nothing to it," the girl explained. "I'll go with you."

That made Monk feel sort of sheepish. He grinned.

"I'll go for you," he said. "Soon as that blasted bucket returns."

They waited. Something seemed to be wrong, for the bucket did not return. A workman, seeing the girl, came running over and explained. "Pete—the operator—is over there at the meeting listening to a fellow named Renwick. There's no one to run this equipment."

That did not seem to stop quick-thinking Chick Lancaster. She indicated the building nearby, where the hoisting machinery was located. "I'll run it," she said.

A few moments later the bucket was at ground level again. Monk climbed in, feeling funny as the steel, barrel-shaped thing swayed beneath his feet. Swayed over a hole fifteen hundred feet deep!

Ham, grinning, announced, "I'd better stay with the girl. She might need me."

Monk exclaimed, "Dangit, I'm gonna—"

But at that moment Ham gave the girl a hand signal from where he stood. She threw a lever and the bucket started down.

Monk, with a start, clutched at the sides of the makeshift car. His breath whistled through his teeth as the shaft walls, black and menacing, zoomed past his gaze.

For Chick Lancaster had failed to mention that the bucket traveled at a speed approaching six hundred feet per minute!

MONK never quite remembered climbing out of the bucket at the base of the shaft. This was all a dream; soon the thing would crash and he would be somewhere in China. He was still so dizzy from effects of the hurtling descent that he staggered around in circles.

Massive rock walls swayed before his vision. Stretching out endlessly to right and left was the eighteen-foot bore that was the greatest water carrying project ever constructed.

And here at the base of the shaft, the tunnel proper widened in a mammoth chamber where machinery could be moved and rock that was brought out of the tunnel, unloaded.

It was just as the hairy chemist was regaining his equilibrium that he saw the walking mummy.

He gulped, stared.

"I'm in hell, sure!" Monk gasped.

The man looked like something ageless. He was so thin that it seemed he surely must break in two as his spindle legs moved. A tunnel overhead light revealed his cracked, brown face, that was like withered parchment.

Monk frowned. He had come down here seeking Hardrock Hennesey. He had also expected to find a few muckers or miners down here in the tunnel. But apparently all were above at the meeting led by Renny.

But this fellow, this mummified apparition—

The figure said in a strange voice, "Come! Follow me!"

Monk gave a start, for that voice was like something from the dead.

But he followed. That was his mistake.

Four individuals moved out from concealment against the rock walls. They piled on hairy Monk. The mummified man disappeared.

Monk swung into action, his powerful fists slamming at ducking heads. Gone was his amazement. These four big men with the ugly faces were something real. They were something you could fight, and so the chemist went to work on them joyously.

Heads snapped on assorted necks. There were grunts of pain. Cries like: "Ouch! Call for help!"

Monk was just getting unlimbered when the four took out in a furious race through the half-dark tunnel. Monk, disgusted, followed.

His short, bowed legs were not quite fast enough to keep up with the escaping four. But he managed to keep them in sight. From his pocket the chemist removed one of the spring-generated flashlights that all the aides of Doc Savage carried.

He switched on the light and could see the running men plainly. And then, abruptly, he couldn't. They had dived into a slight hollow that was a part of the tunnel rock wall.

Monk barged in after them.

And his head slammed against granite and he went down in a heap. Stars exploded. His skull felt like it was split wide open.

Dazedly, Monk felt of the walls. There was nothing except rough rock. No opening. No hideout. Nothing.

Monk perceived this in the racing seconds

The giant masked figure came plunging out
of the misty substance and raced toward Monk!

before unconsciousness overtook him. The slam of his head against solid rock had been too much for even his tough skull. He sat down and went temporarily to sleep.

But something peculiar, a certain warmness, woke him up. He was wet with perspiration and his lungs felt as though they had inhaled burning, scorching hot air.

He swayed to his feet, gasping. He recalled that as he had chased the four through the tunnel, he had passed a bucket of water placed there for workmen, or perhaps overlooked by a water boy.

He staggered through the oppressive heat, located the bucket, bent down to pick it up—then stared.

The water bucket was empty, whereas a few moments before it had been practically full.

Monk started to mutter, "Gollywockus! Maybe I'm seein' things! Maybe that bucket didn't stop… an' I'm dead!"

He couldn't figure it out.

But what he *could* understand was the thing he saw when his gaze went beyond the water bucket and along the shadowy tunnel. He saw the stuff that trailed slowly toward him like seeking tentacles of doom.

Fog!

Grayish, sort of transparent stuff that spread quickly and silently.

Monk gulped. He recalled Hardrock Hennesey's excited words to Renny over the phone. Fog that burned. Fog that made mummies of men! Hardrock had screamed something about it just after he'd mentioned the package addressed to Doc Savage!

Monk, held petrified for a moment, stared at the opaque, misty stuff. Then he started backing up slowly. A thought hit him even as he did so. If he backed up like this, how would he ever get *out* of the tunnel?

While he was worrying about this, the masked figure came plunging out of the misty substance and raced toward Monk. He was a man giant in stature; the fact became obvious as he approached. And the mask over his face was some sort of breathing apparatus.

From behind it, a compelling, deep-timbered voice ordered, "Put on this mask. Hurry!"

It was the unusual voice of Doc Savage!

Chapter V
MESSAGE FROM CHICK

SOMEHOW, Monk got into the protective head helmet that was shoved into his hands.

Then Doc Savage was urging him toward the shaft, the single outlet from the tunnel. From behind the mask, he ordered, "We have about one minute to escape with our lives."

Monk started running. But he was still groggy from the crack on his head. He thought he was making good time, but apparently Doc Savage saw need for greater haste. He scooped powerful Monk up in his arms and ran with him. Ran through the hazy gray stuff that seared the hands, that felt like a puff of breath from a dragon's lungs.

Doc Savage carried heavily-built Monk as though he might have been a child. Standing alone, Monk looked like a pretty powerful fellow. But compared to Doc Savage, he now seemed almost puny in stature.

For the bronze man was a physical giant. Veins in his bronze-hued hands stood out like taut cords. The muscles in his neck showed a remarkable strength found in few men. Though his face was shielded by the breathing mask, a glass front showed the unusual bronze features. Doc's hair was of the same color, only somewhat darker.

He ran as easily and as swiftly as though he might have been carrying a rag doll.

They reached the wider opening at the base of the shaft. Doc set Monk down, whipped off his mask.

He said briefly, "That stuff is spreading. Climb into that thing."

Doc had indicated the huge bucket which was used to carry workmen up and down the fifteen hundred-foot shaftway. Monk tumbled into the thing, pulling off the protective mask, at the same time bubbling over with questions.

"Doc!" he piped in his squeaky voice. "How in blazes did you know I was down here? How did you *get* here?"

"No time for questions," Doc Savage said swiftly. He was in the elevator device beside hairy Monk. He reached out a bronze hand and pulled on a cable that was a signal to those aboveground.

They waited. But nothing happened.

And out of the tunnel behind them something opaque and hazy floated. It appeared like a giant spider's web creeping.

Doc indicated the masks. Monk yanked his back on. From behind his own, Doc Savage said, "The girl—the one named Chick Lancaster—is operating the elevator machinery. She was to wait for the signal."

Monk shuddered, watching the gray stuff that was swiftly floating toward them. Already his hands were seared from passing through just a part of the stuff. He could imagine what would happen if they were completely enveloped by it!

"I hate to admit it," he blurted from behind the mask, "but maybe that girl is crooked!"

Doc said nothing.

And then, without warning, the bucket started upward suddenly. It swiftly hit maximum speed. It almost took the hairy chemist's breath away.

He looked at Doc Savage. But the bronze man was standing as though he might be merely riding in a building elevator to the second floor. His features were calm.

The dizzy flight upward took two and a half minutes. Monk's eardrums cracked at the changes in pressure. His head whirled.

DOC

And then they were climbing out of the thing. It had come to an automatic stop as a "trip" shut off current at the surface landing.

There was no one around. Doc hurriedly led the way to the building that contained the machinery which operated the bucket lift. It, too, was deserted.

Chick Lancaster, the girl, was missing.

IT was Doc who found the note that the girl had left for them. It was tucked beside the switchbox located on the wall, and it read:

> *We think we have located Hardrock Hennesey. If you find this message, follow to the Yellow River Dam, two miles north of here. We'll be at the superintendent's home there. Ham is accompanying me.*

The hastily written note was signed "Chick Lancaster."

Monk looked upset.

"That shyster Ham sure works fast!" he blurted. "No tellin' what he'll tell her about me."

Doc Savage did not comment. His metallic features were expressionless.

Monk suddenly remembered something else. "Where's Renny?" he asked. "He was talkin' to some of the tunnel workers just before I went down in that blasted elevator thing—"

"Renny is still with them," Doc advised. "They have gone to the home of the girl's brother, one of the engineers on this project. It is important to keep the men on the job—regardless of whatever mystery has happened here tonight."

Monk described the mummylike old man he had seen down in the tunnel. He told about the dead man back in the gas station, and of what had been reported before their arrival by Hardrock Hennesey. Something about a farmer who had become a mummified corpse.

The hairy chemist's eyes were wide. "Doc! What the blazes has all that got to do with this tunnel job? Certainly there's no connection!"

The bronze giant was leading the way toward a big limousine parked near the shaft buildings. It was Doc's specially equipped car, a machine that contained bulletproof armor and various scientific devices of the bronze man's own invention. For a moment after Monk spoke, Doc said nothing.

Then he said quietly, "There might be more connection than you think."

Monk puzzled over that for a while. They were in the car now, and Doc took the only road that led north. They passed a road sign that indicated they were on the route to Yellow River Dam.

Monk had imagination. He suddenly blurted, "Doc, you think maybe this tunnel work, this business of boring down there into the Earth, might have unearthed some ghosts?"

The bronze man's gaze remained on the road ahead.

"Ghosts?" he prodded.

"Yeah. You take them guys that dig up old tombs and pyramids... something always happens to them. They die... or get some danged funny disease that nobody can cure. Maybe this is something like that! Goshamighty, there's sure *some* kind of mystery here at this—"

"The mystery at present," Doc put in, "is what was in the package addressed to us. The package Hardrock Hennesey saw in the farmer's car."

"The girl told you when you arrived here?"

Doc nodded.

"Then," Monk said confidently, "as soon as we find Hardrock now, at the dam, we'll know all about it."

"I wonder if Hardrock is the one we'll find," finished Doc, and he lapsed into silence as he drove through the warm night.

The chemist looked at the bronze man swiftly. Doc's comment puzzled him. He could not see where they were going to have any trouble meeting up with Hardrock Hennesey. The girl's note had said she knew where he now was. It was all very simple.

BUT there was nothing simple about the carefully arranged trap awaiting Monk and Doc Savage at Yellow River Dam.

The gigantic unit in the water tunnel system sprawled like a black, bottomless crater in the night. For two miles, the dam spread up and down the mountain valley in which it had been built. A great wall had been completed at the lower end of the dam. Across this was a roadway for automobiles; the road was already in use, though the dam itself was not quite completed.

It was beyond this roadway, atop a hill overlooking the dark, gloomy void of concrete and steel framework, that the superintendent's house stood. It was the house that had been mentioned in Chick Lancaster's note. Lights burned on the first floor behind drawn shades.

Inside, in the basement of the house, a group of individuals who appeared like anything but tunnel workers were holding a consultation.

One man consulted his watch. He said, "Doc Savage and that funny-looking guy left the shaft five minutes ago. They're due here any minute."

The speaker had a hawklike face and nervous hands. He looked toward a big man who seemed to be in charge of the group. Other eyes followed his own.

"Everything's set?" the big man asked.

There were affirmative nods.

"Then this'll take care of that Savage guy," said the leader. He grinned.

The leader had a blocky face, big hands and black, piercing eyes. The thing that made him appear twice as big was the long, bulky raincoat which he wore. There seemed to be no logical reason for the raincoat, except that it was black, and perhaps offered a good means of concealment outside in the dark.

The fellow also seemed to be troubled with indigestion.

He was frequently addressed by the others as Pinky. He was about six foot two.

A man suddenly appeared at the top of a flight of stairs that led down into the basement.

"They're here!" he announced in a hushed voice.

The announcement seemed to be a signal for everyone to move toward the stairs. But instead of going up to the first floor, all gathered in a tight knot just below the door leading to the rooms above.

Pinky said, "You've got the super and Hardrock Hennesey all fixed?"

"And how!" replied the one who had joined them. "Both on the living room floor. Both out cold. Doc and that assistant of his will think they had a fight, and when they go to help them—"

"All right," Pinky rapped. "Quiet!"

Two moments later, a doorbell rang somewhere in the house. It was repeated a moment later.

Then, shortly, there was the sound of footsteps as two men entered the front hallway above. The door behind which the waiting group crouched was right at the end of the hallway, a dozen feet or so from the entrance to the living room.

The footsteps paused in the hallway. Then there came the sound of an exclamation. Monk's words.

"Doc! Lookit! Two guys out cold on the parlor floor!"

After that the waiting group heard footsteps moving into the living room. There followed a sharp crackling sound. A moment later, heavy bodies struck the living room rug, threshed around a moment. Then—silence.

Pinky grinned. "That's what I call neat," he said. "Taking that bronze guy with his own tricks. We planted them little glass vials in the rug. We'll wait two minutes for the knockout gas to evaporate, then we'll go up."

They waited, each man with a gun in his fist. Though apparently there was going to be no trouble from above, none took chances. As one man said:

"You never can tell about that Doc Savage guy. Wish I had a tommy gun instead of this gat!"

Pinky laughed softly. He belched. "Them two birds will be out cold for an hour," he said.

A moment later, at his signal, all proceeded to the upper hallway. They flung into the living room.

It was deserted.

ONE of the gunmen started to exclaim, "Say! What the hell happened—"

And then the sharp sputtering sounds came from beneath his feet, from beneath the shoes of his companions. They were firecracker noises followed by puffs of yellow, bilious-looking gassy stuff.

Big Pinky and the others started choking. A couple of the gunmen fell down.

Another happened to stare toward a far corner of the large room. His eyes goggled. He let out a cry of terror.

It was the first time the fellow had ever seen Doc Savage. He was never going to forget it in all his shady life.

At first, the bronze man did not seem unusually large. It was only when he moved toward the confused, staggering mob of gunmen that he seemed to grow in stature. This was made more noticeable when the apelike fellow appeared beside the bronze man.

Compared to Monk, Doc suddenly became a giant. A giant who was perfectly proportioned. The protective head mask that Doc Savage was wearing made him the more startling.

The helmet contained a glass front, and behind this the unusual eyes of Doc Savage seemed to have a compelling, hypnotic effect. Even as the staring gunman swayed before falling, as a result of breathing the anaesthetic gas, he was to long remember those hypnotic eyes. Of a strange flake-gold quality, they seemed to move restlessly, as though continually stirred by tiny winds.

Others saw Doc and the hairy fellow who was beside him. They tried to get up their guns, to fire at the two. But their arms were suddenly sluggish with leaden weight, and the guns sagged and they all started falling down.

Only Pinky, the big leader in the long raincoat, had had presence of mind enough to leap backward when the gas pellets started exploding beneath his feet.

He streaked through the front hallway, reached the outer door and slammed out into the night.

They tried to fire at Monk and Doc—but their arms were suddenly sluggish with leaden weight, and they started falling down.

Monk followed, looking like some sort of apish monster in his face mask.

But by the time Monk reached the front porch, the big man had faded into the gloom somewhere along the walls of the mammoth dam. The purpose of his long, dark raincoat was obvious. It blended perfectly with the night.

Monk yanked from beneath his coat a peculiar-looking automatic pistol with a drumlike magazine. It was one of the mercy pistols that all Doc Savage aides carried. The weapon made bull-fiddle roars in the quiet night as Monk pressed the trigger.

He aimed the gun in the general direction that the escaping man had taken.

Beside him, his mask now off, Doc Savage said quietly, "He's probably escaped. We'd better take care of these others."

But the assorted thugs lying on the living room floor seemed to be well taken care of. All but one were asleep. The man who wasn't was out in the hallway staggering around. He stared out of bleared eyes as Doc and Monk came back into the house.

He tried to blurt, "What… how—"

Doc said, "You fellows should have checked more carefully on the girl's handwriting before leaving that note."

Monk indicated a room across the hallway. The door to the room was closed.

"We'd better see if Hardrock Hennesey is all right," the chemist suggested.

He and the bronze man had not put on their gas masks again, for the yellowish substance had now disappeared. Its effectiveness only lasted a moment or so.

Doc nodded, glancing at the fellow who was still swaying on his feet before them.

Monk grinned. He said to the man, "Planting them danged gas pellets was a bright idea, fella. Only we just changed them around a little bit so *you'd* get them instead of us!"

Then he let go with a fist that put the man asleep temporarily. Monk carried the man into the living room and dumped him beside his pals.

From the doorway of the room that had been closed across the hall, a thin, leathery-faced man with intense gray eyes appeared. His jaw stuck out like a block of cement and he looked like a taut length of tough piano wire.

Hardrock Hennesey!

Hardrock Hennesey growled, "Where's the damned cuss who slugged me?"

Chapter VI
"J.L."

HARDROCK HENNESEY was the sort of individual who had knocked around the universe long enough to become accustomed to surprises.

And so he looked Monk over briefly. He made no comments about the chemist's homely features. Hardrock, himself, would have taken no beauty prizes.

He did, however, stare at Doc Savage for a moment. The bronze man's remarkable physique caused Hardrock Hennesey's intense gray eyes to widen imperceptibly. But all he said was:

"Thanks for the help, Doc Savage. How the hell did you guys work it?" He waved a hand toward the living room. "Those birds had a nice trap all set for you."

"That," the bronze man explained, "was quite evident from the forged handwriting in Chick Lancaster's note. So we merely rearranged the gas pellets that had been planted in the rug. We put you and the other man in a safe spot, and then waited for results after pretending we had fallen down and been knocked out."

Hardrock shook his head. "Not bad, not bad," he commented.

He led the way back into the room from which he'd appeared. It was a dining room in which Doc and Monk had placed Hardrock and the dam superintendent upon finding them unconscious in the living room.

The superintendent was a tall, wiry man with sunburned features. He was just struggling to his feet when they came into the room.

Hardrock explained that the two persons with him were Doc Savage and a fellow named Monk. It appeared the super's name was Flynn, and he was still mystified as to why he and Hardrock Hennesey had been seized by the gunmen.

Doc directed the tying up of the unconscious men while he made a brief explanation.

"It is obvious," he said, "that someone has an idea that Hardrock Hennesey, here, knows something about a mystery which seems to be centered with this tunnel project."

The hard-boiled little tunnel worker straightened up from where he was tying up a man.

"The hell you say!" he blurted. His eyes were puzzled. "Sure, some damn funny things happened tonight, but that doesn't say they have anything to do with this tunnel job. If they do, I don't know what it's all about."

"The package might explain a whole lot of things," said Doc.

"Package?"

"The package you found in the farmer's car, addressed to me."

HARDROCK jumped. "That's right. Almost forgot about it. But it was gone when I came back!"

"Any idea where it might be?"

The mucker's ageless, leathery face was thoughtful.

"Hell, no!"

Flynn, the superintendent, also had a question.

"How," he wanted to know, "do you happen to be involved in this thing, Doc Savage?"

Monk, too, had a question. His small, bright eyes swung on the bronze man.

"Blazes, Doc!" he piped shrilly. "That's something I was gonna ask you, too? How did you know what was going on up at this blasted place?"

For a brief instant, the bronze man's flake-gold eyes met Monk's. The others missed the glance. But the chemist suddenly understood that there would be an explanation later, when they were alone.

Doc said, "The first thing to do is lock these captives up. We will question them later."

Tall, bony Flynn stepped to a phone, put through a call to the special police. It was this division of the police that did patrol duty on the various shafts in the great tunnel project.

Leaving Flynn to take charge of the trussed-up captives, Doc led the way back to where he had parked his car. He and Monk were accompanied by tough little Hardrock Hennesey.

Hardrock rapped, "By damn, I'm mad!" He massaged a bruise that was on the side of his protruding jaw. "Wait'll I get hold of the geezer that conked me!"

Monk had opened the car door. He turned.

"While you're waiting," he remarked, "maybe you can tell us some more about what happened?"

Hardrock Hennesey had suddenly stiffened. "Say!" he exploded.

"Well?" Monk prodded, watching the tunnel man.

Hardrock was tugging at something in his pocket. "Here's something I *did* find." His gaze swung to the bronze man. "Maybe you'll be interested in it, Doc Savage."

Monk had opened the rear door of Doc's sedan, and the man squatted on the floor there raised up and shoved the gun muzzle in the hairy chemist's face.

"Let's get interested in *this!*" he snarled.

IN the moment that the shadowy figure spoke, Doc Savage whirled into blinding motion. His swinging arm knocked Monk to one side. His left hand caught Hardrock Hennesey in the same instant and pushed him into a tumbling heap down beside the car.

The gun blasted almost in the bronze giant's face.

But in reality, the shot was lower than that, and the slug hit the bulletproof garment that Doc Savage was wearing beneath his clothing. It merely staggered Doc Savage a little.

Astounded, the gunman within the car had been disconcerted for a moment. In that second Doc Savage slapped the gun from the man's fist, seized him by the neck, dragged him out onto the ground.

Monk, howling with rage, took over.

Though the captive was well over six feet, solid and as strong as a bull, hairy Monk slapped the man around until he was weaving on his feet.

The fellow fell down. Monk picked him up, hit him again, held him from falling and snorted, "Brother, now you're gonna answer a few questions!"

The car headlamps were turned on and the captive dragged around in front of the machine.

Monk swore. "You!" he piped.

It was Pinky, the big fellow in the long raincoat. He glared at the chemist, then belched.

Hardrock Hennesey let out a yell and leaped for Pinky.

"That's the punk who slugged me!" Hardrock said. "Let me—"

Doc Savage warned, "Wait! Perhaps this fellow can answer some of our questions."

The bronze man's unusual eyes were trained on the captive, who stood a little apart from them, distinctively revealed by the headlamp glare.

His lips curled. "Nuts!" he said.

Monk grinned.

"Wait a minute, Doc," he started to say. "I'm just gonna—"

The shot from up the hillside beside them was a flat, menacing sound in the hot night. Everyone whirled, but above them there was only the uncertain gloom of the embankment that rose for perhaps a hundred feet above the newly constructed dam.

It sounded like the crack of a rifle, and it was not repeated. But all knew that anyone could have hidden up there at the top of the embankment, fired the shot, then slid off into the night.

Each had jumped clear of the headlights' revealing glow. Monk and Hardrock Hennesey had started to dive toward the hillside. Then they drew up short at the sound that suddenly floated in the night air.

It was a trilling—soft, almost musical; it was difficult to locate the source of the unusual tone.

But Monk recognized it. It was an unconscious thing the bronze man did in moments of mental stress—or perhaps surprise.

Monk whirled toward Doc—and stared.

Their captive, the big, sneering fellow known as Pinky, was swaying back and forth like a man dizzy with the heat. Even as Monk watched, Pinky's legs seemed to give out beneath him and he collapsed to his knees. He was clutching his stomach. From his knees he lurched forward onto his face, groaned once, then lay still.

Doc Savage bent forward. Light revealed the red liquid on the fallen man's back. The rifle slug had entered there, gone clean through the big man's body. He was dead.

Doc Savage straightened, ordered, "Monk, carry him back to the house. Tell Flynn what happened. Then hurry back here."

A quick search of the dead man's pockets revealed that he carried nothing that would identify him—or show for whom he was working.

While Monk was gone, Doc Savage and Hardrock Hennesey climbed the hillside, searched for any clue to Pinky's slayer. Fifty feet back from the top of the embankment, they found where a car had been parked. The tire marks of the machine showed that the rubber was too well worn to leave any kind of identifying tracks. There was no trace of the car or the one who had driven it.

Five minutes later, when Monk had returned, they were driving back toward Shaft 9.

Doc, at the wheel of the car, turned to Hardrock Hennesey. "You said there was something you had found," he prodded. "What?"

Hardrock nodded, reached into his pocket. What he brought out was something embedded in a piece of rocklike substance. It was quite hideous.

It was the shape of a hand, and it had claws.

DOC had stopped the car momentarily. He was examining the object as Hardrock explained.

"Found that down in Shaft 9," Hardrock said. "It's a claw that can be used to slip over the hand. Like brass knuckles, in a way, but damned if I ever seen anything quite like that."

It was Doc who said, "A form of fighting weapon used hundreds of years ago." He looked briefly at Hardrock. "You say you found it down in the tunnel?"

The tough little mucker jerked his head.

"Damned right I did. An' something else."

"What?" Monk demanded.

"Evidence that the new tunnel has passed through something damned peculiar down there!" Hardrock offered. "Something that looks like an old ocean floor. People must have lived down there thousands of years ago."

Monk scratched his head. "You been drinking?" he prodded.

Hardrock snorted.

"Wish I had!" the mucker exclaimed. "Wait'll I show you some other stuff I found."

They proceeded to Shaft 9. They located Renny, and the giant-sized engineer reported, "I think I've got the workmen talked into returning to their jobs. But not until morning. They're all upset by what's happened tonight."

Monk stared around. "But where are they now?"

Renny looked worried.

"Searching for the girl," he announced in his booming voice. "She's missing."

Hardrock Hennesey stuck out his jaw. "If anything happens to Chick, I'll cut the throat of the guy—"

Monk's eyes had narrowed. "Hey!" he exclaimed. "Is Ham still with her?"

"He was," Renny replied.

Hardrock frowned. "Who's this guy Ham?" he demanded.

"A shyster!" hairy Monk announced. "Betcha he's already got that girl Chick convinced—"

Doc Savage interrupted with, "Renny can stay up here and operate the lift machinery. Also, he can watch for the girl or Ham. We'd better get started."

Just as they reached the huge bucket that would lower them swiftly below ground, Monk remembered the mysterious gray stuff that was like fog, the thing they had encountered down in the tunnel.

He mentioned it to Doc.

But Doc Savage indicated the masks he had brought along from his car. "We'll have to take that chance," he said.

Hardrock was already in the bucket with Doc Savage. Monk followed, looking somewhat worried.

He said, "Doc, I think we're taking an awful—"

The bronze man had just straightened up from picking up something off the floor of the shaft lift. What he held was a girl's small handkerchief. In one corner were the two initials, "J.L."

"Jane!" Hardrock Hennesey cried.

"Jane who?" Monk asked.

"Lancaster. That's Chick's handkerchief. Her correct name is Jane!"

Monk grinned. He no longer appeared worried about going below.

"Come on," he piped, "I just want to see that blasted shyster Ham!"

But what they were to find was something else again.

Chapter VII
STRANGE WORLD

AT the base of the great shaft, they stood listening a few moments. They had seen no trace of the peculiar grayish fog upon stepping from the steel bucket.

There was something awesome, something tremendous, about being down here fifteen hundred feet beneath the Earth's surface. Curved walls hemmed them in. The tunnel stretched right and left like the yawning, dark mouth of a Gargantuan serpent.

Except for the distant whisper of air being pumped down through the ventilating system, there was an abysmal silence, profound, sort of chilling.

Monk shrugged off the creepy feeling, grinned and said, "Well, Hardrock, where do we start looking for the rest of this antique claw of yours?"

Hardrock Hennesey had been listening intently. He moved to the tunnel wall, pressed his ear flat against the surface for a moment. His leathery face screwed up and he appeared thoughtful.

"Funny!" he commented.

Monk watched him. "What's funny?"

"I don't think there's anybody down here," Hardrock said. He looked at Doc Savage. "And yet there was Chick's handkerchief!"

Monk muttered, "Wait'll I get that guy Ham!"

Doc said nothing for a moment. Then, quietly, "Why would the girl come down here?"

Hardrock Hennesey shrugged. "She has the run of this place. Maybe she and that Ham discovered something. Or"—Hardrock's intense gray eyes looked worried—"maybe they've been tricked!"

"That occurred to me," was Doc's significant remark.

It was a toss-up as to which way they should go. As Hardrock explained, "I was talking to one of the miners earlier. The south bore from here extends three miles; the north bore almost four. If they *are* down here, they might have gone either way."

Doc nodded. "Which way to the place where you found this?"

The bronze man indicated the hand with the claw, which the little tunnel worker had turned over to him.

"Back here," Hardrock said, indicating the north extension of the tunnel behind them.

Doc suggested that they might as well proceed that way first. At least, they would investigate the thing Hardrock Hennesey had located.

The bronze man was using one of his flashlights, though the tunnel itself was dimly lighted by the electric bulbs. Doc's eyes explored the floor of the big tunnel as they walked along.

Behind them and before them, their footsteps made weird sounds as they echoed and reverberated through the tunnel. When anyone spoke, the words went trailing away into the distance, echoing like strange voices from a netherworld.

Each man carried a gas mask, held ready in case the uncanny-looking fog should be seen again. But they saw no trace of it.

As Hardrock explained, "Dammit, I've been working in tunnels for thirty years. Never saw anything quite like it either above or belowground. You could see through it, and yet you couldn't. You just imagined you could!"

Doc Savage said nothing. His alert eyes were constantly probing ahead. His ears were sharp for the slightest foreign sound.

Once Monk exclaimed, "Blazes! This looks about where I slammed my head into that blasted wall. Wait a minute!"

The chemist moved to the side of the tunnel, started a search. He remembered where he had seen the running thugs. He looked around for several moments as Doc and Hardrock Hennesey waited.

Scratching his head, he joined them again. "Maybe I was having hallucinations!" Monk remarked.

They continued. They covered perhaps a mile of underground passageway. They saw nothing, heard no one moving ahead.

It was just about this point that Doc Savage picked up the object off the tunnel floor.

Monk stared. "Gollywockus!" he piped.

Hardrock Hennesey squinted and couldn't believe his eyes.

What Doc Savage held was a spearlike weapon that was like nothing Monk had ever seen. It was made of stone that was harder than flint. It was crude. It looked like a weapon that might have been used in the era of cliff dwellers.

Doc held the spear up before the flashlight glare, and all saw what he indicated.

There was blood on the head of the spear, and it was still moist.

DOC SAVAGE stood looking at the strange weapon, his eyebrows slightly knitted together. It was Hardrock who said:

"Somebody's been struck—and with *that!*" His eyes were wide. "But who—what *kind* of person would use an implement like that?"

Monk blurted, "Maybe a cave dweller!"

"Don't be crazy!" Hardrock started to say. And then he stared, his eyes getting wider. "Say! Do you really think—"

Doc interrupted them.

"Perhaps we should look farther into the tunnel," he suggested.

Monk was first to lead the way. His homely features were worried-looking. He piped shrilly, "Blast it! Maybe Ham and the girl are hurt!"

That appeared to be the thought of all as they quickened their pace and hurried through the seemingly endless eighteen-foot bore that passed through the Earth. A muck-car track stretched through the entire length.

Even at the fast pace they were traveling, it was some time before they reached the northern end of the bore. Then they came upon the mucking machines and equipment near the tunnel head. There was evidence that the miners and muckers who had worked here had walked off the job in a hurry. A "powder monkey" had left a case of dynamite lying dangerously in the open, near the tracks where the muck cars passed. Drills and jackhammers had been dropped and lay carelessly about.

In the tunnel head itself, work had been hastily stopped, and the huge platform where the drillers had been working was strewn with tools.

Strangely, they had passed no one, seen no moving thing.

Monk stared at Doc Savage. He exclaimed,

"Goshamighty, *somebody* musta got hurt with that spear. But where is he? An' who *did* it?"

Apparently there was no answer for that.

DOC SAVAGE moved among the machinery and equipment located here at the tunnel head. His eyes flashed over things briefly. He obviously found nothing that startled him.

Doc's eyes were thoughtful, though, when he came back to Hardrock and Monk. He looked at the little tunnel worker.

"You were going to show us where you found that hand with the claw," Doc reminded.

Hardrock gave a slight start. "That's right!" he exclaimed. "Forgot all about it when we found that spear. Come on."

He led the way back through the tunnel bore. Following him, Monk gave the bronze man a questioning glance. The glance said that perhaps this Hardrock Hennesey was not a person to be trusted.

But the expression in the bronze giant's eyes told Monk nothing.

A quarter of a mile back through the tunnel, Hardrock paused, studying the rock walls. This was a section that had not yet been cemented over, as the entire tunnel would be before completion.

"Let's have that light," Hardrock asked, indicating Doc's flashlight.

Taking it, he sprayed the powerful light ray up along the curved wall. About on a level with his head, he held the light beam steady for a moment on the wall surface. Then he moved it back and forth slowly in a horizontal plane.

"Do you see that?" he prodded.

Doc Savage had stepped closer. He was examining the vein of earth revealed by the moving light. Then he was digging into the rock substance with his powerful fingers.

A piece of stuff that looked like sand turned to rock came loose. The bronze man studied it intently. A bit of substance crumbled beneath the great strength of his crushing fingers. Something like a small, petrified shell dropped into the bronze giant's palm.

Doc said thoughtfully, "It appears that, hundreds of years ago, this level down here was originally the Earth's surface. This was the original sea level."

Hardrock Hennesey jerked his head. "That's what I figured!" he cried. "And this is just about where I found the claw thing."

Monk was a chemist, not an archaeologist. He stared, blurted a question.

"Doc! You mean people used to *live* here in this blasted place?"

"When it was the Earth's surface," Doc said. "That was before the Glacial period, before this whole area was changed by some earth movement."

Monk breathed, "Golly!"

Hardrock put in, "They've found such a situation on other water tunnel jobs. On one leading into New York City, down about a thousand feet they found where elm trees—or trees like them—had once been growing. People must have lived there at one time."

Monk looked at the clawed-hand thing protruding from the bronze man's pocket, and his little eyes bulged.

"Kind of spooky!" he said.

But not more spine-chilling than the horrible, weird cry that came from somewhere ahead of them. Drifting through the miles of underground tunnel, it gained volume, was magnified into a dreadful scream of terror.

It was Hardrock Hennesey who said in almost a whisper, "It... it sounds like a guy... *dying!"*

THEY ran for ten minutes toward the source of the cry. The sound came once again, closer this time. There seemed to be more of a dreadful wail to the sound.

Monk was sweat-soaked. He wiped at his brow as he ran. "Whew!" he complained. "Thought it was cool down here a little while ago. But I'm dang-blasted hot now!"

Even the bronze man's metallic features were beaded with moisture, though Doc showed no other effect of the race through the tunnel. He was well ahead of the others. And thus it was that he was first to draw up short and call out a warning.

"Watch out!" Doc Savage rapped.

Monk and Hardrock Hennesey shortly flung to a stop behind him. Both stared ahead.

Monk, puzzled, piped shrilly, "What is it? I don't see anything."

"Watch!" said Doc.

And then, slowly, the thing became obvious to the others. Monk squinted, and Hardrock Hennesey seemed to give a slight shudder.

He cried, "The fog!"

It didn't look like a fog, at first. Drifting slowly, sort of translucent, the stuff might have been a mirage. It floated like thin morning mist on a mountain top.

Monk's small eyes were straining. He suddenly yelled. "Doc! There's somebody *moving* in that stuff!"

But Doc Savage had already seen. He whipped out an order.

"Hold your gas masks in readiness!"

The bronze man, his own mask in his hand, moved forward with blurred speed.

And as suddenly he stopped, as though he had smashed into a solid wall of rock. He backed up slowly. Ahead of him, the opaque substance slowly became a solid mass of grayness.

The opaque substance became a solid mass of grayness and intense heat against the faces of Doc and Monk and Hennesey!

Doc motioned Monk and Hardrock Hennesey back. All were aware now of an extreme heat that beat against their faces, that caused their hands to smart. The heat quickly grew more intense.

They kept moving backward, staring, and Monk understood why he had been perspiring so a moment earlier. It was *this*—some uncanny thing that was unapproachable.

Hardrock cried, "It… it was like that where the farmer died. It's the same thing!"

Doc Savage's eyes were intent. They tried again to locate the object that he had seen moving within the mass. But he could not see beyond the gray pall.

They all heard the scream.

Frantic, utterly terrible, it held them rigid a moment. And then the stuff was pressing closer, driving them still farther backward. They were helpless before its searing heat.

They were helpless to aid whoever was *within* that death fog.

It was Hardrock Hennesey who yelled. "Somebody's dying in there!"

Doc did not answer. He made an attempt to move forward, but was literally hurled back by the fiery heat that lay ahead.

And then, for the first time, Hardrock Hennesey showed fear. He grabbed the bronze man's arm, pointed toward the gray wall that blocked them off.

"Listen!" he screamed. "What'll we do? That's *the only way out of here!"*

Monk rapped, "As if we don't know it!"

It was obvious that they were trapped.

Chapter VIII
ESCAPE

THE gray-looking substance continued to spread, and Doc Savage, Monk and Hardrock Hennesey were forced to keep retreating. But after a while the fog stopped moving, remaining motionless in the air. It hung there like smoke trapped in a small pipe.

The bronze man's eyes flickered. "Perhaps now," he said quietly, "we can escape."

Monk gulped. "Escape! How? Not through that stuff!"

Doc directed that the two were to wait for him. They were to remain clear of the death fog. He would return as quickly as possible.

Doc left them, running back toward the northern end of the tunnel.

"What's he going to do?" Hardrock Hennesey asked, worried.

Monk shrugged. "No tellin' what Doc's ever going to do. We'll just have to wait."

They waited in grim silence, their eyes on the motionless gray fog, a hundred feet down the tunnel away from them.

Once Monk remarked, "I'm gonna blast that guy if we ever get outta here!"

"Who?"

"Ham. Betcha he's already got a date with that Chick Lancaster!"

Hardrock said nothing. He looked at Monk, scowled. They sat there with their chins cupped in their hands and thought about dying. Neither could see how they could possibly escape from here.

Doc Savage's return gave them both somewhat of a start.

It did not seem possible that the bronze man could have run to the tunnel head and back so swiftly. Doc was not even breathing hard.

But a rigid, two-hour daily set of scientific exercises kept the bronze giant in perfect condition at all times. The exercises had been followed since childhood. In fact, the bronze man's entire life was the result of scientific training.

Hardrock Hennesey jumped up and stared at the object the bronze man was carrying. "What're you going to do with that?" he prodded.

For answer, Doc passed a length of wire to the hard-boiled little tunnel man. "Get this ready," he directed swiftly.

What Doc held was a stick of dynamite. Hardrock was preparing the fuse and wire that would be strung to that single piece of dynamite.

Monk looked worried.

"Blazes!" he piped. "You'll blow us to hell and gone, Doc!"

"There's hardly enough here for that," explained Doc.

Ordering them to stand back, and putting on his mask, Doc ran forward toward the fog screen that blocked them in the tunnel. He approached as close as possible to the stuff, set the dynamite stick, played out the wire as he returned.

Then he ordered, "You'd better lie down."

In the next moment, Doc set off the blast.

For seconds afterward, Monk was certain that the tunnel walls were smashing down all around them. But then he discovered it was only the terrific racket shattering against his eardrums. The detonation went rolling back and forth through the bore. Dust blinded their eyes. And then, finally, there was silence.

They stared toward the fog stuff. It was gone. The tunnel was clear.

Doc Savage led the way. They passed what had once been the body of a man. Doc Savage motioned them on, as he paused momentarily to examine the victim.

There was not the slightest chance of recognition. The man's head, legs and arms were missing as a result of the explosion. But there was enough of his clothing left to reveal that he must have been a tunnel worker, probably sent down here to look for them, but who had been caught in the death mist.

Ten minutes later they were aboveground.

And there, with giant Renny, they found Chick Lancaster and well-dressed Ham.

MONK howled with rage.

"You blasted shyster! What's the idea of walking out on me?"

Ham smiled coolly. With him were the two pets, Habeas and Chemistry.

"Who ran out on *who?"* Ham demanded. He smiled fondly at the girl. "I've been helping Chick, here, search for Hardrock."

The girl's pretty blue-green eyes, seeing Monk's frown, looked worried. She touched Ham's arm.

"Careful," she cautioned. "He has a mean look on his face!"

The lawyer grimaced. "That's no mean look," he said, "that's his face!"

Doc Savage had been talking to Renny and Hardrock Hennesey. He left them to come over to the girl.

Chick Lancaster's pretty face was suddenly flushed, and she was looking at the giant bronze man out of admiring eyes. All women fell hard the first time they ever met Doc Savage. All learned, later, that Doc avoided falling in love with a girl.

It wasn't because he wasn't human, or because he didn't have a heart. For Doc, with all his scientific training, had as much feeling as the next man. But he controlled those emotions. He believed that because of his dangerous career—that of righting wrongs and punishing evildoers—he should never ask a girl to share that existence with him.

And so, now, he merely nodded to lovely Chick Lancaster and said, "We have been trying to find you. There is something which you can explain."

The red-haired girl gave a little sigh. She felt suddenly somewhat self-conscious standing before this unusual person.

"Explain?" she asked. "Explain what?"

"Why you wrote to the governor of this State?"

Monk and Ham looked quickly at the bronze man. This was the first they had heard about Doc Savage having previous information about Chick Lancaster.

The girl was startled.

"You… knew… *that?"* she said.

Doc nodded. He turned his steady gaze to Monk. "That's why the phony note from Pinky and his gang did not fool me. It was not in this girl's handwriting."

Monk looked puzzled.

"But how did you get hold of *her* letter, Doc?" he asked.

"From the governor of the State. It was sent to me." Doc looked back at Chick. "You wrote to the governor telling him of trouble that was happening here. You hinted at something mysterious."

Monk got in another question before the girl could reply.

"Doc, you mean the governor *asked* you to investigate?"

Doc nodded again. "The request," he said, "was sent to me several days ago."

It was something that surprised everyone. It convinced them that there was something of utmost importance connected with the mystery. But what, they did not yet know.

Doc was waiting for the girl's answer. She suddenly stared past them all, looked at the man who was approaching. She said:

"Perhaps my brother can explain better than I."

RAYMOND LANCASTER was a man about forty, with flame-red hair and freckles, and eyes that were as sharp as flint steel. For obvious reasons, he was usually called Reds. He was one of the leading engineers on this new water tunnel job.

Reds Lancaster had already met big Renny, who literally towered above the man's small, wiry figure. Lancaster was introduced to the others, informed of Doc Savage's request. He suggested that all adjourn to one of the nearby buildings.

A few moments later, he was explaining:

"Trouble started as soon as we began work on the dam."

"What dam?" Monk put in. He was holding Habeas in one arm, scratching the pig's ear with his hand.

"Yellow River Dam. There were accidents. More than the usual amount." Reds Lancaster, as he talked, played with some sort of chain that held an engineering society key. The chain dangled from the pocket of his expensive whipcord breeches. He was dressed in similar fashion to his sister, Chick Lancaster. "But accidents are a thing you can try to prevent. They are something real."

He stopped jiggling the chain, and the key on it hung straight down, motionless. "But this mystery that happened tonight, this other thing… well, it's uncanny. How *can* you fight a thing like that?"

Doc asked: "Have you any theories at all?"

The wiry, alert little engineer was thoughtful a moment. Then he jerked his head. "Yes."

"What?"

"I think it is a direct blow at the governor of this State. I think the whole thing has something to do with him. Call it a menace against his career. Someone is trying to ruin him."

Ham, Monk, Hardrock Hennesey and big Renny stared at the red-headed engineer.

Ham said sharply, "That doesn't make sense! What has the appearance of a mysterious fog, the finding of mummified men, got to do with the governor?"

"That," said Reds Lancaster quietly, "is what we have to figure out." His eyes looked suddenly tired. "This stuff about mummies and weird fogs is nonsense. It *has* to be!"

Monk snorted suddenly. "Yeah?" he demanded shrilly. "Well, brother, just wait until *you* get into some of that stuff!"

Someone looked at Hardrock Hennesey. "How about it, Hardrock? You had a narrow escape?"

All had heard by now about the tough little tunnel worker being trapped by the fog at the gas station. Hardrock had not explained how he had escaped death at that time.

He took a hitch at the overalls that were too large for him, said, "Pinky and those mugs of his grabbed me just before I almost burned up from the heat of that stuff. They put my clothes on that dead farmer's body and left him there in my place. They wanted to make it look like it was me."

He indicated the clothes he was wearing. "That's why I'm wearing that dead guy's clothes."

"Why did they want you?" Ham put in.

"Because they thought I had a package that had been addressed to Doc Savage."

Monk frowned. "Didn't *they* have it?"

Hardrock shook his head

"Hell, no! It's just disappeared, and no one knows where it is."

Everyone had suddenly started talking at once. It was the bronze man's voice that halted them.

"Just a minute," he said quietly.

He looked at Renny. "Monk and Ham will remain with you. Get all workmen back on their jobs first thing this morning. You might call in the mine police to help patrol the tunnels and shafts. Hardrock can help. Perhaps he can learn something."

Doc looked at the engineer, Reds Lancaster. "You'll cooperate?"

"Certainly. We're losing thousands of dollars a day on this job. We've got to find out what's wrong!"

Renny said in his booming voice, "What are you going to do, Doc?"

"It appears," said the bronze man, "that an interview with the governor might be advisable. I should be back here by tomorrow."

Doc explained a few more things he wished his aides to do. He started for the door.

Someone exclaimed, "Where's the girl?"

Chick Lancaster, it turned out, had left. No one knew where she had gone.

Doc Savage went out into the cool, damp air of early morning. Gray sky was showing in the east, beyond the buildings of Shaft 9.

He went back to his big limousine and swung open the door. He had a long drive ahead, and there was need for hurry.

Chick Lancaster, looking bright and excited, sat in the front seat of the bronze man's car.

She said, "I'm going with you. There's something you should know about."

Chapter IX
TRAIL TO TROUBLE

APPROXIMATELY five miles north of Yellow River Dam, Doc Savage became aware that another car was following him and the girl.

For the past mile they had been winding through the narrow, steep grades that passed over mountainous country which cut off a valley beyond. It was necessary to reach that valley before the main State road would be encountered. Once reached, the main highway should take them to the capitol in two or three hours.

But now, through the trees behind them, Doc caught an occasional glimpse of the trailing car. He picked up speed. The other car did likewise. He slowed down. The trailing car fell back.

Doc looked at Chick Lancaster and said quietly. "We might have a little trouble, unless you can stand a lot of speed."

"Trouble?"

The bronze man nodded to the rearview mirror. "We are being trailed."

For two long moments, the girl's blue-green eyes watched the mirror. Then she spoke quietly.

"I think you're right."

Threat of danger didn't seem to terrify this girl as it might some women.

"We can get away from them," Doc said confidently, and he opened the car up.

And what Chick Lancaster observed in the next few moments was a demonstration of driving that astounded her. The road wound and reversed and dipped up and down steep grades. Doc drove almost with relaxation, and yet at speeds that were terrific.

Ten minutes later, the girl looked across at him, grinned and commented, "That's that. We've lost them."

They were now climbing an unusually steep grade that swung over the last remaining hillside before the valley beyond.

Doc started to say, "Someone apparently—"

He paused, his gaze flicking to the dashboard of the car. The car was slowing. It sputtered, came to a stop partway up the hill.

Chick Lancaster's eyes were wide. She had followed the bronze man's gaze to the dashboard needle indicator.

"We're out of gas!" she exclaimed.

"It seems," Doc added, "that someone figured it out carefully. They left just enough gas in the tank so that we would get stalled in this hilly country."

Behind them, at the start of the hill, a car motor roared. It was the sedan that had been following them.

Doc, tense, was suddenly giving swift directions to the girl. As he talked, he yanked up door handles that locked the doors from inside. He did this to all but the door beside him.

"You'll remain in the car," Doc said hurriedly. "There is no possible way they can reach you. You'll be safe."

"But—!"

"I'll be back."

Doc Savage reached into a compartment that was located in the dash. He removed a package that was about the size of a one-pound box of chocolates. Slipping the package beneath his coat, he stepped out of the car.

For the first time, the red-haired girl looked scared.

"Please!" she exclaimed.

Doc's words were clipped. "Lock the door after me!" he ordered. "You'll not be harmed. *Don't try to leave the car.*"

He slammed the door behind him, heard the door handle lock as the girl pushed it up from inside.

He also heard the slugs that whined close as he disappeared into the surrounding woods.

Heads were protruding from the big sedan. A man was aiming a pistol and firing in the direction the bronze giant had taken.

The driver of the trailing car—a beefy fellow with a heavy, unshaven face—brought the machine to a stop fifty feet beyond the bronze man's car.

HE said, "What the hell!"

There were four other men in the machine beside the driver. They looked like the kind of individuals employed in dock strikes.

All were carrying guns, and all raced toward the bronze man's car.

The beefy man laughed harshly. "Some guy, this Doc Savage. He ran off and left the dame!"

He grabbed the car door handle. Then he stared. The handle would not budge.

He rapped on the window, glaring at the girl seated inside the machine. "Open up!"

For answer, Chick Lancaster coolly thumbed her nose at the big fellow who needed a shave.

With a snort of rage, the big man backed off, raised his gun and fired at the car window. He fired high enough that the shot would go over the girl's head, but at least it would scare her into unlocking the car doors.

Instead, the five thugs themselves got a shock. The tiniest of marks appeared on the window as a result of the slug striking. The glass did not even web.

The big leader tried shooting at another window. He got the same results.

With a curse, he waved a fist at the girl inside the car.

She merely returned his glare.

Suddenly, one of the other men grabbed the burly fellow's arm. "Hey!" he yelled. "Maybe this is a trick. They say that Doc Savage is pretty smart."

That seemed to hold them all rigid. They swung, stared toward the woods where Doc Savage had vanished.

"Spread out!" the leader rapped. "That bronze guy's in there *some* place. Get him!"

With guns held ready, all five men advanced on the woods across the road. Shortly they disappeared beneath the enshrouding foliage.

From behind the protection of the bulletproof car windows, Chick Lancaster watched.

And five minutes later she heard the roar of guns and the yelling and the wild trampling of underbrush. Men came tumbling out onto the road, piled back into the sedan parked behind Doc's car. The burly-looking fellow was last to appear. He leaped behind the wheel of the car, got the motor started, and almost yanked out the clutch as he sent the car racing up the hill.

None of the men seemed any longer interested in Chick Lancaster. The only thing that apparently worried them was to escape with their lives.

A moment later, black, dense smoke billowed out of the woods at the point where the five men had emerged. It was blinding stuff that shut off Chick Lancaster's view of the spot.

As she stared, a figure appeared out of the black cloud.

It was Doc Savage.

The girl opened the car door, exclaimed. "Mercy! What has happened?"

"They thought the smoke things were bombs," Doc said. "We have succeeded in reversing the game of trailing one another."

"Trailing?" The girl's pretty eyes were puzzled. "You mean you are going to trail *them?*"

Doc nodded. He was now busy taking a two-gallon can from the rear section of the limousine. It was a can of gasoline.

Chick Lancaster climbed out and watched Doc Savage as he dumped the gas into the tank.

"But how?" she demanded. "How do you ever expect to trail them? They'll be miles from here by the time we get to the State road and get more gas."

Doc finished dumping in the gas, put the can away, climbed behind the wheel. From beneath the dashboard of the car he swung out what looked like a small aerial direction-finder. He turned a switch, waited a moment, then said, "Listen."

The series of signals came from a small boxlike

affair located near the small aerial. As Doc Savage started up the car he explained:

"Those signals are coming from a small short-wave transmitter placed in their car. We should be able to trail them."

Amazement was mirrored in the blue-green depths of the girl's wide eyes.

"But how in the world did you work that?"

"While they were trying to get into this car, the device was planted in their own. In the trunk on the rear."

Chick Lancaster recalled the package Doc had removed before leaving the car.

"The candy box?"

"Yes."

Chick Lancaster sat back on the seat and heard the steady signals coming from the car far ahead and decided that this bronze man was a fellow worth knowing.

FACTORY whistles were blowing for the noon lunch hour when Doc Savage passed through the outskirts of the State capital. The steady stream of signals were still coming from the small box located in his car.

Chick Lancaster said, "Why would they be coming *here?"*

"It might be interesting to find out," offered Doc.

They had seen no trace of the car, and yet, by following the signals emanating from the device which the bronze man had placed in the trunk of the other car, they had been able to keep the other machine within reach. From the intensity of the signals, Doc Savage judged that the other machine was not more than a mile ahead of them.

They passed through city traffic, came to a wide boulevard that led into the heart of the city. Far down its length was the golden, shining dome of the capitol building.

The girl's eyes widened. "Do you think," she asked, "they would be going there?"

Doc's eyes were thoughtful. "We'll see."

For a moment, the signals faded. Then they picked them up again. The bronze man frowned slightly. At the next intersection, he swung right, proceeded for three squares. The signals were stronger again. Doc turned left on a through highway that passed out of the city.

"I guess those men aren't stopping here after all," the girl said.

Doc drove in silence. Shortly they were passing an exclusive section of large estates. Houses became more scattered. What few there were appeared only briefly through the trees of broad, sweeping lawns.

The road curved. High stone walls replaced hedges and lawns. It was impossible to see the homes now.

The signals suddenly became very strong in their ears. Doc's unusual flake-gold eyes were sharp. When the signals suddenly started to fade again, he slowed the car and turned around in the roadway.

The girl looked at Doc.

"What is it?" she wanted to know.

"We have passed the other car."

"But there was no side road, no place where they could have turned off!" the girl exclaimed.

DOC was proceeding slowly along the road. Directly before the entranceway of a huge estate, the signals became strongest, Doc noted the name of the estate as he swung the car into the graveled drive that wound beneath old elms.

Chick Lancaster suddenly gave a start.

"Do you know what place this *is?"* she exclaimed.

Doc nodded.

"The home of Governor Bullock," said the bronze man quietly.

"But—"

Doc held up his hand, indicated the huge house of block stone ahead. The gravel drive swung beneath a porte cochere of the house. The signals were still plain in Doc's car.

But there was no sign of a machine parked before the governor's mansion.

Doc drew up, stepped out of the car and mounted the steps. There was a screen door; beyond this a door which stood open. The man lying on the hall floor behind the screen door was moaning and trying to get to his feet.

Doc Savage flung the door open, hurried into the hall, was quickly helping the heavy man to his feet. The costume of the man showed that he was a butler.

There was a nasty red welt on the butler's forehead. For a moment he stared dazedly at the bronze giant. Then his gaze sharpened and he exclaimed:

"You're Doc Savage! You're the man Mr. Bullock was expecting!"

Doc said, "What has happened?"

The butler was trembling. "Some men, some ugly fellows, were here just a few moments ago. They struck me when I told them Mr. Bullock was missing since last night. They wouldn't believe me!"

Doc's eyes flashed. "Missing? How do you know?"

"Mr. Bullock left here for an important conference at his executive office last night. He has not been seen since!"

"And the men that were here a few moments ago?"

"Gone!"

Doc swung toward the doorway. "You'd better bathe that head," he said, and started out.

"Wait!" the butler called, and he was suddenly

handing a long white envelope to the bronze man. "Mr. Bullock left this last night, saying to give it to you if you called while he was out."

Doc started to open the envelope, remembered the signals that they had still heard as they drove into the estate. There was still the trail of the five men to follow.

He put the envelope in an inner pocket, hurried back to the car and got the machine started. He followed the drive that circled the mansion and cut down through a wooded lane beyond the estate.

The signals were abruptly very loud again.

Chick Lancaster cried, "They must be very close!"

Doc rolled to a stop a dozen feet before a rustic wooden bridge. The bridge formed part of the roadway, and spanned a brook that was part of the estate.

The girl was suddenly out of the car beside Doc Savage. Through the open side window of the bronze man's car, the transmitter signals were very loud.

Frowning, the girl said, "That's queer! How can the signals be so strong when their car is not even in sight?"

They were at the bridge. Suddenly Doc's gaze veered off to the side. In the next split second he had shouted the warning.

"Look out!"

With blurred speed, Doc swung the girl's trim figure into his arms and leaped backward.

The bridge before them went up into the air in a shuddering, earth-rocking blast.

Chapter X
THE BIG PEOPLE

THE house was one story high, badly in need of paint, and looked like something ordered from a mail order catalogue. The name on the tin mailbox outside the gate said:

ZEKE BROWN

Reds Lancaster, engineer, pointed at the house and said, "This is where he lived. Alone. He must have learned something, and because of that he died."

Monk and Ham had stepped out of the engineer's car. Learning that both were interested in all movements the farmer, Zeke Brown, had made before his mysterious death, the girl's engineer brother had obligingly offered to show Monk and Ham where the man had lived.

It was four o'clock in the afternoon, and the day was hot. The two pets, Habeas and the runt ape, had climbed out of the car and were lying down in the grass, to cool off.

Monk, frowning, muttered, "Blast it! I'd like to know what Zeke Brown had in that package for Doc."

Reds Lancaster was swinging his car around in the roadway. He leaned out and said, "There's a new shift going to work at the shaft at five. I'll have to get back. I'm putting Hardrock Hennesey in charge as walker."

Ham ignored some remark that Monk was making, looked at the engineer and asked, "Walker?"

"Superintendent in the tunnel," Lancaster explained. Sweat stood out on his freckled face. The collar of his flannel shirt was open and his necktie pulled down, a wet, tight knot over his chest.

He added: "If I can be of any help, let me know."

He left them there and headed back toward Shaft 9.

Monk had started toward the house. Habeas got up out of the grass and ran after him.

Ham and the pet chimp followed. The lawyer was saying, "I don't see where you expect to learn anything here, dunce."

Monk had found the kitchen door open, was pushing inside the house.

"Listen," Monk rapped, swinging on his partner, "we've checked on all Zeke Brown's movements on the day he died, haven't we?"

Ham frowned. "I hate to agree with you, ape, but the answer is yes."

"And we learned, as far as everyone knows, that he didn't leave his home all day?"

Ham nodded.

"And yet," continued Monk, "Zeke Brown had a package which he was gonna mail to Doc. He went out last night to mail it. And half an hour after he left this house he was dead. Maybe we can find some blasted thing here that will show us what he was gonna mail."

Ham shrugged. He started to say, "I might as well humor you. Otherwise—"

He paused, listening. Monk, too, was peering curiously toward a hallway that divided the house. They were standing in the kitchen, and the sound came from across the hall, from what was apparently a bedroom.

It was a creaking; steady, frequent.

Monk suddenly swung toward the hall. Ham held his sword cane in a ready grip as he followed.

In the doorway of the other room, hairy Monk drew up short, craned his short neck, exclaimed, "Well, I'll be a ring-tailed baboon!"

The old fellow sitting in the creaky chair, rocking, must have been all of ninety years old. He had skin like leather that has been in a fire.

He looked up at the homely chemist and said, "Have you seen them?"

"Seen what?" Monk demanded

"The people?"

"What people?"

"The people that lived here in the ground. The big people looking like giants."

Monk gulped. "What the blazes!" he piped shrilly.

The old fellow kept on rocking in the creaky chair.

HAIRY Monk stood staring at the old fellow in the chair.

Ham did likewise.

The two pets, the pig and Chemistry, stuck their heads between Monk's bowed legs and looked also.

"Crackpot!" was Monk's comment, looking at his partner.

"Crazy as a bedbug," agreed Ham.

For the moment, they forgot that they were mad at each other.

The old brown-looking fellow stopped his rocking, glared at the two and said, "Maybe you'd like to see one?"

"See what?"

"One of the big people."

Monk looked at Ham, grinned, whispered, "We'll humor him."

They stood aside while the bent old fellow got out of the chair, led the way through the kitchen and out of the house. He followed a path that led to the old barn. The barn, which had once been red, looked so decrepit that it was about ready to lay down on its side.

The old man went inside. The place was shadowy, smelled of old hay. Somewhere a bee buzzed listlessly in the heat of late afternoon.

The old man proceeded to a pile of straw in the back of the barn and started shoving some of it to one side. Suddenly the pig, Habeas, let out a snort and backed away. Chemistry scrambled up a nearby ladder.

Monk said shrilly, "Blazes!"

The skeleton was about eight feet long. The size and shape of the bone structure indicated that the skeleton's original owner must have been a person at least nine feet tall.

The skeleton had been carefully concealed by the straw.

"You see?" the old fellow said.

Monk stared. "Whew!" he whistled. "I'm glad that guy ain't *alive!*"

Ham was bending down, examining the skeleton.

"I can show you another one," abruptly put in the old man.

Monk was interested. He was thinking of the thing they had seen down in the tunnel—evidence that, centuries ago, there had been another form of life in this locality. A coastal region that had been fifteen hundred feet below where they stood now.

"Where's this other one?" he prodded.

"You come with me," the withered old man suggested.

Ham was still bending over the skeleton. He looked up at Monk. "I thought we were going to look over the house," he said. "You wanted to find out about that package Zeke Brown was going to mail to Doc."

"I'll be back," Monk said. "First, I'm gonna find out what else this old geezer has found."

Monk followed the old fellow out of the barn and across a field. They reached a wooded area beyond, and the old man kept on going, following a trail that led deeper and deeper into the woods. It was cooler in here, and the sun was kept out by the heavy top growth of the trees, which made the place look as though the sun had gone down.

Later, the sun had gone down and the old fellow was still walking, setting a good pace for one so old.

Monk complained, "Hey, grandpop! When are we gonna reach this other guy?"

"Soon now," the old man said, and he kept plodding ahead.

It grew darker. Silence lay like a heavy blanket over the wild section. Monk was about ready to say the hell with it, and return, when the old man paused and pointed ahead.

"This is the place," he said.

It was a small clearing. Evening dusk made everything shadowy and vague. The old man pointed to a pile of carefully placed rocks that looked not unlike an altar. On this rested the indistinct, long form.

Monk stalked across the clearing and bent down to examine this second skeleton, and the thing got up and took hold of the hairy chemist's neck.

IT occurred to Monk, in the next wild moment, that what had hold of him was no skeleton. It was a human figure, about the biggest the chemist had ever tackled, and the fight that followed was terrific.

The big man bounced the chemist on the skull with something that felt like a large, round rock. But it proved to be a fist.

With a roar of rage—Monk always made bull roars when really mad—the chemist tore free of the fellow's powerful hold and started swinging his fists.

He slammed into his assailant and let go with smashing rights and lefts.

And the big man merely let the blows roll off his barrel chest and laughed. He laughed harshly and bounced another fist off Monk's head.

Monk sat down on his hind quarters. He leaped up again.

And was immediately knocked off his feet.

The chemist spun around, dived behind the rock pile and got two good-sized rocks in his fists. He let them fly. The big fellow got back in the shadows and ducked low, but Monk kept picking up the rocks and hurling them in the general direction of the fellow's indistinct form.

Somewhere back in the woods there sounded a cackling laugh. The old geezer!

Wild with rage at being tricked like this, Monk let a couple of rocks fly toward the source of the sound.

A rock came back and hit him in the chest, knocking him flat. Monk crawled to his feet dizzily, stayed in a crouch behind the rock pile and was more careful from then on. Nevertheless, he kept up his barrage of hurtling rocks. He kept it up until his arms grew weary and he was forced to stop for breath.

And then, puzzled, he listened.

There was no sound in the dark clearing. No rocks were flying back at him. He was, apparently, alone.

He crept forward cautiously, hoping he might find an unconscious form. A moment later, Monk swore.

For all he found was a large rock pile across the clearing. He had practically moved the stone pile from one spot to another, in his wild barrage.

Monk stood there swearing for two minutes without repeating himself once.

And then the light hit his homely features and Ham's voice said:

"I always figured you were crazy. Now I know it!"

HABEAS, the scrawny pig, raced across the clearing ahead of Ham. He leaped up into the chemist's arms and licked his face.

Ham said, "For once, you hairy mistake, that ungainly animal showed sense. He got worried right after you'd left and kept pestering me. So I followed."

Monk exclaimed about the fight.

"The guy musta been a mate to that one back in the barn!" he muttered.

"You mean—"

"Like a giant," Monk continued. He picked up two large, round stones and glared off into the woods. "Come on. We'll find them."

Ham said, "Wait! We've got to hurry back."

"Why?"

In the flashlight glow, Ham's face was suddenly worried.

He said, "Reds Lancaster called that farmhouse. Renny heard something from the State capitol and asked him to get us as soon as possible. Lancaster is going to meet us back there at the farm."

"What's the trouble?" Monk demanded.

Ham was already leading the way back through the woods. There was anxiety in his words as he went on, "I don't know what it is. But that girl's brother seemed mighty worried about something."

They set a fast pace, the two pets running along behind them. The moon was up by the time they returned to the dead farmer's house. They saw the red-headed engineer's car parked in the roadway in front of the place.

Lancaster hopped out at sight of them. His wiry, alert form was tense.

"We've got to hurry!" he said.

"It's something about Doc?" Ham prodded.

The engineer nodded, motioning them toward his car.

"Chick called from the capitol. It seems she and Doc Savage were almost blown up near a bridge on the governor's estate. She was knocked out by the blast."

"And so?"

"When she woke up, Doc Savage was missing."

Chapter XI
THIRD DEGREE

THE hotel room was stifling hot, and for a good reason. All windows of the large room had been closed tight and the shades drawn. Outside in the night the thermometer registered eighty. Inside the stuffy room, with the lights turned on, it was well over ninety.

Pretty Chick Lancaster sat tied in the straight-back chair and perspiration dripped off her smooth, high forehead. Her auburn-red hair was moist against her forehead; little curls of it clung damply against her neck.

But her blue-green eyes were bright and blazing.

She glared at the circle of men grouped around her and snapped, "For the hundredth time, you can go to hell!"

"Little spitfire!" one of the men said wearily.

The fellow's shirt was open at the neck and his sleeves were rolled up. The shirt stuck like wet sheeting to his shoulders. He had a hard, cruel face.

The other four men with him were equally as hard-looking. They also appeared disgusted.

They all stared at Chick Lancaster, and one said, "Maybe she doesn't know where the bronze guy is. Maybe she's just givin' us a stall."

For several hours now, the questioning had been going on. The men took turns firing questions at the girl. They were pretty good at it.

They should be. At various times in their questionable careers they had all been in police lineups and been given the third degree.

A bridge lamp had been tilted so that the bright light hit Chick Lancaster in the face. Her features were flushed from concentration of the light. A tiny vein in her smooth throat throbbed.

But her chin was held high and her gaze was fiery. She had steadily refused to answer any questions hurled at her by the five thugs.

One man snapped, "Dammit, we gotta find Doc

Savage. That was the big boy's orders!"

"Maybe *you* can make her talk?" someone asked.

"Maybe I can," said the man in a quiet, flat voice.

Heads turned to look at him. The fellow had an axe-shaped jaw and there was something about his eyes that made you uneasy.

Chick Lancaster, hearing the tone of his voice, stiffened imperceptibly. She saw the man stare at his fingernails, then polish them on his shirt sleeve. He looked at his nails again and then up at the others.

"I got some pliers down in the car," he said significantly.

He held his fingers up to the light and looked at the nails again.

Chick Lancaster shuddered. She had heard of torture methods used by crooks. She had heard of pliers being used to pull out fingernails.

Horror took hold of her. She was terrified because she did not know what she would do if they tried such methods. *She did not know where Doc Savage was!*

For when the blast had demolished the small bridge on the governor's estate, she only remembered being swept up into the bronze giant's arms, as he made an attempt to pull her clear of the danger. And then the blast had knocked them both flat and she had recalled nothing more.

Nothing, that is, until she woke up in the sedan with these five thugs. And now, for hours, they had been questioning her about the bronze man's whereabouts. After dark, she had been carried, gagged, up a fire escape of this hotel. She had screamed once the moment they had taken the gag out of her mouth. And a man had laughed.

"Yell your head off, baby," someone had said. "No one in *this* place is gonna ask questions. They know better."

And now—

The hatchet-jawed man who had mentioned the pliers started toward one of the windows. It was one containing a fire escape outside. He turned back and said, "I left the car down back in the alley. I'll be right back."

His companions waited quietly, staring at the girl.

She felt suddenly faint, thinking of what was going to happen when the cruel-faced man returned. But she gritted her teeth and sat there with her hands clenched behind her back, where the wrists were tied tightly together.

"Better decide to talk, babe," one man said. Sweat made his face appear like pasty dough.

"Joey doesn't fool," put in another.

Joey was apparently the one who had gone down the fire escape. He had not bothered to close the window, merely pulling the shade down to the sill behind him.

It rustled slightly in a hot, languid puff of breeze that drifted in from the night. The men continued to sweat as they watched the girl. One swore.

The shade rustled again and a man looked up and started to complain, "What the hell kept—"

Various things then happened, none of them expected.

Standing just inside the window, Doc Savage, looking like a great bronze statue, said, "You should have kept Joey inside."

THE four men dived for guns at the same instant the bronze giant dived for them. They would never be able to understand how Doc Savage moved a dozen feet while their hands were only moving inches.

Doc hit the group before the guns were clear of shoulder holsters. Furious action followed. Two men fell down. They didn't get up again.

A third tried to slug the bronze fellow. He never saw the fist that lifted him off his feet as it cracked beneath his jaw. He landed in a heap beside the first two.

The fourth man tried to dive for the hall door. Fingers seized his throat, and pressure touched a certain nerve. He went quietly to sleep.

Doc Savage turned his attention to the red-haired girl. Untying her, he said quietly, "You should have stayed at the shaft with your brother."

The girl stood up from the chair, moving her slender arms to restore circulation. She smiled fondly at Doc Savage, exclaimed, "I wouldn't have missed this for the world!"

The bronze man made no comment. His metallic features were expressionless. He had already turned to start tying up the four men with the cords that had been used on herself.

Chick Lancaster shrugged and gave a little sigh. This bronze fellow was certainly different from most men. She couldn't figure him out.

She asked, "What happened back there by the bridge? All I remember is—"

"We were knocked down," Doc explained. "You were merely dazed for a few moments."

"But—"

"They must have needed something out of the trunk. That explains how they found the miniature shortwave radio transmitter. They put the transmitter a hundred yards down the bank of that brook and set the trap. They captured you while I was down there looking for the transmitter."

Chick Lancaster's blue-green eyes were wide.

"Trap? You mean, we were supposed to be killed there at the bridge?"

Doc nodded.

The girl stared at Doc Savage. "I'm beginning to understand the kind of dangerous life you lead," she said.

Doc had all four men tied up. He picked up one man, set him in an armchair, then took something that looked like a small hypodermic needle from a vest beneath his coat. The captive's shirt sleeve was already rolled up, so Doc Savage merely stuck the needle of the gadget into the man's arm and pressed a small plunger.

Watching, wondering what this was all about, Chick suddenly remembered something.

"Look!" she exclaimed. "I just thought. How did you happen to *find* me?"

DOC looked up at the girl. "The police were given the license number of their car two hours ago," he explained. "It was located in this neighborhood just a little while ago. A few minutes ago I caught Joey entering the car."

"And the police?"

"They were merely requested to let me know where it was last seen."

The girl stared. "Then you have connections with the police here?"

Doc merely said, "We have worked with the police of various large cities at different times."

He did not explain that he was an honorary member of the F.B.I. and the New York City police department; that in practically every city through the country, he would gladly be given a free hand to do what he chose.

The fellow who had been administered the drug was suddenly mumbling.

"What did you do to him?" Chick queried.

Doc stated several long words. "In short," he added, "truth serum. We will try to find out what he knows."

The man's eyes were open. At first, he looked at the bronze man sort of vaguely. Then his eyes widened and he said, "I'm supposed to kill you. You're Doc Savage."

"Why are you supposed to kill me?" Doc prodded.

"Because they are not sure just how much you know."

"Who?"

"The rest of them—the guys I'm working with."

"And who's that?"

The man answered the questions readily enough.

"Oh, Joey and Louie Heller and the Kid. All of 'em."

Doc Savage frowned slightly. Names of ordinary hoods and gunmen were not what he was seeking. What he needed was the name of the bigshot, the person who might know about the strange mystery that had hit Shaft 9 and why it had done so.

He asked: "Who is behind you? Who is paying you?"

The captive shrugged. "We call him Lefty. That's all I know about him. But he's working for someone still bigger."

"Who?"

The man was obviously now trying to avoid answering the questions. He looked suddenly pale, frightened. But the words came out against his will.

"I heard Lefty say something about... about Governor Bullock."

Chick Lancaster gasped. "No! It *can't* be!"

Doc looked at their captive. "Governor Bullock?"

"Yes."

Doc questioned the fellow further, but learned nothing. The captive only knew what he had overheard Lefty say. Lefty had merely hinted that their pay was coming from the State capitol itself.

Doc gagged the man, as he did the others—they were showing signs of returning consciousness—then stepped to the phone located in the room.

He called police headquarters, identified himself, reported that there were four thugs tied up in the room and a fifth in a car down in the alleyway.

He hung up.

The girl was still stunned. "I can't *believe* that it is the governor," she said. "I happen to know him well. Why, he's—"

"It might be a good idea to see him," suggested Doc.

"But how? That butler told you he was missing. He—"

Doc reminded Chick Lancaster of the note that had been handed him at the governor's estate.

"It was a message saying to meet him at the Morley Hotel," Doc explained. "Governor Bullock is hiding out there. His life has been threatened."

The girl gasped. "But if he *is* behind this mystery, why would he be in hiding?"

Doc said, "That is why it might be interesting to see him." He stepped toward the fire escape window, motioned the girl to follow. It was obvious that Doc wanted to avoid detection as they left the hotel.

He paused before helping the girl outside, and said, "But first there is something else. A phone call to the shaft revealed that you are in the custom of staying at the Plaza Hotel when on trips to this city. I called them, and the desk clerk said there is a package there for you."

"Package?"

"Yes. A package for me, but sent in your care."

"What could it be?"

Doc said, "We had better hurry."

Chapter XII
THE PHOTOGRAPH

THE package was about six inches square and a half inch thick. Chick Lancaster handed it to Doc Savage with the comment, "What *can* it be?"

The bronze man was seated behind the wheel of his big car. He had waited, because he had not wanted to be observed, while the red-haired girl had gone into the hotel where she was in the habit of stopping while in the capital city.

Doc unwrapped the package while Chick Lancaster watched. Inside, two pieces of cardboard protected a photograph that was new and glossy. It was about the oddest-looking picture either had ever seen.

Chick exclaimed, "Heavens! What *is* it?"

Doc was gazing intently at the photograph. He said nothing for a moment.

It was a view that might have been taken in some sort of tomb. Weirdness best described it.

Rock walls formed a background for what was some kind of ancient chamber. Crude weapons leaned on the wall. On the rock floor, a skeleton lay in a grotesque position. Off to one side there was a huge thing that looked like great slabs of marble embedded with crude wooden spikes.

The man was pressed between these body-piercing slabs. It was evident that he had died hideously.

But Doc Savage seemed more interested in the size of the skeleton shown lying on the rock floor. From his vest pocket he took a small rule. He measured the length of the picture and the size of various ancient objects shown in the torture room. In his mind, he calculated the size of the skeleton. He remarked:

"No person living today would be as tall as that."

The girl gasped. "What does it mean?" She was pointing at words printed across the bottom of the picture. They read:

MEN SHALL DIE WHEN THEY
DISTURB THE BIG PEOPLE

Doc Savage was holding the photograph at various angles beneath the dashboard light. There was something like a shadow across one corner of the picture. The shadow did not seem to be a part of the view that had been taken of the strange chamber.

The girl shuddered. "Heavens! What a horrible thing! Where do you imagine it was *taken?"*

"If we knew," the bronze man said quietly, "it might explain a lot of things."

He made no further comment. He locked the photograph up in a dashboard compartment of the car, put the car into speed and headed for the Morley Hotel, after asking Chick Lancaster which direction it was.

It was almost ten thirty when they stopped on a side street beside the tall structure where Doc Savage had mentioned the governor was in hiding.

Doc said, "Perhaps you had better wait here."

But the girl's eyes flashed. "Nothing *doing!* I'm going with you."

There was enough determination in her voice to show that time might be wasted in trying to dissuade her from going. Doc shrugged, and climbed out. He locked the car and they entered the hotel by a side entrance.

The bronze man headed directly for an elevator that was standing open on one side of the large lobby. The car, except for the operator, was deserted.

Doc said, "A friend is ill. Would you take us right up?"

The operator quickly closed the doors and Doc and the girl had the car to themselves.

But in the hallways of the fourteenth floor, she looked at him and asked, puzzled, "How did you know—"

"Governor Bullock is registered here under the name of Samuel Jones," Doc explained. "He is in Room 1401."

Room 1401 was at the end of a long, carpeted hallway. Doc knocked quietly on the door, stood waiting.

After a while a voice asked cautiously, "Yes?"

Doc Savage looked at the girl. She nodded.

"That sounds like the governor, all right," she whispered.

The bronze man said, "This is Doc Savage."

The door immediately opened and they stepped inside.

And immediately men with guns stepped out from where they had been pressed against the walls and covered Doc Savage and the girl. One said harshly:

"We kinda thought you'd fall for that fake letter!"

BECAUSE the red-haired girl was so close beside him, Doc Savage hesitated a moment before whirling into action. In that instant, guns were jammed into his spine and at least half a dozen men had him covered.

Chick Lancaster was seized by two other men. She started to scream. Immediately a hand was slapped roughly over her mouth and she was swept off her feet. She was quickly carried through a foyer and into a larger, inside room of what appeared to be a suite.

Doc was urged inside, also. Two of the men remained behind him, two on either side. They were taking no chances on this bronze fellow.

The girl was being tied up and gagged. Doc was treated in like manner. There were so many guns covering him that he had little chance of trying for a break. Besides, there was the girl to think of.

Someone went through the bronze man's pockets, found his car keys.

"This'll be good," the man said. "We'll use his machine. No chance of being grabbed now in that hot car."

Apparently Doc and the girl were going to be transported to some other point.

While the other gunmen waited, two men left the apartment. One was only gone two moments. When he came back, he said:

"Well?"

"Everything's fixed. We've got that guy on the freight elevator well greased. We'll take them down that way. Jimmie's gonna have the bronze guy's car waitin' in the alleyway out back. Come on."

While one man remained in the hall as a lookout, Doc and the girl were carried out by the others, hurried to a large service elevator around an ell in the corridor, placed inside and taken to the ground floor.

A dimly lighted freight entrance was revealed when the car came to a stop. The two captives were removed to an areaway behind the hotel. It was here that Doc's big limousine was pulled up.

The girl and Doc were dumped in the rear of the car. Two men climbed into the seat; three others got into the driver's section. Those who did not get into the car grinned down at the bronze man where his great form was jammed in on the wide floor.

"Be seein' you, Savage—in hell!"

THE driver spoke to one of the men who were remaining behind. "You know where to meet us?"

"Yeah. You better get going."

"O.K."

The car rolled off into the night. The windows had been closed, and it was stuffy inside the car. The girl, Chick, was crowded between the two big men on the back seat. Each man held a gun. They watched Doc Savage more closely than they did the girl.

Doc was flat on his face on the floor of the machine. His hands had been tied behind him. His ankles were tied also, and yanked backward and upward so that they were tied to the ropes encircling his wrists. A gag was in the bronze man's mouth.

The driver wheeled the big car carefully through city streets. He took no chance on being stopped by a traffic cop. Ten minutes later they were beyond the street lights and rolling through open country. The windows of the machine were opened.

Someone said, "Whew! I was damned near roasted!" as a breeze came in the windows and took away the thick stuffiness inside the car.

Doc Savage, with his teeth, kept working at the floor mat that was just beneath his face. His movements, so as not to arouse suspicion, had to be slight. He worked for perhaps twenty minutes before he had the corner section of the mat rolled back beneath his perspiring face.

His teeth closed over the tiny hook located there and he pulled on it carefully.

It was about a half hour after this, as the car was passing through a particularly lonesome stretch of country, that the plane came down out of the air and circled them and started dropping the magnesium flares.

THE flares were bright enough that everyone in the machine was quickly blinded. The driver yanked on the brake, howled, "Holy hell! I can't *see!*"

"Turn around, you sap!" someone yelled. "It's some kind of trap!"

The driver started to swing the machine around in the roadway. He let out a shout. Behind them, another flare must have been dropped—for the space back there was a blinding sheet of white.

The car was completely surrounded by the curtain of intense whiteness, so brilliant that it was impossible to keep the eyes open for more than a moment at a time.

Suddenly, beyond that sheet of whiteness, a plane motor sputtered and died. Almost immediately there was a shout and a racket like a bullfiddle roar.

The car driver slammed open the door and cried, "Me, I'm gettin' the hell outta here!"

That seemed to be the general idea of his partners. All piled out and ran like confused blind men through the white, burning magnesium glare.

There was the sharp crack of pistols. Over this, more of the bulfiddle roaring sounds. And then, quite distinct, a voice that howled:

"Yeo-o-ow! I got me a blasted polecat!"

Chapter XIII
GOVERNOR MISSING

IT was hairy Monk Mayfair who had yelled. Running from the plane toward the blinding white light, one of Doc's machine pistols in his hand, he had crashed into someone, a fellow wiry, slender and quick-moving. The magnesium glare was too intense to make identification possible.

But Monk got his huge hand on the man's coat and started thumping away on the captive's head with the butt of the gun.

It was Ham's voice that yelled, "Wait! You've got the wrong person!"

Monk thought it was a huge joke. "I should have hit you harder," he squealed.

The arrival of two of the escaping thugs from the car momentarily stopped the argument.

Monk grabbed a man. Ham had his slender sword flashing. Everyone started fighting enthusiastically. Three minutes later the two thugs lay sprawled on the ground and the two aides were trying to locate Doc's car in the blinding white light.

Somewhere ahead, Renny's voice roared, "Here it is, Lancaster. Come on!"

Ham and Monk, though they were blinded, moved toward the sound across a rough field. The two pets, Habeas and Chemistry, ducked in and out between their legs, also blinded by the light.

The four men—Ham, Monk, Renny and the girl's engineer brother, Reds Lancaster—had been flying toward the State capital when they had picked up the peculiar signal from Doc Savage's car. They had been using the fast plane left in the gas station field when they had arrived at Shaft 9.

The signal was a shortwave code transmission that had automatically gone on the air when Doc had pulled the tiny hook in the floor of the car. The hook had switched on a small transmitter concealed beneath the floorboards of the big machine, and was only one of the scientific gadgets that Doc Savage had built into the unusual automobile.

Trailing the steady source of code signals, Renny—who had been at the controls of the plane—had located the bronze man's car speeding along the stretch of lonely highway. He had dropped low, released the magnesium flares that had blinded the car driver and his associates.

There was the sound of voices from somewhere within the curtain of dazzling whiteness. Monk squinted his eyes as he ran through the rough field, trying to see. He saw Ham just ahead of him. And then, abruptly, he couldn't.

Monk yelled, "Hey! Where are you?"

A form raised up in front of him. Ham!

MONK exclaimed, "Blast it! Where am I going?"

Spluttering, the lawyer said, "Into the river… I've just come out!"

The words came too late for Monk to check his waddling, fast stride. He plunged off a two-foot-high embankment and sprawled into the water. The water was only waist deep, apparently a shallow stream that cut through the fields.

Monk came up snorting with rage. He glared at Ham, wading toward the opposite bank.

"I'm gonna flatten you for not letting me know that water was there!" he muttered.

Ham ignored the remark. The brilliant glow was dimming somewhat now; ahead, he had seen the car parked in the roadway just beyond a low fence.

Monk followed. The pets, looking like scared, wet chickens, scrambled after him.

Ham and the hairy chemist reached the car about the same time as huge Renny. The brilliant flares had dimmed enough now so that all could see.

Doc Savage had just stepped out of the car. He was helping the girl, Chick Lancaster, out of the rear seat.

Chick Lancaster stared at Doc Savage, gasped, "You were not *really* helpless, then? Why, you just now untied yourself!"

Doc merely said, "It was possible that they might have led us to where Governor Bullock was either waiting for them—or a captive. When I saw they were not going to do this, I figured we ought to try to seize them."

Doc explained briefly to the girl about the signal transmitter located beneath the car.

"Renny," added Doc, "had orders to come to the capitol tonight if we had not returned. I took a chance on catching them somewhere en route."

The girl's green eyes were wide. "But how did you know we were headed back toward the shaft?"

Doc raised his hand briefly, indicated a small compass that was a part of his wristwatch. "It was quite obvious as to the direction we were going," he finished.

Big Renny had been staring around. He asked abruptly, "Where's Lancaster?"

"My brother was *with* you?" the girl asked.

Renny, his long face as gloomy-looking as ever, nodded.

"He's been helping us all he could," explained Renny. "He came along tonight because he was worried about you."

They all started a search in the vicinity of the car. And a few moments later, all returned and gave the same report.

Lancaster, obviously, was missing.

MONK remembered the two men that had been knocked out and left back in the field. He started to say something about going back to get them, then looked at red-haired Chick Lancaster. He grinned at his partner Ham.

"You'd better go, shyster," he piped. "There's something I gotta tell Chick." He smiled fondly at the girl.

For Monk had gotten over his first suspicions of the girl. If she was trying to help Doc Savage, she must be O.K., in his opinion.

He stepped toward her now and said, "I've been worried about you."

Chick Lancaster gave Monk a warm smile. Then her lovely eyes clouded. She gripped the chemist's burly arm.

"What *could* have happened to my brother?" she asked worriedly.

"Maybe he's chasin' some of those crooks," was Monk's theory. "He'll be all right. He looks like a guy who can take care of himself."

Doc Savage said quietly, "We had better make a more complete search. Monk can bring back the two men who were knocked out. Chick had better wait in the car."

Monk sighed as he looked hopefully at the girl. "See you later, babykins," he said, and motioned to Ham.

"Come on, shyster."

Ham, his custom-tailored clothes clinging to him wetly, looked as though he was going to cut his hairy partner's throat as soon as he got him in a dark spot.

Still arguing, they returned to the spot where they had left the two men in the field—and found no one.

Monk stared. "Them danged polecats musta been found by the other guys who escaped from Doc's car!" he muttered.

They searched the field. They climbed a stone wall that separated this field from another beyond, a smoother stretch of ground where the bronze man's plane had been brought down by Renny. They even went to the plane to make certain that everything was O.K. The two aides finally returned again to Doc's car. The bronze man and big Renny had returned also, and they too reported no success in locating Reds Lancaster.

The girl, they found, was asleep in the rear of the car. It had been hours since any of them had had any rest.

Doc Savage was thoughtful a moment. Then he said:

"There is an angle to this that is very peculiar."

Doc told them the mystery concerning the disappearance of Governor Bullock, of the things that had occurred in the capital city. As yet, he had made no comment about the queer photograph sent him in care of the girl.

Renny suddenly boomed, "Holy cow, Doc! If the governor is mixed up in this thing, why would he have called you in to investigate?"

"Smoke screen," Ham, the lawyer, put in quietly.

HAM explained. "He could have called in Doc in order to throw suspicion from himself."

The bronze man's features were thoughtful.

"There is something that all of you should know about," he said abruptly. "It changed the whole aspect of the mystery."

"What?" Renny wanted to know.

"Governor Bullock practically financed Yellow River Dam and most of the water tunnel project used in conjunction with it. That would hardly make him out a crook now."

"Then how do you explain his disappearance?" asked Ham.

Monk had a word to say before Doc could answer.

"How do you explain anything in this blasted mystery?" he demanded. "The giant skeleton thing, that death fog, those guys changing into mummies!"

Doc looked at Renny. "Have there been any more accidents at the shaft?"

The big engineer shook his head. "Nothing happened today," he said. "Everybody's back on the job."

The bronze man had apparently reached a decision. He motioned them into the car. The pets were already in the front seat.

"There is an answer to this thing somewhere in the State capitol," Doc said. "All of you return to the shaft. Perhaps you will find a trail to Lancaster. And you might try to find out who mailed the photograph."

All three stared.

"You mean," asked Ham, "the package that was missing from the farmer's car?"

Doc nodded. "It was a photograph, taken recently and readdressed to me in care of Chick Lancaster."

The bronze man got the photo from the car, showed it to the three aides.

Monk jumped. "Blazes!" he squeaked. "That's the same kind of giant skeleton we saw back in the barn."

"Barn?" asked Doc.

Monk told about the old fellow who had tried to trick him. He described the skeleton hidden in Zeke Brown's barn.

But Doc Savage seemed more interested in Monk's description of the ageless-looking old man whom they had met at the farmhouse.

"Find him," Doc ordered. "Look for me back at the shaft some time before tonight."

Leaving them with the girl and the car, he disappeared toward the field where the plane had been set down. A few moments later, all heard the motor roar as the fast craft took to the air, circled once, then headed off toward the capital city.

It would be daylight in another hour.

Monk remarked, "Goshamighty! I just thought of something! I just remembered we didn't see Hardrock Hennesey all day. Now I wonder what's happened to *him?"*

Chapter XIV
HARDROCK FINDS A CORPSE

THERE were two others who were interested in finding tough little Hardrock Hennesey.

The two were working on the muck machine down in the tunnel below Shaft 9. Powerful fellows, they wore the work clothes and metal helmets of muckers. They had gone to work on the midnight shift that same day, when a call went out for additional labor to help rush the tunnel job to completion.

Around them now there was noise and sweating and swearing. Air drills yammered in the hands of miners up on the platform of the tunnel head not far beyond them. An hour ago, the tunnel had been cleared while a blast had been set off. Now the miners and the muckers were back in the bore cleaning out the cracked rock and muck. It was mostly rock.

One of the two men leaned on his shovel and spoke to the other. He almost had to yell above the racket.

"You know what?" he shouted.

His partner—a close look at the two men's raw-red hands would show that they were not used to this kind of labor—leaned on his shovel also and said, "Well, what?"

"I think that little Hardrock Hennesey has learned something. I just heard from one of the nippers that Hardrock is up there in the north extension of the tunnel. An' there ain't no guys working up there tonight!"

The other big fellow looked worried.

"Hell!" he exploded. "Maybe he'll find that—"

His partner nodded. "That's what I was thinking! We better investigate."

They dropped their shovels, approached a tunnel foreman and one man had a fit of coughing. He pressed his hands to his chest.

The other said to the foreman. "The dust has got him, boss. I'll have to take him up."

The first workman kept groaning and holding his hands pressed against his chest.

"All right," snapped the foreman. "Take him up."

Silicosis—a disease of the lungs caused by inhaling quartz dust—kills more tunnel workers than actual accidents. The foreman took it for granted that one of the two muckers had an attack of the disease now.

The two men hurried through the tunnel. After a while they were clear of the work gangs. They proceeded swiftly until they had reached the beginning of the long north extension from Shaft 9.

Here, work was practically completed. The report was that, tomorrow, the northern end of the bore would be blasted through to meet the tunnel from Shaft 10. And Shaft 10 was the last unit connecting with Yellow River Dam, the huge supply unit in the great project.

A nipper had just alighted from the bucket, having come down from aboveground. The "nippers" were the apprentices who kept the miners supplied with drills. They handled steel.

One of the two big muckers asked, "You seen Hardrock Hennesey, kid?"

The nipper waved a hand toward the north bore. "He's up there. He went in just as I was going out, about twenty minutes ago."

The two murmured something and hurried on.

They covered the four miles to the tunnel head. They passed no one. When they had gone as far as they could, one looked at the other and stared.

"Hardrock isn't here!" he exclaimed.

His partner, for a big man, looked scared. "That means," he stammered, "that... maybe he's found it!"

"Come on!" rapped the other, and they started running back through the tunnel bore.

Halfway to the base of the fifteen hundred-foot shaft entrance, they slammed into Hardrock Hennesey.

Hardrock eyed the two and said, his jaw thrust it, "I've been looking for you two buzzards."

There was a fight.

HARDROCK HENNESEY, as a kid, had been raised on the sidewalks of New York, in a section near Tenth Avenue. More than once bigger kids had beat him up, for Hardrock Hennesey had always been a pretty small guy.

And so he had learned, as he grew up, that there are other things to use besides fists. Because most men were usually bigger than himself, he generally went prepared.

What he used now was a pipe wrench yanked from the pocket of his too-big overalls. He sailed into the two big fellows like a Spitz dog going after two overgrown mongrels.

The wrench flew, and the two thugs let out assorted yells and Hardrock Hennesey got himself worked up to some nice plain and fancy swearing.

One man was slammed up against a hard rock wall of the tunnel. The other got hold of Hardrock Hennesey's arm and tried to twist it so that it would break and the wrench would be knocked free.

But the little tunnel worker sank his teeth into the big fellow's wrist. Howling with rage, the man sprang clear. Hardrock hit him with the wrench. He fell down, moaning.

The other one had come running back into the battle with his fists flailing and his head pulled down like a wrestler's. Hardrock tapped the man on the head with the heavy wrench, stepped aside as the fellow fell atop his inert companion.

Hardrock Hennesey spat out tobacco juice, put the wrench back in his pocket and said for the benefit of the surrounding grim walls, "About time I got those Doc Savage guys, I reckon."

When the sun was well up in the sky later that morning, Hardrock Hennesey located Monk, Ham and the big fellow named Renny asleep in the limousine of the bronze man. The car had been run beneath some willows at some distance from Shaft 9. It was a good shady spot where the sun would not bother them when it started to get hot.

Hardrock woke everyone up and announced, "I got something to show you."

Monk climbed out of the car, looking disgusted and sleepy. Ham and Renny followed.

Renny asked, "What is it?" in his blasting voice.

"IT'S about that farmer, that Zeke Brown, who turned into a mummy. I know what he had found out."

"What?"

"You won't believe it unless I show you," said Hardrock Hennesey. "But I got wise to it when I followed an old buzzard that looks old enough to be Meth—what the hell was his name?"

"Methuselah," supplied Ham.

"Yeah—him," agreed Hardrock.

Monk was suddenly interested. He described the brown, leathery-faced old man who had tricked him at the farmhouse.

"That's the bird," said Hardrock. "Well, come on, and I'll show you something."

Hardrock suggested that they drive, and they all piled into the car. The pets, Habeas and the runt ape, were asleep on the floor in the rear.

Hardrock Hennesey gave directions, then looked worried and asked, "Where's Chick Lancaster? She all right?"

"We made her go home and get some rest," said Ham.

Chick and her brother, Reds Lancaster, lived in a rented house about a mile away from Shaft 9.

The route Hardrock Hennesey pointed out led away from the construction center, followed a dusty country road that ended in a meadow some distance behind the farm of Zeke Brown, deceased.

They got out and Hardrock led the way across a pasture. Habeas, the pig, immediately chased Chemistry across the field.

Summer heat had dried up the ground until it was like a baked, hard mud. They walked for some time, came to a hollow that dipped down beneath some trees.

Hardrock Hennesey indicated some dried-up tracks in the hard earth. "Zeke Brown musta been looking for a strayed cow," he said. "There's the prints."

"So what?" Monk demanded in his squeaky voice.

The little tunnel worker gave the chemist a cool look, led the way farther into the hollow. It became a crevice between ridges of land. Well into the opening, Hardrock suddenly paused and pointed at something hardly a dozen feet away from where they stood.

"What do you think of that?" he asked.

All stared.

The opening was a three-foot-wide crack in the earth. Cautiously, they moved forward and stared over its edge. The bottom of the thing was approximately twenty-five feet below them.

Big Renny studied the split in the ground a moment and then commented, "Some earth vibration has probably caused it."

"You ain't seen nothing," put in Hardrock Hennesey. "Wait a minute."

He moved off beneath the nearby trees, returned quickly with an armful of rope. He was paying out the rope as he returned, having, apparently, tied the other end to a tree trunk.

"Wait'll you see what's at the bottom of this place!" he exclaimed.

He caught hold of the rope, lowered himself over the edge of the crack, and slid downward. Shortly, the others followed.

In the bottom of the crevice, they all noted that it seemed to follow a well-defined fissure in the rock. Hardrock led the way.

It became darker and they appeared to be dropping lower at each step; and after a while the little tunnel worker took out a flashlight and indicated the way.

They had proceeded for perhaps twenty minutes. They were below ground now, and it was cool and dank in the narrow passageway. Hardrock suddenly paused and said, "Here it is."

He pointed the light ahead.

Monk exploded, "I... ah... Jehoshaphat!"

The others merely stared.

The place had been widened into a sort of small room. And what was in the room was enough to create the horrors.

It looked like a medieval torture chamber. Crude, ungainly contraptions for tying up a person were built into the rock walls. There were sharp implements made out of quartz and stone.

On the floor there was a skeleton as long and as big as the one Monk had seen in the barn. A giant!

But the most awesome sight of all was the torture thing to one side of the roomlike space. Created of two crude slabs of granite, the machine held stone spikes that had been ground down to needle points.

A man was in the machine, and red liquid had oozed from his body and dried on the stone spikes.

Monk had a hard time getting out words. He blurted, "I... ah... Blazes! This is the same place shown in the photograph *that was sent to Doc!"*

Hardrock was staring intently at the dead man in the spike device. His intense gray eyes widened and he stared at his companions.

"Holy hell!" the tunnel worker gasped. "That... that guy in the machine! It's Jackhammer Edwards. A miner! He... he disappeared from the shaft a couple of days ago, I heard!"

Monk, curious, walked over and examined one of the hooks embedded in the rock wall. It, too, was of stone, as though made back in the dark ages.

Tugging at the hook, he exclaimed, "That old fellow might not have been so cracked after all. He kept talkin' about the big people."

The chemist turned and stared at the others. His

homely face was puzzled. "Jeepers! What kind of people *did* live here in the Earth?"

Monk had been holding to the stone-hook thing in the wall.

Suddenly Ham looked past Monk and yelled.

"Look!" the well-dressed lawyer rapped.

A foggy, vaporous spray was coming from tiny openings in the stone ceiling of the room. It spread, lowered swiftly, becoming like a grayish mirage. The room, within seconds, grew terrifically hot.

Monk let out a yell and leaped toward the others. "The fog!" he howled.

He started toward the opening where they had entered the room. And staggered backward as though he had been slammed with a massive fist. His homely features were blistered and his huge hands burned.

"We're trapped!" squalled Monk.

The opaque fog was fast growing more dense in the room.

Chapter XV
TUNNEL OF DOOM!

LATE that same afternoon, every newspaper in the State was carrying black headlines. Word about the mystery centered around Shaft 9 and Yellow River Dam had leaked out. Also other facts.

A capital afternoon sheet ran the following:

GOVERNOR MISSING

Mystery Surrounds Tunnel Project as Strange Fog Causes Deaths and Terror

Capital City, August 3rd.—Though various State officials deny the fact, it has been learned on good authority that work on the ten-million dollar Yellow River Dam and tunnel project has been stopped. A series of queer accidents have occurred on the construction job. Workmen, it has been stated, speak of a weird fog that appears and which turns men into mummies. Others even speak of a queer race of people that have been unearthed, and now men are too terrified to enter the various shafts.

This newspaper recalls a warning given months ago when Governor Bullock first broke ground for the mammoth Yellow River Dam. At that time, a committee of leading State businessmen and politicians held out for a site to be used in an adjacent valley to Yellow River. The site was considered more advantageous. But Governor Bullock, through a bond issue, had financed the site for the present dam and adjoining water-tunnel outlet. At the time, as many will recall, there was considerable argument over the entire thing.

And now, surprisingly, and as the mystery spreads at Yellow River Dam, it has been learned that Governor Bullock cannot be located. There have been hints of swindle. Has the people's money been invested in a project that is worthless? What has happened to Governor Bullock?

Doc Savage, a remarkable person who has solved baffling mysteries the world over, is reported to be at Yellow River Dam investigating. At this writing, Doc Savage could not be reached.

There was more, and at the very end of the newspaper story there appeared a box announcement set in boldface type.

BULLETIN

Three Doc Savage assistants are reported missing in tunnel mystery. The three men, accompanying a tunnel worker named Hardrock Hennesey, apparently were seen last at an early hour today. No trace has been found of them since. More details will be given here as soon as they are received.

Oddly, Doc Savage himself was in one of the very newspaper offices from which the foregoing information was released. It was the bronze man himself who asked that the articles be toned down. All facts concerning the tunnel mystery were not given to the public.

Two of the officials of the paper were on the committee that opposed Governor Bullock and his Yellow River Dam project. Doc had talked to them, and the others. One man in particular, a Colonel Henry Bishop, was returning to Yellow River with Doc Savage tonight. It was he who insisted that Governor Bullock was a crook.

While Colonel Bishop awaited Doc Savage in the executive offices of the paper, the bronze man went to the dark room of the newspaper and made a request. He would like to have use of their largest photographic projection equipment.

The request was quickly granted. Alone in the room, Doc Savage did a peculiar thing. Using special apparatus, he projected the photograph of the torture chamber onto a huge silver screen. He magnified the picture until it was "blown up" to a hundred times its regular size.

For a long time, Doc studied the projection. He seemed particularly interested in a shadow that was cast on one side of the picture. Just before Doc switched off the projector, his unusual trilling sound filled the quiet room. Apparently he had made some discovery which interested him.

Sometime later, accompanied by Colonel Bishop, Doc Savage was returning in his plane to Shaft 9.

Colonel Bishop, politician and part owner of the *Sentinel,* was a man in his late forties. He looked like an unassuming clergyman rather than an aggressive State leader and a person reputed to be worth a million dollars.

He wore somber black and a flowing black tie. He had pale, almost scared-looking eyes that stared widely out from behind thick-lensed eyeglasses.

When Doc Savage brought his fast plane down swiftly for a landing in a field near Shaft 9, thin Colonel Bishop clung to the sides of his seat and looked as though he was going to be sick. This giant bronze fellow's dynamic personality sort of frightened him.

They had no sooner landed, and climbed out, than a man whom Doc Savage had been seeking met them.

Reds Lancaster, the girl's engineer brother!

DOC inquired, "What happened to you last night?"

Lancaster was tense and excited. Apparently he knew the newspaper publisher, for he spoke to the man briefly. Then he turned his attention to the bronze man.

"I trailed two of the crooks almost all night," the wiry-looking engineer exclaimed. "I've found something!"

"What?" asked Doc.

"Peculiar animallike tracks, down in the north bore of Shaft 9. There's something damned queer we've hit down there. No wonder most of the workmen are terrified!"

"We'll investigate," Doc Savage said.

At the shaft, they met the girl, Chick Lancaster. The lovely red-haired sister of Reds Lancaster looked tired and pale.

She spoke to the bronze man about Monk and the others.

"We've searched everywhere for them!" Chick gasped. "And we can't find a trace of where they went. Hardrock Hennesey was with your three assistants—Monk, Renny and the one who is so nice—Ham."

Naturally the bronze man did not know about the four men being trapped by the weird fog. He said, "They are perhaps trailing something. All are capable of handling themselves."

But the mystery of their disappearance had even affected the tunnel workers. Hundreds of men milled about near Shaft 9, their faces grim in the glare of the floodlights at the shaft opening.

Only a few had been persuaded to stick to their jobs. As Reds Lancaster explained bitterly:

"We're blasting through the north end of No. 9 tonight. No. 10 is completed and hooked into Yellow River Dam. We're going to make a test."

"Test?" Doc prodded.

"Water is going to be released through the system," explained the alert, red-headed engineer. "We blasted through the southern end of No. 9 this afternoon. We're rushing things in an attempt to prove that the project is O.K., and before the rest of the muckers quit. We've *got* to!"

Chick Lancaster looked suddenly horrified. "You can't blast tonight!" she cried. "Perhaps those men—the ones with Hardrock—are down there some place!"

Reds Lancaster moved to his pretty sister's side, squeezed her slender arm. "Nonsense, sis. The tunnel has been searched from end to end. Besides, we can't wait any longer."

Colonel Bishop, his pale eyes wide, had been standing saying nothing.

He abruptly blurted, "I think I'll go up to your house, Lancaster. This… this whole thing gives me the horrors!"

He disappeared into the night.

Doc looked at the engineer. "But about these funny tracks you saw down there—" he started.

"Come on," suggested Lancaster. "I'll show them to you before we blast through."

A few moments later they were descending the fifteen hundred-foot shaft in the bucket. The girl, Chick, had wanted to go with them, but her brother had argued her out of it.

Twenty minutes later, Doc Savage was being shown the peculiar tracks in the earth of the tunnel.

SEVERAL workmen had come down with them. The men carried powerful flashlights, battery affairs that sprayed light as bright as day over the tunnel walls.

The prints were like the tracks left by a man's bare feet—only twice as large. They appeared in some of the soft muck of the tunnel floor.

Lancaster asked, "What do you make of them?"

Oddly, Doc had not been examining the tracks closely. Unobserved, his interest seemed to be more intent on the walls of the water tunnel.

But now he looked at the tracks, turned to a mucker and said, "You might give us a little more light here."

Behind Lancaster and the bronze man, who was bending down examining the earth, the workmen swung the light beams across the tunnel.

From where he crouched, none could observe the bronze man's gaze. It had flicked quickly to the tunnel wall beyond, was studying what appeared to be a large, grotesque shadow visible there. No one else observed the shadow, for Doc was careful not to lift his head too high. All thought he was studying the footprints on the floor.

But suddenly, the bronze man's trilling sound filled the bore. Musical, like distant winds stirring, it floated on the dank, close air.

A mucker gasped, "What was that?"

Others stared around.

No one had noticed the slight movement of the bronze man's lips as he made the unusual sound, an unconscious thing he did in moments of startling discovery.

Doc straightened up, said, "The tracks are very

interesting, but obviously faked by the man responsible for this trouble here."

Muckers stared at Doc Savage. Reds Lancaster looked spellbound.

"You mean," he stammered, "there is… is something *explainable* about all this mystery?"

Naturally," said Doc Savage quietly. "In fact, something has been made vividly clear to me."

Doc Savage would make no further explanations. It was his policy never to tell what he knew until he had a case completely solved.

But one thing was clear to those accompanying him now: Doc Savage, obviously, knew what the tunnel terror was all about.

Reds Lancaster was suddenly saying, "We'll have to hurry. We'll have to get out of here. The blast is scheduled for ten o'clock."

They had fifteen minutes in which to get aboveground!

LANCASTER'S auburn-haired, worried sister was waiting for them when they reached the surface. The bronze man drew the girl to one side.

He made a quiet request. He would like to know where there was a phone that could be used in private.

Chick Lancaster directed him to a community store that was located near the shaft. "There's a private booth in the back," she explained. "Old Milt is so deaf he wouldn't be able to hear you anyway."

Doc disappeared into the night. Oddly, he did not wait for the blast that was going to be set off in a moment or so.

In the store, within the private booth, the bronze man called a number in New York City. He talked several moments, then got the operator again and called another number. The bronze man made three calls in all.

When he came out of the store his metallic features were grimly thoughtful. He looked around for the girl, saw her running toward him.

Her face was white. She was trembling as she ran up to the bronze giant and cried frantically, "Reds—my brother—"

For a moment, it appeared as though she was going to faint.

Doc seized the girl's slender arms, demanded, "What's happened?"

The girl choked out stark words. "The blast… in No. 9… they've set it off!"

"Yes?"

"And Reds… he's missing. *Someone saw him go down in the shaft just before the explosion!"*

At the shaft opening, there was yelling and confusion. Steel-helmeted miners and muckers were grouped around the shaft opening, staring out of horrified eyes at the bucket that had just been raised from the tunnel.

It was empty.

Doc Savage looked, said nothing. But he seized the girl's arm. "Come on," he said quietly. "From now on, you must stay with me. Your life is in grave danger."

The girl's eyes were wide with amazement. *"My* life? But what about my brother?"

She drew back in horror as she realized Doc's purpose. The bronze man intended going below, into the tunnel.

"That explosion!" Chick Lancaster cried. "The water will be coming through. Oh, my God! Poor Reds—"

It was then that the bronze man made a strange statement.

"I don't think there will be any water," he said. "We will be able to enter the tunnel. Perhaps we will locate your brother."

Men protested as Doc and the girl climbed into the lowering device.

But Doc held up a bronze hand, said, "If we cannot get into the tunnel, we will signal you. The bucket can be then brought up again."

He motioned to the bellman, and then he and the girl dropped out of sight.

Someone said, "He's doomed!"

Chapter XVI
THE DEAD AND THE LIVING

THEY found the mummified man when they stepped out of the bucket at the base of Shaft 9. He was lying beneath a huge muck machine, his body mangled.

Chick Lancaster, showing the courage that was part of her makeup, rushed forward as some detail about the man's clothing riveted her attention. She bent to look before the bronze man could stop her.

And then she had whirled away from the spot, terrible screams coming from her throat. She flung herself against Doc, beat at his great chest.

"It's Reds!" she sobbed wildly, and her slim body was suddenly quivering with choking sobs.

The man beneath the muck machine wore whipcords and a flannel shirt and high-top leather shoes. From a pocket of the whipcords was visible a length of watch chain; attached to this a small gold key with the name of a well-known engineering society. It was the key and chain that the girl's brother had always worn.

The rest of Reds Lancaster was unrecognizable. His hands, face, entire body—as Doc learned after a brief look—was a thing of dried-up, parchment-like skin. Shriveled, as though by terrific heat that could have only come from one source.

The fog!

Doc examined the corpse's fingernails and skin ridges near the eyes.

Gently, Doc led the girl to one side. He went back and inspected the muck machine. A brief examination showed the bronze man that the machine had been tampered with, so that it would collapse the moment anyone turned on the power that operated it!

Abruptly, reaching their ears, there came a distant thumping, a sound as though someone was pounding on a solid wall of some kind.

Doc listened. He moved across to the girl and touched her arm. He said, "I realize how you feel. But I must ask you to come with me. You are not safe alone for a moment."

Chick Lancaster was too stunned to protest. She allowed the bronze man to lead her away from the gruesome sight of the crushed, mummified man. They headed northward through the great bore of the tunnel.

But even in her grief, Chick Lancaster's brain was clear enough to prompt a question.

"I don't understand," she said. "That explosion! That water that should be released from No. 10 bore! Why hasn't it been released?"

As they hurried through the tunnel, Doc, from time to time, had been glancing at his wristwatch. He drew up short now, held out his arm for the girl to see. Visible was the small, accurate compass which he had shown her once before.

"The tunnel should lead true north," he said. She nodded, her eyes still misted.

"Look!"

SHE stared at the compass needle.

"But what—" she started to ask.

"Magnetic north!" Doc said. "The tunnel has not followed the original line plotted by the engineers. It tends to a slight curve west of north. There has been a mistake."

"Mistake?"

"They use a plumb line in the shafts composed of a heavy weight attached to a cable, which is lowered down the shaft, is that right?"

The girl nodded. "They use that to make certain the tunnel follows a straight line."

"Exactly," agreed Doc Savage. "But—that weight was magnetized by someone. It threw the calculations off. I examined one of the plumb line devices yesterday."

Chick Lancaster was stunned by the information. She quickly understood why no water had been released into this tunnel from No. 10 by the explosion of the tunnel head.

"The two tunnels do not meet!" the girl cried.

Doc nodded.

They had been hurrying through the tunnel as they talked. The thumping sounds had become louder. Suddenly, they appeared to be right beside them.

Doc paused, swung around. One of the spring-generated flashlights was in his bronze hand, for the vague tunnel lights were too dim to reveal much of the rock walls.

Doc started to say, "It was just about here Monk cracked his head on what he thought was a—"

Then he stopped. The girl, too, stared.

It was as though the dynamite blast of such a short while ago had found a weak spot in an earth fissure. For the rock wall had split. There seemed to be some sort of opening!

Doc plunged forward, the light in his hand. The girl followed. And before their intense gaze they both saw the heavy slab of rock that had swung aside as though it were a door of sorts.

Both peered past the opening.

"Good heavens!" cried the girl, her eyes wide.

Doc led the way past the crack in the wall. The place beyond was a huge, underground cavern. A great domed ceiling met their gaze. The vaulted passage stretched off to the right and left, and somewhere in the distance was the faint sound of water moving over stones.

And something else.

The thumping sound was loud now, as though someone were hammering on something.

The girl had started to move into the underground cavern. She turned back as she noted that Doc had paused, examining the wall through which they had entered.

Doc had taken out a penknife, was probing at the surface of the wall.

An exclamation escaped his grim lips.

"GLASS!" he said.

"What—" the girl started.

"It is not a rock wall of the tunnel at all, but a glass section painted over to resemble rock. It is an opening through which anyone could have entered—or escaped—from the tunnel."

Chick Lancaster stared. "But—"

Doc was bending down, picking up something that had been hidden behind the door. Moisture dripped from the domed ceiling over their heads as he moved, and ran down his corded neck.

The object the bronze man clutched was a cylinder, an aluminum-colored object about the shape and size of a small oxygen cylinder used in hospitals. There was a valve at the end of this thing, and Doc gave it a turn.

Immediately a vaporish, gray-white gas came from the nozzle. It touched the bronze man's hand, burned like hot fire into his flesh.

Doc jerked the valve closed, whirled the girl

away from the spot. The odor of the escaping, foglike gas identified a chemical that he well knew.

"What is it?" Chick cried.

Doc waited until the small amount of escaped gas had dissipated. Then he moved carefully back to where it had struck the wall that was moist. The wall was absolutely dry!

And there was a livid, small burn on the bronze man's hand.

He said, "The formula is complicated, but briefly—it is a chemical that destroys water, breaks it down into its two components, oxygen and hydrogen. And in doing so, terrific heat is generated. Enough of that stuff would even dry the moisture out of a human's body."

Chick Lancaster gripped the bronze man's arm. She was trembling. "It… it explains the… the mummies!" she said.

Doc Savage nodded. The girl covered her face with her hands, thinking of the body they had just seen back by the muck machine.

The thumping sound from within the underground cavern had abruptly faded. Doc was straining his ears, listening.

He started to say, "We might—"

And then the yell came. A roar, rather, floating back from some distance. A voice that called:

"Holy cow! Monk! Ham! Look what's here!"

Doc and the girl raced through the great underground cavern. From time to time their feet struck loose sand. It was as though they were on the hard packed beach of a section that had once been at sea level.

They ran toward the sound of Renny's voice.

Chapter XVII
DANGER OVERHEAD

THE four men moved with weary steps. For hours they had been pushing their way through the vast underground caverns. For hours they had been without food. They had about given up hope.

Monk, his homely face gloomy, said, "You know what?"

The three men trailing behind him drew up short and looked at the hairy chemist's bedraggled appearance. The three men were Ham, big Renny and little hard-boiled Hardrock Hennesey. Even Ham's usually natty attire was soiled and torn.

Hardrock Hennesey spat, remembered that there was no tobacco in his mouth, swore and said, "Maybe we oughta go back to that torture room place and try our luck at getting out the way we came in."

Monk jumped.

"Not *me!*" he piped shrilly. "We had a close-enough escape as it was. It was blasted lucky we found that way out of the room and into this cavern."

Renny nodded. "We'd better keep on the way we're going."

They were using a single flashlight. Above their heads moisture dripped from the great domelike ceiling of the underground passage. A dampness, a raw coldness, had got into each man's bones, and they were shivering.

Powerful Renny carried a heavy stone which he had picked up a couple hours ago. From time to time, he moved close to one of the rock walls and banged the stone against the surface. He had hoped to find some spot that might show a fissure by which they could get out. He had not been lucky.

The four kept walking.

Monk muttered, "I wonder if there really are some of them big people still living in this crazy world down here?"

Ham snapped, "Shut up. I'm trying not to think about it!"

Their steps lagged. Renny took the lead, being of more powerful build than the others. It was he who was carrying the light, and he got some distance ahead of them. They seemed to be climbing now, and the giant engineer's hopes had quickened. Thus he had forged on ahead.

And when his booming voice shouted back to them, all stood still for a moment in stunned silence.

"Holy cow! Monk! Ham! Look what's here!"

MONK, his bowed, short legs carrying him along furiously, for all his weariness, was first to reach Renny's side. The others arrived shortly behind him.

Renny was squeezed into a narrow crevice where there was barely room for his massive shoulders. His gloomy face turned back to look at the others. He yelled:

"There's something—here—ahead—that looks damned modern, or I miss my guess. Looks like a pipe!"

They all squeezed in behind Renny and urged him forward.

The round, huge thing gleamed in the light ray. They reached it. It was a pipe—a steel waterline pipe about eight feet in diameter. By the merest chance, Renny had spotted the thing at the end of the narrow defile leading out from the cavernous underground space.

They immediately started following the pipe line. At points it was necessary to crawl on hands and knees, to squeeze through knothole spaces.

They proceeded perhaps half a mile, and found that the pipe ended in a room that was apparently some sort of valve gate in the water system.

An iron ladder led upward. They scrambled up the ladder, opened a huge steel cover. They were suddenly out in the night air.

For a while, it was difficult to get their bearings. But Renny, who knew more about engineering than the others, was first to figure out where they were.

"Holy cow!" he bellowed. "It's the dam. We're in some kind of sluiceway that runs off one side of the thing!"

High, concrete walls bordered them in on either side. The walls were higher than that found around any prison!

Ahead, a broad apron of concrete angled upward. Up, up! It stopped at a sheer cement wall that rose as high as the side walls themselves.

Behind them, the wide apron of concrete dropped downward in a spillway that ended at a drop-off a hundred feet above jagged, huge rocks.

All stared.

Monk voiced their thought. "How the blazes we gonna get outta this place?" he wanted to know, puzzled.

From far above their heads, the harsh, cold voice from atop the wall rapped: "That's just it. *You aren't!"*

They all craned their necks upward. The flashlight that Renny was holding outlined the wiry, alert figure of the man standing up there looking down at them.

It was the engineer brother of Chick—Reds Lancaster!

A MOMENT later, another figure appeared beside that of the red-headed engineer. A man of about forty, wearing glasses and black clothes and a flowing black tie. He was extremely thin.

Hardrock said, "Who the hell is *that* guy?"

None could have known that it was the man who had accompanied Doc Savage from the State capitol—the newspaper publisher-millionaire, Colonel Bishop!

But all were certain of *one* thing. They had been tricked. The expression on the two men's leering faces above said that they planned death for these Doc Savage men and little Hardrock Hennesey.

Reds Lancaster had made a motion with his arm. A moment later there was a sound like a rushing of wind through swamp willows. What followed almost immediately held all four men momentarily frozen with horror.

Water. Tons and tons of water, suddenly appearing at the top of the spillway, hurtling down upon them.

Water that was being released from the storage lake that was Yellow River Dam!

Ham screamed a warning.

"Back inside. Hurry!"

They tumbled back into the opening that led into the valve gate room. They slammed the heavy, round steel trapdoor over their heads. There was a heavy dog-arm arrangement that sealed the lidlike affair tightly in place.

Water was pouring through even as powerful Renny grabbed the levers and screwed the lid up tight.

Above them now, ominous in sound, water rushed past the slim steel protection and made the noise the sea makes against the side plates of an ocean liner.

At the bottom of the ladder, below them, Doc Savage said:

"It was lucky Renny called out your names while you were back in the cavern."

They looked down. They saw Doc and the girl, Chick Lancaster!

Monk, without thinking, started to yell: "Doc! Blazes! Guess who's behind this thing? He's up there on the wall and he's—"

Some expression in the bronze man's magnetic eyes stopped the hairy chemist from completing the statement. Doc was standing just a little in front of the girl.

He said, "The man's name is Colonel Bishop."

The girl gasped. "Bishop? The publisher? Why, good heavens, he's a friend of Reds—" She remembered the accident at the muck machine. "He was a friend of my brother—"

She was suddenly in tears.

Doc Savage was listening to the sounds of the tons of water overhead. His metallic features were grim.

Ham yelled down, "We'll have to go back, try to find some way—"

But the bronze man was suddenly shaking his head.

"There is no way back," he pointed out. He indicated the girl. "We located a clever entrance from the tunnel into the underground caverns. Later, we went back to examine it again. It had been automatically sealed by some electrical device, apparently operated from aboveground."

Hardrock Hennesey stared at Monk. Ham looked at big Renny. And they all knew that as long as that spillway was open above their heads, they were trapped. They could be kept down here for days—weeks.

DOC SAVAGE had suddenly motioned them down from the ladder. He had moved toward a heavy steel door on one side of the concrete-walled room. He turned back a moment and directed:

"You will all wait here. There's just one chance that the main sluiceway valve can be shut off—if the water in the dam is not too high to block off this passage."

He disappeared beyond the door, entering what was obviously a passageway beneath the great dam itself.

They waited. Ham, as gallant as ever for all his bedraggled appearance, held the girl's slim hand. He heard her story about the death of her brother, at the base of Shaft 9. He listened in silence and said nothing, but his eyes met those of his companions.

He, like Monk, Hardrock Hennesey and Renny, had seen Reds Lancaster a moment ago with their own eyes.

It must have been an hour later that they all stiffened, listening. The rush of water above them had slackened. It slowly dropped to a murmur. It finally stopped.

Renny yelled, "Doc's got it shut off!"

He piled back up the ladder, unloosened the heavy dog-arms, put his weight against the round trapdoor.

It lifted upward and water dribbled down his shoulders and gloomy-looking face.

But the way out was clear.

A light beam hit their faces as they came out into the night air. Doc Savage's voice called down to them.

"Grab the rope. Come up one at a time."

They tied the rope around the girl's slender waist first. They saw her pulled upward to safety. Renny, Ham and Hardrock Hennesey went up next.

When Doc dropped the rope down the last time, Monk didn't wait to be pulled up. He scrambled up the thing hand over hand like a happy monkey!

Atop the sluiceway wall, off to their left, they saw something in the dark night that held them momentarily rigid.

Two men, fighting, along the very edge of the great retaining wall of Yellow River Dam! While two hundred feet below, bellowing and waving their fists angrily, was a mob of tunnel workers from Shaft 9. The workmen held flashlights and flares. Obviously they were yelling at the two fighting men atop the great wall which towered over their heads.

But on top of the dam wall, the light was too vague to make identification of the two fighting men possible.

Monk was all for getting over there and investigating.

It was Doc who held him back. The bronze giant indicated the girl, whose face was still pale from the ordeal which she had been through.

He told Monk, "Take her up to the superintendent's house." Doc indicated the house overlooking the big dam, the home where Flynn, the superintendent, lived. "She has taken a slight chill," Doc said. "Hurry."

The assignment was one which hardly displeased the homely chemist. He lifted the girl into his arms and hurried off.

Doc swung back to the others.

"She must never know," he ordered

Ham asked: "You mean, that her own brother, Reds Lancaster, was behind this mystery?"

The bronze man nodded. For one of the few times ever observed by anyone, slight lines of fatigue showed around his remarkable flake-gold eyes.

"Yes, that," said Doc. "Also, that he was merely a dupe for the *real* villain—Colonel Bishop."

Everyone stared.

As Doc Savage talked, his eyes were on the two men battling high up on the dam. He suddenly started in that direction, saying quickly, "We can figure out what to do with Lancaster *after* we rescue him. It appears that he and Bishop have split."

Renny, racing after Doc Savage, exclaimed, "That's *Bishop* up there fighting?"

Doc nodded, and as he swung up to grasp a ladder that led onto the wall, the others ran after him.

Chapter XVIII
DEATH FOR TWO

THE distance to where the two men were struggling furiously near the sheer edge of the dam wall was perhaps two hundred yards. Doc and the others were almost to the spot when the bronze man drew up short, pushed the others back

"Listen," he said warningly.

They all heard the shots. The gunshots that were accompanied by curses and loud yelling from below the wall, from the tunnel workers momentarily out of sight of Doc and the others.

The workmen, enraged, were shooting at the two fighting men—Lancaster and Colonel Bishop. The two crooks had been spotted, and now men were intent upon killing them!

Little Hardrock Hennesey wanted to get his hands on Reds Lancaster. He tried to get past the bronze man. Powerful Renny yanked him back.

Renny bellowed, "Fool! Do you want to get riddled with those bullets?"

They could hear lead smacking the wall of the dam, close beneath the feet of the two struggling figures. The slugs richocheted off the concrete, went screaming upward into the night.

For the moment, Doc and the others could do nothing. To move nearer to the fighting pair of men meant danger of being hit by a stray bullet. And so they stood tensely and watched.

A powerful spotlight being used by one of the workmen below the dam wall hit one of the struggling figures. It outlined the thin figure of the black-clad publisher—Bishop. The man's flowing black tie was in shreds; he was now without his glasses.

As they watched, Ham demanded, "But how is Bishop tied into this thing?"

Doc said, "Bishop owns practically all the property in the valley sponsored by the politicians opposing Governor Bullock. By throwing suspicion on the governor, and also creating a menace here so that the work would have to be stopped, he would force them to use the other site. Thus he would clean up a fortune when they came to buy the property."

"But Lancaster?" Ham prodded. "What about him?"

"Lancaster owes Bishop forty thousand dollars. Years ago, Bishop helped him out of some sort of mess. Now he is forcing Lancaster to pay off. The girl informed me tonight that her life has recently been threatened. That was Bishop's trick to force Lancaster to do his bidding."

As he talked, Doc had moved closer to the two. So intent were they upon slaughtering one another that neither had noticed the approach of the bronze man and his partners.

But more bullets arrived over the top of the dam wall. They whined past the ears of everyone. Doc and the others were forced to crouch low.

Lancaster and Bishop were rolling around in a tangled heap now, dangerously near the edge of the wall. Miraculously, the bullets missed them.

As they all watched tensely, Doc added another bit of explanation. "A phone call to New York revealed that Bishop was the owner of most of the property they would be forced to use. Of course, he was working through a false name, under a fake company."

Suddenly, before their eyes, a peculiar thing happened.

Colonel Bishop, with a frightful yell, swayed to his feet, clutching his thin chest. In his right hand was a gun. His own, apparently.

Obviously he had tried to use the gun on Lancaster. But the quick-moving engineer had managed to twist the weapon away from him. Bishop had shot himself.

He swayed. Even Lancaster looked amazed that such a thing could have happened. Perhaps he had not meant to kill Bishop. At least the expression in his wide eyes now said that he was startled. Unmindful of the shouts from below, he watched the wounded man.

And then, without warning, Bishop threw his toppling body against the engineer. In his last weak step forward, he knocked into Reds Lancaster.

Lancaster made a frantic attempt to catch his balance. His hands pumped the air as though he was making a frantic attempt to grab something. In the next instant he went backward over the wall and disappeared from sight. A scream floated above the yelling from below.

Bishop crashed into a broken heap at the very edge of the wall.

Doc and the others leaped forward. Disregarding the moaning man at their feet, they stared down the sheer length of the wall. They were in time to see Lancaster's tumbling body strike the outward curve of the dam, two hundred feet below. It struck, bounced, then slid like a limp rag doll along the remaining seventy-five feet of dam footing. A wide swath of red fluid, revealed by the spotlights, was left behind the body.

Every bone in Lancaster's body must have been broken by the plunge.

MONK had arrived back from the superintendent's house in time to witness the death plunge of Lancaster. He stared now in awe.

Puzzled, he asked, "Doc, while we were waiting for you to shut off that water, the girl told us her brother died back there in the tunnel. She even said—"

"The person she saw," said Doc, "was the old fellow who tried to lead you into a trap earlier. I estimated his age from the ridges in his fingernails and from the crow's feet around his eyes. Lancaster saw that he was almost trapped. He was going to vanish from the picture. And so he made it appear that he had died. What he did was kill off that old fellow who had been working for him throughout."

Mention of the withered old man made Monk remember the giant skeletons and the horror chamber. He asked about that. Renny and Ham were bending down over the dying man.

Doc Savage said, "When the girl was with me in the underground caverns, she happened to mention the old Indian mounds that used to be near here. They unearthed some of the stuff when they first excavated. The Mound Builders left weird collections. Lancaster used the stuff to make it appear some race of people were still living there in the Earth. In fact, there was an old museum near here once. It is now closed. Investigation will probably disclose that things have been stolen from the place."

Bishop, dying, had been propped up by powerful Renny. The man's dimming eyes sought the bronze man's. He muttered weakly:

"The photograph… I mailed… did not fool you!"

Doc shook his head. He said. "There was a shadow across one edge of the picture, Bishop. In your own newspaper building that photo was enlarged many times. Tonight, down in the tunnel, a workman's flashlight happened to cast an enlarged outline of Lancaster's profile on the tunnel wall. It matched, identically, the profile revealed by the enlarged shadow in the photograph. Lancaster took that picture, and inadvertently his own shadow was cast on a wall as he made it."

Monk suddenly remembered something. He made a dive toward the dying man. The chemist wasn't very particular whether the man was dying or not. Bishop was the real villain, and there was something he should know.

"Hey!" squalled Monk. "Betcha *he* knows about the governor!"

Doc pushed Monk back as he said, "Governor Bullock is safe at our New York headquarters."

Monk stared. "But how—" he started to demand.

Explaining another of the phone calls he had made tonight, Doc Savage said, "He went there because his life had been threatened." Doc told them about the letter handed him by the dazed butler at the Bullock estate. "The letter the governor *really* left explained that he was going to our headquarters. He had previously phoned and asked me to investigate this mystery. But his letter was switched for another by thugs who knocked out the butler."

The dying man gasped, "Has... *anyone* ever... outwitted you... Doc Savage?"

Monk started to blurt, "Brother, *nobody* fools Doc—" And then he paused.

Colonel Bishop was dead.

LATER, following a circuitous route from the small valley below the dam, the tunnel men arrived at the spot where Doc and the others were grouped around the dead man.

One of the arriving men exclaimed, "Lancaster's dead. He tumbled off this wall—"

Doc Savage nodded. And then, holding up his hand, he made a brief speech. It was probably one of the most impressive speeches the bronze man ever made. He said:

"Lancaster, in a way, was a dupe for this man here." He indicated the dead newspaper publisher. Briefly he explained how Bishop was behind the mystery. He went on, "Lancaster is dead, but his sister believes he died down in the shaft. It is best that she always thinks that."

Doc mentioned the fight between the two men behind the mystery. "At the very last, Lancaster must have turned against Bishop. He had realized his mistake. And so now, and for all time, it is best that his sister know nothing of his connection with the real villain. Since he is dead, no good can be gained by making her suffer further."

There were shouts of "Bravo!" from the tunnel men. All liked Chick Lancaster. She was the kind of a girl who inspires admiration in brave men. All agreed to Doc Savage's suggestion.

Preparations were made for the removal of Lancaster's broken body, lying at the base of the great dam. Someone asked the bronze man:

"But what about that fog that turned guys into mummies?"

Doc told of finding the cylinders of chemical hidden in the cavern. He explained how the chemical broke down water and at the same time generated terrific heat.

"The heat," Doc pointed out, "was so intense that it literally baked a man's body. The chemical is also poisonous. Bishop planned on using it in the water system of the dam to make it worthless—in case his other plans fell through."

Tall, angular Flynn, the superintendent of the dam, arrived accompanied by the two pets, Habeas and the chimp.

Monk let out a joyous shout. Ham grabbed his pet.

The superintendent said, "They were just delivered to the house. They wandered back to the shaft tonight, half starved. But they had been fed."

Monk petted Habeas. Ham held the chimp in his arms.

The hairy chemist suddenly remembered the girl. He asked:

"How's Chick?"

"Got her wrapped up in bed with plenty of blankets," the superintendent said. "She's O.K. now. In fact, she's been asking for you two."

Monk beamed, and Ham looked pleased, also. They led the way back to the house. In the lower hallway, they waited until the superintendent had gone upstairs to see if the girl was awake.

She was.

MONK'S homely features split in a wide grin that threatened to dislodge his ears.

"Chick likes Habeas," he piped in his squeaky voice. "I'm gonna go upstairs and cheer her up!"

Ham pushed his burly partner aside. He gave Monk a frigid stare.

"She likes *me!*" Ham said icily. "Not that scrawny pig! Get out of my way!"

They both went up the stairs, arguing.

THE END

INTERMISSION by Will Murray

Doc Savage battles home-grown threats in these two novels written in the 1940s.

William G. Bogart appears to be the primary author of our first selection, *Tunnel Terror*. It was logged in the Street & Smith pay book as his work on January 25, 1940, but his name was subsequently X'd out and that of Lester Dent typed in its stead.

Since Bogart had been a subeditor under John L. Nanovic until leaving to freelance in 1938, this was an understandable mistake. Lester Dent had moved back to La Plata, Missouri at this time, and the storyline was probably hashed out in the S&S New York offices between Nanovic and Bogart. No outline exists among Lester Dent's manuscripts, indicating that he may not have had even a supervisory role in the creation of this tale. Yet the text contains a number of Dentian flourishes. Had Bogart learned to ape the original "Kenneth Robeson," or did Dent touch up his prose during one of his frequent visits to the S&S offices in New York?

Whatever the case, Bogart was writing as a Dent ghost, and so Lester was paid for the manuscript, splitting his fee with the writer.

The minor industry that was *Doc Savage* magazine was going full blast in January of 1940. Within days of *Tunnel Terror* landing on Nanovic's desk, Lester turned in *The Awful Egg*, while Harold A. Davis submitted *The Purple Dragon*.

The next month, Bogart delivered *The Awful Dynasty* and Alan Hathway penned his first Doc entry, *The Headless Men*. It's entirely possible that Street & Smith, receiving the first sales reports on *The Avenger* magazine, which also carried the byline of "Kenneth Robeson," was again planning to go twice-a-month with *Doc Savage*.

As had happened back in 1935, the plan fizzled. Instead, Street & Smith revived *The Whisperer* that Fall.

Submitted under the working title of "Hell and Hardrock," *Tunnel Terror*, which ran in the August, 1940 issue, is typical of Bill Bogart's Doc Savage output. He often exploited the threat-to-industry theme, possibly because he was not as imaginative as other ghostwriters, and these were areas that could be researched. The present novel is another example of this.

Editor Nanovic blurbed *Tunnel Terror* in typical fashion:

> In our next issue, we will have Doc and his gang go through some really exciting experiences in a huge tunnel-building job. The tunnel is not a tunnel in the true sense of the word, since it is a water conduit. But it is as large as a total job would be, and many times longer than any practical tunnel might be. There are a number of such projects going on all over the country right now; for water supplies for great cities, for drainage, for irrigation, and for other purposes. The dangers which beset the men working under such conditions are tremendous. When, as happened in this case, some evil influence is at work, the dangers are multiplied by many times; the result is a tense, thrill-filled situation that makes a better-than-usual Doc Savage exploit. You will thrill to "Tunnel Terror," complete in the next issue.

Nanovic delved deeper into the subject, in the issue showcasing the novel:

> There are certain types of jobs which carry with them a great deal of color and interest. Mere mention of such jobs immediately brings you visions of exciting, life-risking episodes.
>
> Perhaps the most exciting of such jobs is that of tunnel building. Whether the tunnel is under a river or through a mountain, or a long, underground connection for water source or anything at all, that glamour and interest exist. That is why we feel that the novel in this issue, "Tunnel Terror," is one that will really give you something to thrill over. Not only are all the accepted risks and dangers present in this job of constructing a huge tunnel project, but Kenneth Robeson, with the masterly hand that he uses on all his Doc Savage novels, puts into the story all the interest, suspense, and punch that you find in every one of these successful stories. Such a combination is hard to beat—and we know that every line of "Tunnel Terror"… to the very end, will give you just one thrill after another.

William Bogart went to great lengths to obscure this story's setting, placing it in the "West," but not naming the state, and calling its capital, "Capital City." But there are a few significant clues, specifically mention of the "Yellow River Dam" associated with the tunnel construction. That project appeared to be based upon the Denison Dam, which was built on the Texas-Oklahoma border, in which the Red River was dammed, creating the artificial Lake Texoma.

Construction of the Lake Texoma Dam, as it is also known, began in 1939. It was completed in 1943, so it perfectly fits the timeframe of the novel. Apparently, *Tunnel Terror* takes place in Texas.

One of the most intriguing elements of this story was the discovery of mysterious human bones of giant size in the underground tunnel project, which are associated with the mound builder culture of Native American Indians. While these ancient mounds are most associated with the plains states, some have been found in Texas, home of the Caddo culture.

Newspaper accounts going back to at least the eighteenth century recount the discovery of giant skeletons unearthed all over the United States, often as tall as twelve or more feet in height, and some possessing unusual characteristics such as double rows of teeth, or six digits on hands and feet. These bones are often associated with Native American burial sites.

Bogart never quite explains these giant remains, but they appear to have been introduced into the story to build up its mysterioso atmosphere. It's also possible that further explanations were cut from the text by an overzealous S&S assistant editor.

Appropriately, civil engineer Renny Renwick is the lead aide of this story. Curiously, Ham Brooks is spotlighted on the cover. The intention was to showcase each of Doc's five aides on 1940 covers. Monk had already graced the cover two issues previous to this one. But after Ham's turn came, the practice ceased. A sales decline in 1940 may explain the sudden change in plans.

Our second story, *Once Over Lightly*, has a strange and convoluted history. It begins in 1946, a year in which Lester Dent was trying to break out of the pulp magazine ghetto and become a hardcover and slick magazine scribe. He had hopes of leaving Doc Savage behind him, with William Bogart carrying the ball. Bogart was busily writing the monthly novels during that summer, while Lester banged out some mystery novels for Doubleday's Crime Club imprint.

The germ of the idea was a memo Lester penned that year:

> Transfer "Monk and Ham" feud to two girls in a detective yarn. They can be stooges in a detective agency."

Trying to get a toehold in the better-paying slick magazines, he embarked on "The Mystery of the Barking Duck," about Miss Mary Olga Ten Eyck, whose initials form her nickname, "Mote." Mote is affiliated with the N.W.W.F.B., or the National Wailing Wall for Frightened Businessmen, and is an attractive blonde. As the story opens, the Foundation is in a dither about the resignation of an important member, Miss Grizella Jones, aka Jonsey, who appears to be the key to the whole Foundation.

Seven pages into the draft, Dent abruptly changes course and starts afresh, this time calling the story "The Mystery of the Immodest Mouse." Mary Olga Trunnels and Jonsey are now ex-WACS fresh to Hollywood and looking for a break. Ensconced at a desert hotel, they become embroiled with some curious characters, including updated versions of his retired pulp protagonists, Genius Jones and Click Rush, the Gadget Man.

Around May, Dent sent a 67-page partial for this humorous mystery novelette to his New York agent, Willis Kingsley Wing, for evaluation, signing the work "Formar Savage" as a gesture to his breaking away from his Doc Savage obligations.

When he didn't hear back, Lester wrote again:

> Did you get a tentative start I sent you titled, I think, Mystery of the Immodest Mouse? If it's off too much, I want to use it in a Doc Savage, and if not, I'd like to go on to it.

Wing had mixed feelings about the manuscript, admitting that it had been a fun read, but noting that by the time the finished story reached print, the premise of two returning WACs would be pretty dated. He also remarked, "The suggested pen-name has significance to you, I suspect, but it is so patently a phony name I think you better give some thought to a better one."

That was the end of the career of Formar Savage. Dent shelved the idea temporarily.

When Doc Savage shifted to bi-monthly frequency, Bogart was out and Lester resumed his responsibilities to Street & Smith as "Kenneth Robeson," inaugurating a group of Doc Savage stories told in the first person. His Doc Savage sabbatical had lasted only six months.

Not until April of 1947 did Lester return to "The Mystery of the Immodest Mouse," re-outlining it as a Doc Savage narrative related by his former protagonist. Dent called it *Once Over Lightly*, and it was finally published in the November 1947 *Doc Savage Science Detective*.

Here is how editor Babette Rosmond blurbed it:

> "Why should I be involved? It's a matter for the local sheriff," said Doc Savage.
>
> He was wrong.
>
> It was a screwy hotel—but then the whole set-up was screwy, including a girl named Glacia and an inheritance that nobody quite understood—except that it led to sinister results.
>
> You, too, will wonder about Keeper and the mystery surrounding him—or it...as you follow this new Doc Savage novel, ONCE OVER LIGHTLY.

One suspects that the title was a sly reference to that fact that Lester retyped the original story, completing the narrative and transforming it into a Doc entry. He probably expected them to change the title anyway. But they didn't.

Of course, *Once Over Lightly* wasn't merely a retyping job. After all, the Man of Bronze had to be brought into the action. For his new opening, Lester reached back into his personal history, and replicated the time when he was a young pulpster, back in 1930. One day, he received a surprise telegram from Dell Publications in New York City, suggesting that he quit his day job at the Associated Press and relocate to write full time on salary.

As you will shortly read, Mary Olga Trunnels is faced with a similar offer. *Once Over Lightly* was one of the last of the first-person Doc Savage novelettes, and the final we have to reprint. Enjoy it. •

ONCE OVER LIGHTLY

by Kenneth Robeson

Chapter I

OUT of a clear sky came this telegram. It read, MISS MARY OLGA TRUNNELS: IF YOU ARE MAKING LESS THAN HUNDRED A WEEK QUIT YOUR JOB. I HAVE BETTER ONE FOR YOU. FINE SALARY, LOVELY SURROUNDINGS, WONDERFUL PEOPLE.

It was signed, GLACIA.

That didn't sound like Glacia should sound somehow, so I wired back: HAVE YOU TAKEN TO DRINK?

This should have drawn a sassy answer, but it didn't. It got this:

WIRING YOU TRANSPORTATION. JOB IS SUPERB. HONEY YOU MUST COME.

—GLACIA.

The telegrams were coming from a place named Sammy's Springs, California, and it did not seem to be on the map. A place called Sammy's Springs sounded as if it belonged in California, but it still wasn't on the map. I looked.

Being a conservative girl sometimes, and also still feeling that all this didn't sound quite like Glacia, I tried the telephone. The operators seemed to have no trouble finding Sammy's Springs.

"Glacia," I said. "What has gotten at you? Have you married a monster, or something?"

Glacia had a voice that went well with champagne and little silver bells, and she used it to tinkle pooh-poohings at me. Then, speaking rapidly, she told me in five different ways that it was a wonderful job out there, and asked me four different times to come out in a hurry.

"I'll rush down and wire you a plane ticket this instant," Glacia said.

"Why should *you* wire the ticket? Why not let the purveyor of this wonderful job do that? And by the way, who is my future employer?"

"Oh! You're coming! Fine! Wonderful! Oh, I'm so delighted!"

She kept saying this in various ways for a while, then said well this was costing me money, long-distance calls didn't come for nothing, and goodbye and she would meet the plane with bells on, then she hung up. She hadn't told me who the job was with, nor what it was.

I decided that it had been Glacia I was talking to, because it was Glacia's voice, but that was about all. Glacia hadn't demanded a cent of grease for getting me the job. Not like Glacia, that wasn't. She wasn't one to do a favor without getting her bite, and she was brazen and hardheaded enough to have it understood ahead of time that she would want a cut.

I lay awake for a while trying to figure it out, and about midnight, just before going to sleep, I began to wonder if Glacia hadn't sounded scared, really. Still, it would take quite a fright to jolt a dollar out of Glacia's mind.

The next morning, I went to work at the office, and waited for Mr. Tuffle to make a mistake. Mr.

Tuffle was my department boss, and could be depended on for a mistake every day. He was the vice president's son-in-law, which put him in a position where he could blame his subordinates for his stupidity. I began to think he was going to miss today just to spite me, but about two o'clock he came over to my desk roaring to know where the Glidden Account papers were and why in hell I hadn't turned them in on time. I had turned them in on schedule, and further than that, I knew just where he had misplaced them the afternoon he rushed off early for a game of golf. I went to his desk, dumped the drawer contents on the floor, grabbed out the Glidden Account papers, and raised hell myself. I carried the stuff into Mr. Roberts' office, raised more hell, and got fired.

That took care of the embarrassing matter of having to quit the job without the usual two-week notice. Incidentally, it did the office morale some good. They gave me a party that night.

Glacia had wired the airline reservation herself. I inquired about that, and she was the one who had sent the ticket.

The plane was one of those super-duper four-motored stratosphere jobs. It got me to Los Angeles in less than ten hours, and they were paging me over the public address system there. I was wanted at the reservations counter, the loudspeaker was saying.

"Oh, yes," said the reservation clerk. "This gentleman is waiting for you."

The gentleman was a very tall Indian, with two feathers in his hair. He was having trouble with one of his feathers, which was cocked forward over his left eye. He straightened it, and looked at me.

"Ugh!" he said presently. "You the one, all right. You answer description." And then he asked, "You got heap strong stomach?"

"I don't know about that, Hiawatha. Why?"

He put a large copper thumb against his own chest. "Name is Coming Going," he said.

"Glad to meet you, Mr. Going," I said. "Now why this interest in my stomach?"

"Got lightplane," said Mr. Coming Going. "Supposed to fly you like a bird to place named Sammy's Springs."

"Oh," I said. "You mean that you are a pilot who has been employed to furnish me transportation the rest of the way to my destination?"

He nodded. "That would be long-winded way of saying so," he admitted.

"Who hired you? Glacia?"

Coming Going lifted his eyes as if he were looking at an eagle, and whistled the wolf-call.

"That would be Glacia," I said. "All right, let's get my suitcases and be on our way."

"Ugh," he said, and we got my suitcase. He must have expected more in the way of baggage, because he seemed favorably impressed.

"Squaw with one suitcase!" he remarked wonderingly. "Wonders haven't ceased." Then he examined me again, with more interest than before, and said another, "Ugh!"

That "Ugh!" was the end of his conversation for the trip. I found out why he was interested in whether or not I had a strong stomach. The plane he had was a little two-place grasshopper affair, sixty-five horsepower, the pilot seated ahead of the passenger. A kite with an engine. We flew for three hours over desert and mountains and the thermals and downdrafts tossed us around like a leaf. My stomach stood it, although there were times when I wondered.

The only comment Mr. Going had on the durability of my midriff was another, "Ugh!" after we landed. It was slightly approving, however.

Glacia came running and screaming, "Mote! Darling! You did get here! How divine!"

Glacia was blonde, small, lively, and wonderful for gentlemen to look upon, with hair falling to her shoulder, widely innocent blue eyes, a tricky nose, and other features to nice specifications. She did not look as if she had a penny's worth of brains, although she actually had some—in an acquiring fashion.

I told her she was looking wonderful—she was—and then asked what about this job, and didn't get an answer. I got a lot of conversation, the gushing sort, but no specific data on the job.

Glacia had a car waiting. A roadster. Seen after dark, the color of the car wouldn't put your eyes out, but now the desert sun was shining on it, and it nearly blinded me.

"You must have taken some fellow for plenty, honey," I said.

Glacia had no answer to that, but plenty of other words, and we got in the roadster and drove through mesquite, cholla cactus, yucca cactus, barrel cactus—I didn't know one cactus from another, but Glacia gave a running comment on cacti as we drove—and after a few miles it became evident that we were approaching a rather odd sort of civilization.

"You'll love this place, dear," said Glacia.

We got closer.

"For God's sake!" I said.

"There!" said Glacia. "I told you. Quaint, isn't it?"

"You mean this is a hotel?"

"Yes."

"But what—"

"Oh, it isn't a bit like the ordinary hotel," Glacia explained. "That's probably what makes it *the* place to be seen. Lots of Hollywood people come here. Nothing around here is supposed to be quite commonplace."

I could see that it wasn't commonplace. The buildings were made of native stone and enormous logs in an utterly bizarre architectural plan, like one of those hairbrained plans that artists think up for the magazines when they are handed a story of a visit to Mars or some other planet to illustrate. The structures hadn't been skimped on size, either, I discovered, when we drove into a tunnel-like portico that would have accommodated a locomotive.

There was a whispering sound, a big door closed quietly behind us, and we were greeted by a rush of cold conditioned air that seemed approximately zero. Outside the temperature must be past a hundred.

"You'll love it," Glacia said.

"You're not," I said, "implying that this is going to be my place of residence?"

"Certainly. Why not?"

"There's a slight matter of dollars involved. Or don't they use them for legal tender around here?"

"Oh, that's taken care of," said Glacia.

"Is it? You don't say. I'd like to know—"

What I wanted to know about was this job, which was rather elusive it seemed to me, but three more Indians stalked out of the place and without a word captured my bag and disappeared inside with it. Two Indians carried the bag. The other walked behind them. They hadn't made a sound.

"Do they scalp anybody?" I asked.

"They're bellhops. Don't be silly," Glacia said.

"What do they charge you for a room around here?"

"They don't call it a room. You're a tribe member. That includes your lodging, food, recreation, everything."

"Don't beat around the bush, dear. I asked you the charge—"

"Nothing—for you. It's taken care of."

"Just the same, I'm not going to sign the register."

Glacia laughed, and I found out why. There wasn't any register, or if there was one, I never saw nor heard about it. This hotel, or resort, or whatever you would call it, was the screwiest spot imaginable.

My room was swell. Glacia managed to deposit me in it without telling me what the job was, and then skipped, saying, "You'll want to scrub up, honey. You look like you'd been pumped here through a pipe." Which was more like Glacia. She normally wasn't a very civil person, to people she could bulldoze well enough to call them her friends. I'm afraid I belonged to that category.

The room had a stuffed buffalo in it, but otherwise it was normal. The walls were pastels, blues mostly, and the furniture was what one would probably find in the forty-dollar-a-day suite in the Waldorf. But the buffalo rather dominated the place.

I went to the window to see whether the scenery was in keeping. It wasn't. The scenery was all right, a swatch of authentic desert equipped with the varieties of cactus Glacia had named, sand dunes, mesquite, probably sidewinders and scorpions, too. The mountains were not far away; they were remarkably dark mountains that tumbled and heaved up to a startlingly cyanite blue sky, and if there was a shred of vegetation, I failed to see it. The scenery was unique in a bleak, tooth-edging way. It didn't look at all genuine, but then that wasn't unusual in Southern California.

The scenery seemed to have an effect on me, though, or perhaps it was the hotel. Or wondering about this job. I showered and changed, and didn't feel any more confident, and tried to find a telephone to get in touch with Glacia. There didn't seem to be any room telephones. I went into the hall, and an Indian, presumably another bellhop, was passing, and I asked him, "What about room phones? Don't they have any here?"

"Ugh," he said. "Takeum buffalo by horn and talk to him." He walked off.

I yelled, "Listen, Pocahontas, what room is Miss Glacia Loring in?"

"Mink," he said, not looking back and his feathered headdress not missing a bob.

So I went looking for mink. The suites weren't numbered either, it seemed, but were designated drawings of different animals and birds on the door panels. The place was screwy enough that this touch seemed quite sane and practical.

Glacia had changed to a bathing suit. It was small, a dab here and there. Not enough to do her figure any harm.

"Angel," she cried at me. "I want you to meet Uncle Waldo!"

"Whose Uncle Waldo?"

"Mine."

"I didn't know you had one," I said. "Listen, you beautiful wench, if you're trying to pass some antiquated boyfriend off as—"

"Oh, don't be so stinking moral," she said.

"He's really your Uncle?"

"My mother's brother. God help her," Glacia said.

That should sort of prepare me for anything, I thought. I hadn't known Glacia's family too well when I was a kid growing up in Kansas City, because we lived in the part of town where we had backyards and washings were hung there. The Lorings had lived four blocks over, not a great distance, but quite a long way measured in the snobbery scale. Glacia Loring and I ended up attending the same high school, and we must have found something in common—as I recall, we were both going to become actresses at the time, and got together in school theatricals—and we saw quite a lot of each other.

Were we friends as kids? I don't know. I doubt it, but it would depend on what the definition for friendship was. We were together a lot. We fought over the same boys, and got stuffed at the same soda fountains. I suppose we sort of rubbed off on each other. I toning Glacia down a little, and she giving me more glisten. But I don't know about that, either. I do know my mother didn't approve of Glacia's folks, and Glacia evidently had similar trouble at home, because she never took me there.

Not that Glacia's folks were snobs. They were screwballs. They just plain resented common sense, and they maintained that the conventional and the ordinary was slops for pigs. I think Glacia's mother and father were married in an airplane circling over Kansas City as a publicity stunt, and I knew that her grandfather on the maternal side had maintained that he, not Peary nor Cook, had been first to discover the North Pole, and that he had sued, or threatened to sue, both Admiral Peary and Cook for daring to lay claim to the Pole. This old fellow would be the sire of Glacia's Uncle Waldo, if there was really such an individual. And since Uncle Waldo was a sprig on such a goofer-tree, anything might be expected of him.

It might have been the cockeyed hotel, but I expected to find Uncle Waldo covered with monkeys. I wouldn't have been surprised, anyway.

What I met was a nice-looking old gentleman, not much taller than I am, an old gaffer made of oak and weather-cured hide. He wore tan flannel trousers with sandals, and a terrific checkered shirt. He was sitting in the bar which overlooked a swimming pool, and he was the only person in the place with a glass of milk in front of him. He looked me over.

"A seaworthy seeming craft," he remarked.

That didn't sound too much like a compliment, but I gathered it was. He had no more to say until he had given Glacia's scanty bathing costume a disapproving nose-wrinkling, and watched me order a drink. I ordered ginger ale with nothing in it, because my stomach was still in some doubts about what to do over the lightplane ride. Apparently, what I ordered met with approval, because Uncle Waldo got around to dropping an oracular opinion.

"She'll do," he said.

Glacia blew out her breath.

"Darling," she told me. "Now I can tell you about the job. It's working for me."

"For you!"

"Oh, don't look so shocked. What's so bad about that?"

"I don't know what's tough about it," I said. "But I'm sure something will develop."

Uncle Waldo chuckled. This sounded like a steam engine snorting once.

"The pay is good," Glacia said hastily. "You'll get fif—" She paused and examined my expression. "Eighty a week," she corrected.

"That's too much," I said. "Or is it?"

"Don't be so damned suspicious," Glacia said.

"So there's something I should be suspicious of?"

"Of course not!" She didn't sound convincing, although she tried hard enough.

"What is this job, baby?"

Glacia evidently had an answer all ready, but suddenly decided I wouldn't believe it, and got busy trying to think of another. While she was doing that, Uncle Waldo summarized the job.

"You hold niece's hand," Uncle Waldo said.

He meant Glacia, of course. By holding Glacia's hand, I hoped he didn't mean what I thought he meant. Anything that would make Glacia want her hand held probably wouldn't be easy on the nerves.

Chapter II

THE job had a snake in it somewhere. But two days passed and nothing happened and I was lulled into a condition that might be called a somewhat puzzled peace of mind—the kind of an attitude where you don't think you'll have to swim, but you take your bathing suit along just in case.

The two days had incidents enough in them, but they weren't significant incidents. Except, it later developed, one incident was going to lead to something. For I saw Doc Savage.

Glacia was with me at the time. We came into the lobby and there was an air of hush and bated breaths like the Second Coming.

"The redskins must have arisen," I said.

"It's always like this when he's passing through," said Glacia.

"What do you mean?"

"You'd think," said Glacia, "that if he wanted a vacation, he would go where no one knew him… Still, that place would be hard to find, I guess."

At this point the magnet for all the gaping interest appeared. He was a bronze man with flake gold eyes—that description sounds a good deal more casual than it should sound, probably. But that was all he meant to me at the time. A bronze man with flake-gold eyes. I did notice that when he passed near another person or a piece of furniture to which his proportions could be compared, there was the rather odd illusion that he became a giant. Not quite seven feet tall, but almost. Otherwise he was just an athletic-looking bronze man with gold eyes. Striking. But nothing to fall over on your face about.

Not until he had passed through the lobby and was gone did it seem permissible to resume breathing.

"Well, well, quite an effect," I told Glacia. "Who might he be?"

"Don't you know?"

"Should I?"

Glacia looked at me as if she considered me thoroughly stupid. "You mean to tell me… ?" She shook her head wonderingly.

"Has my education been neglected?"

"You evidently forgot to put on your brains this morning," Glacia said. She seemed genuinely disgusted. "That was Doc Savage."

"So?"

Glacia's eyes popped a trifle. "I honest-to-God believe you've never heard of him."

"Am I supposed to have?"

Glacia said she could cry out loud, said a couple of other things not complimentary, and added, "You must be ribbing me, dear."

"Just be nice for a change and tell me who he is?"

"Doc Savage, the Man of Bronze, the righter of wrongs and the nemesis of evildoers."

The way Glacia said it was odd, and I looked at her. She had put considerable feeling into it, not as if she was irked at my not knowing who this fellow was, but as if it was a personal matter with her—as if Savage himself was a personal matter.

"Oh, a detective," I said.

Glacia said, "Not so you would notice," without bothering to shake her head.

"G-man, then?"

But Glacia shook her head and said, "Skip it, baby." And the rest of the afternoon she was rather sober.

Later that evening, I found my redskin pilot, Mr. Coming Going, near the swimming pool. He wore a swim suit and two feathers, was having trouble with one of the feathers drooping over an eye, and was sitting with his legs cocked up on a table, watching female guests disporting in the pool.

"Ugh!" he said to me.

From that beginning, I worked the conversation around to Doc Savage, and asked for information about the star guest. I had touched a sympathetic chord, because Mr. Going's eye brightened. He said "Ugh!" a couple of times enthusiastically, changed to perfectly good Kansan City English, and told me that Doc Savage was a noted celebrity, a righter of wrongs and punisher of evildoers.

"I got that same line from my girlfriend-employer," I said. "But it sounds a little screwball."

"That Savage fellow is no screwball," said Coming Going. The glint in his eye was probably admiration—not for me, but for Savage. "What gave you such an idea?"

"That evildoer nemesis and wrong-righter stuff," I said.

"It's straight."

"Gadzooks. It sounds like strictly from the place where the bells hang."

"Well, that's what he does."

"You mean that's his profession?"

"Yep."

"How does he make it pay off?"

Coming Going shrugged. "I'm not his historian. Strikes me you should have heard of Savage. How did you miss it?" He gazed at me with more approval than he had evidenced hitherto. "You seem to be a pleasantly ignorant wench. The type I admire, incidentally."

I noticed that Mr. Coming Going had blue eyes. "Just how much Indian are you?" I asked.

He pretended to be alarmed lest we be overheard. "My pop once bummed a cigarette off Chief Rose Garden, but don't tell anybody on me."

"What tribe did Chief Rose Garden belong to?"

"Kickapoo, I guess. He was selling bottled Kickapoo Snake Oil off the tailgate of a wagon that stopped in our village for a while."

I left Mr. Coming Going without being certain whether I was being kidded.

That night, Glacia asked me to share her room. Somehow I did not seem at all surprised when she did so, which must mean that I had sensed something of the sort coming. Glacia was off-handedly high and mighty about it. "You'd better move in with me, and cut expenses," she said. And added, "I've already had your things brought to my suite."

It was all right. After all, she was paying me—she really was; I'd collected the first week's pay in advance—and she was entitled to give the orders.

About ten o'clock, Glacia said something else that seemed a bit odd. "I'm going to say good night to Uncle Waldo," she told me.

"If I'm not back in half an hour, will you check up?"

"What do you mean, check up?" I asked.

She said angrily, "Just see why I haven't returned! You ask too many questions!" She flounced out, slamming the door.

I went over to a chair and dropped into it, waiting for the clock minute hand to move half an hour. And presently I noticed that I had instinctively or for some other occult reason selected a chair facing the door. My hands seemed to have a peculiar unrest of their own—they wanted to hold something, and the fingers were inclined to bite at whatever they gripped, the latter objects alternating between the chair armrests, my knees, a handkerchief and an Indian warclub that I chanced to pick off the table.

The warclub, it presently occurred to me, was out of place. It didn't belong in the room, which was otherwise a fine modern hotel room. The screwball atmosphere of the hotel didn't extend to any of their suites—except for one little touch like a stuffed buffalo or something of that sort. And that reminded me—I looked around for the screwball item in Glacia's suite. But there didn't seem to be anything, because the warclub wasn't enough of a zany touch to qualify.

Presently I was worrying because there wasn't a stuffed buffalo or the equivalent in the place. The logical conclusion to be drawn from that was: I must be getting a loose shingle. The nutty desert resort, and the intangibility of my job, might be getting me.

Twenty minutes later, I decided I was scared. There was no other emotion that would quite account for my goose bumps. Frightened. Why? Well, Glacia wasn't back yet. But that didn't quite account for it. Something was giving me the feeling—feeling, indeed! It was more than an impression. It was utterly conviction—that there was considerable danger afoot. Where the notion came from, I hadn't the slightest idea.

In the next five minutes—Glacia had been gone twenty-five now—I formed a sound notion of what was making the roots of my hair feel funny. It was this—it didn't make sense, but it was this—something was waiting around to happen, and it was something violent. I had arrived at the desert resort and found an air of suspense, of expectancy, concealed waiting, tension, fear, danger and God knows what more. How did I know I had found these things? Somebody would have to tell me.

I was in the right mood to jump seven feet straight up when the door began to open with sinister slowness. It had been twenty-nine minutes since Glacia left. The door to the hall opened a fractional inch at a time. I didn't jump straight up or straight down. I just turned to stone.

Nobody more dangerous than Glacia came in. She gave me a rather odd smile.

"It's fate. Why don't you go to bed?" she said.

"What for?" I asked. "I won't sleep."

But evidently I did sleep. I think I did, anyway, because there was a period when nightmares and nighthorses galloped through a zone of muted terror. And once I possibly sat up in bed and looked for Glacia and she was gone. I say possibly, because I'm not sure; I only know that I lay back—granting that I ever sat up in the first place—and worried for a long time through a ghastly series of dreams about what I should do about Glacia being gone. Then finally I got the answer—I should get up and find her. Whereupon I awakened, unquestionably this time, and looked, and there was Glacia asleep where she should be on the other bed. I didn't go to sleep again that night. It wasn't worth the effort. I was scared of the dreams, too.

The sunlight was splattering in through the windows when Glacia arose, showered, wrapped a housecoat about herself and said, "I'll see how Uncle Waldo is feeling."

"Is he ill?"

"He wasn't quite himself last night," Glacia said vaguely, and left.

She came back with her face the color of bread dough that had been mixed two or three days ago.

She said, "Uncle Waldo is—is—" She gagged on whatever the rest was and arched her neck, all of her body rigid. She held that for a moment. Then she said, "His face—his brains are all over his face."

Then she went down silently on the floor. Fainted.

Chapter III

HE was a short, wide, furry man with one of the homeliest faces ever assembled, and he wouldn't have to be encountered in a very dark place to be mistaken for an ape.

"Oh, Yes," he said. "Another female admirer. We comb them out of the woodwork every morning.... Well, what do you want?"

"I wish to see Doc Savage," I said.

"That's not hard to arrange. Doc will be passing through the lobby at nine-fifteen. Just be on hand. I understand they're thinking of putting up grandstand seats."

"Aren't you funny?"

"Not very," he said. "Just sarcastic. Look, baby, do you think it's very ladylike to pursue—"

"I want to talk to Doc Savage."

"I know. But it will be harder to arrange. Still, some do. It happens. One did in his car yesterday, and assaulted him with a pair of scissors. It scared the hell out of me, but she only wanted to cut off the end of his necktie, which she did."

"Stop being a stuffy fool!" I said.

He grinned faintly, examined me with more interest, and whistled his approval brazenly. "If I thought being sensible would get me anywhere with you—"

"There's a man dead," I said.

"Uh-huh. It happens every—" He paused, his head jutted forward and down and turned sidewise. "You levelling?"

"He's dead."

"Natural death?"

"I wouldn't say so."

"Where?"

"Here in the—I can't get used to calling this silly ranch a hotel," I said. "His name was Loring. Waldo Loring."

He nodded and said, "Oh, that. Yes, I heard one of the guests had been killed in an accident."

Accident. That was right. That was what the hotel had said it was, which was about the only normal thing I had seen about the hostelry so far—hoping to make their guests think a murder hadn't been committed. So they had said it had been an accident.

"The accident," I said, "was an Indian warclub. It happened several times to his head. There was quite a change made."

He considered this, and there were some subtle changes in his manner, somewhat as if a racehorse had heard the rattle of fast hoofbeats.

"Now I want to talk to Doc Savage," I said.

"I'm Monk Mayfair. I'm Doc's right hand and catchall. Won't I do?"

"Listen, I've told you—"

"Oh, all right, but you'll just get tossed into the wastebasket, and I'm the latter. Doc is on a vacation out here." He paused and looked at me thoughtfully. "I guess you won't be satisfied until he tells you that himself, though."

He went away, leaving me in the living room of a suite which was clearly one of the larger ones. I looked around for a stuffed buffalo or the equivalent, and was peering behind things when Monk Mayfair reappeared and asked dryly. "You hunting something?"

"Stuffed bison," I said. "But I suppose you'll do for a substitute."

After he scratched his head without thinking of a reply, he escorted me into another room where Doc Savage was making a coffee table and room-service breakfast look small by sitting before them.

Monk said, "Doc, this is Miss—"

"Mote," I supplied. "Mary Olga Trunnels, formally."

"She hunts buffalo, but thinks I would do as a substitute," Monk added. "Mote, this is Doc Savage."

Doc Savage arose, gave me a surprisingly pleasant smile, and indicated a chair. But, probably lest I get any idea the visit was to be on a social plane, he said, "Monk tells me you have a matter of a dead man and a warclub."

"That sounds a little like hello and goodbye," I said. "Am I dismissed already?"

"Not at all. What gave you that idea?"

"I just got a long lecture on lady necktie snippers and wastebaskets from Mr. Mayfair. I gathered I was only to be permitted a bow, and that just to humor me."

Perhaps he thought that was entertaining. I couldn't tell. His bronze face was handsome, but already I could see that it only showed the emotions he wanted it to show. So the fact that his smile flashed again might mean nothing.

He said, "Mr. Mayfair is watchdog today. He prefers to watch pretty girls. I presume that was the gist of his lecture."

"That wasn't its gist," I said. "But it might have been the hidden meaning."

Monk Mayfair took a chair. He didn't seem disturbed.

Doc Savage said, "If you have the idea I don't care to listen to your troubles, perish the thought." He picked up the coffee percolator, asked me if I could use some, and I said I could.

"I'm Mary Olga Trunnels, and up until a few days ago I was employed by the Metro Detective Agency in New York City. It's a private investigations firm, doing all sorts of jobs that detective agencies do, but mostly insurance company work," I said. "Have you got time to listen to me begin the story that far back?"

"Start as far back as you wish," he said.

So I began still earlier, in Kansas City when Glacia Loring and I were brats together, and gave him a picture of the nonconforming background Glacia had. I carried the briefing down to a couple of years ago, when I had last seen Glacia—she had quit a modeling job in New York to come to Hollywood and be a movie star, without having achieved the latter, however—and skipped the intervening time. Then I told him the events of the past few days, and they seemed rather flat, somehow, except for the death of Waldo Loring.

"I think Glacia really hired me as a protector," I said, "because I happened to be working for a detective agency, and she felt that sort of job qualified me."

"I gather Miss Loring hasn't flatly told you that?"

"No. Intuition and guesswork told me that. But I know a scared girl when I see one, and Glacia is scared."

"Of whom?"

"I don't know."

"Then I presume you don't know what is behind it?"

"Look, I haven't been Girl Friday around a private detective agency for better than three years without learning a little about human nature. Glacia is terrified. I'll stick by that. She is doubly scared now, but she had it before her Uncle Waldo was killed. I can't cite you case and example for proof, but I do know how it feels to sit on a volcano when it's getting ready to erupt, which is the way it has been the last couple of days."

"What about the deceased man, Waldo Loring?"

"Waiting. Secretive and waiting. I had the feeling he was a hunter in a jungle full of wild and dangerous game, a hunter standing behind a tree with his rifle cocked. Waiting to shoot, but at the same time not knowing what instant one of the wild animals might pounce on him. Last night one of them pounced."

Doc Savage tasted his coffee. "Let's leave your intuition a little more out of it," he suggested.

"No. Because I wouldn't have much left," I said. "And I know my intuition. I'll bank on it."

"Did Glacia discuss her Uncle Waldo with you?"

"Never... Of lately, nor before. I didn't know she had him."

"He wasn't around previously, then?"

"No. I got the idea they'd only met recently—that is, Glacia hadn't seen him for a number of years, and he had looked her up a few days ago at the most. Uncle Waldo had been a seafaring man, I think. He talked like a sailor. A real one, not a phony. I would guess him as not a navy man, but a commercial sailor, and an officer, perhaps the captain of a freighter."

"Is that entirely guesswork?"

"Deduction, my dear Watson. I know the difference between navy and commercial jargon. Uncle Waldo was commercial. You can spot a man used to commanding by his manner—at least I can. That meant Uncle Waldo was an officer on a ship. And officers on passenger liners develop polite manners. Ergo, he was a freighter captain."

"A freighter captain waiting for something to happen to him," Savage said dryly.

"Or waiting to make it happen to someone else, if he could get in first lick."

"You mentioned an Indian warclub in the room occupied by yourself and Miss Glacia Loring. Was that the instrument used on Uncle Waldo?"

"I don't know. But the warclub is gone."

"You also mentioned a nightmare last night during which you thought Glacia had left the bedroom."

"I'm not sure about that."

"I would mention it to the police anyway," Doc Savage said. "The warclub. The nightmare. Both items."

"I'm mentioning them to you," I said uneasily. "Isn't that enough?"

"I hardly think so."

I slapped the coffee cup down on the table. Some of the coffee sloshed out. I jumped up. "You mean you're not going to help me?"

"Help you?" His bronze face registered a great deal of astonishment, all for me. "Good Lord! This is a matter for the local sheriff. A murder. Why should I be involved? Particularly when I'm on vacation."

Why should I involve him? A question of great logic. I could look a long way and not find an answer. But he had sat there for fifteen minutes and let me recite my troubles, and so I told him just what I thought about it. My thoughts of the moment, worded just the way they came to me.

"My, my," said Monk Mayfair. "Language."

"So you two let me in here and big-shot me!" I said. "I don't know why I didn't expect that, but I didn't. All right—I've entertained you for a quarter-hour. Now you can go ahead and enjoy your day without further help from me."

Doc Savage did not say anything. He was examining the inside of this coffee cup, and his neck seemed a little deeper bronze.

Monk Mayfair got up hastily, said, "Mote, you seem to be a capable article, and I wouldn't want you to—"

"With that funny face," I yelled at him, "You don't really need all those wisecracks. You're hilarious enough without them!"

I left them. There was a chair in my way, and I kicked that. The door was too heavy to slam well, but I gave it a good try.

Chapter IV

THERE was a tall sunburned man wearing dungarees and a checkered shirt in front of the door of the suite in which Glacia's Uncle Waldo Loring had died.

"What body?" he said. He listened to me explain that I knew about the body because I was an employee of the dead man's niece. Then he said, "Oh. I see. Well, what do you want to know?"

He had a deputy sheriff's badge pinned to the pocket of his shirt. From the same pocket dangled the paper tab on the end of the string that was attached to his tobacco sack. He had been holding a stick of sealing wax over a blazing match. Now the wax got soft, he jammed it against a strip of paper he was sealing across the keyhole, and implanted the impression of a coin, which he took from his pocket, on the soft wax.

He added, "The deceased is still in there. The Sheriff called in a crime laboratory guy from Los Angeles. The expert can't get here until this afternoon. I'm sealing the suite meantime. What did you want? Anything out of the room? If so, you can't have it."

"I just wanted to know what arrangements had been made about the body," I said.

"No arrangements. The arrangements we hope to make is to put the pinch on somebody for murder. The Sheriff said that. The arranging is his job, and I'm glad it is. Me, I would be baffled."

He didn't sound much like a native of the desert, so he probably was. He said his name was Gilbert. He showed me the coin he was using to seal-mark the wax. It was an early California gold piece, worth about ten times face value as a collector's item, he said. It was his pocket piece. Then he said he would finish waxing the lock in a minute, then why shouldn't we have a drink?

I said no, thanks, and left.

Now I wasn't angry. I was getting a little scared. I had been put out with Doc Savage because he hadn't jumped to our aid, but that had evaporated. The anger had drained out of me, and the hole had filled up with something that could get a little worse and be terror.

I went to our room. Glacia was sitting in a chair, her purse open on her lap and both her hands in the purse.

"You feeling better, honey?" I asked.

She took her hands out of the purse. She was a trifle clumsy doing so, and a small blue .25-caliber automatic pistol slid out on her lap. She had been sitting there holding it. Gripping the gun and watching the door.

"I feel all right," she said.

She didn't look it—her gay, crisp, alert, predatory blondness was awry. She was like a china doll that someone had been carrying in his pocket.

"Who were you going to shoot?" I asked.

She jerked visibly. "Nobody. Don't be ridiculous." She jabbed the gun back into the purse, and threw words out. "Where have you been? Why did you run off and leave me?"

"Baby," I said, "you'd better not hold out on me any longer."

Her head came up, and her eyes tried to meet mine, but couldn't. "Don't be such a fool," she mumbled.

It was obvious that she wasn't going to open up. I didn't pick at her, because it would have done no good. I dropped in a chair and waited. Glacia got hold of herself with an effort—you could see her doing it, like a sparrow drinking water. She would look at me, take an intangible drink of what she probably supposed was my calmness, and her throat would tremble. But it trembled a little less after each look.

When she had herself nailed down again—proving she wasn't scared enough to lose her head, at least—she conducted mining operations in the purse. It wasn't a little blue lady-gun this time. It was an envelope. In the envelope was a key.

"Uncle Waldo gave me this to keep for him," she said, displaying the key. "It's the key to the hotel safe deposit box downstairs."

I didn't know that the zany hostelry supplied their guests with private boxes, but it did not seem a bad idea, and some hotels did it. After hesitating, Glacia got around to explaining why she was showing me the key. "Will you go downstairs with me and we'll look in the box?" she asked.

"Glacia," I said. "Why did you hire me in the first place?"

She looked hurt, and sounded a little like a kitten mewing for its milk as she said, "You're such a competent person, Mote. You—you're the kind of advisor I need. Stable. And not afraid."

"You want advice?"

"Yes."

"Then take the local law along when you go down to investigate Uncle Waldo's box."

Still like a kitten—with its tail stepped on—she yowled, "That's ridiculous! I'll do nothing of the sort! Why should I?"

"Murder is a tiger that doesn't care who it scratches," I said, probably stupidly. "You start searching a murdered man's safe deposit box, and you're likely to get scratched plenty."

"It's mine, too. Some of my jewelry is in the box," Glacia said.

She didn't say it cunningly, so I supposed it was true. Anyway, she wasn't going to take a policeman along, and if I didn't go, she would eventually work up the courage to go by herself. So we went downstairs, me wondering if she really had any jewelry in the box, and how she would lie out of it if there wasn't.

They let her have the box without an argument, but she did have to sign a slip. I got a look at the slip—the box was in her name as well as Uncle Waldo's. That made it partly all right, or enough all right that they wouldn't jail us immediately. Let's hope.

Sure enough, Glacia dug out a piece of jewelry. An amulet studded with rhinestones and worth all of thirty cents, probably, on the Woolworth market. But I knew it was hers, because she had worn it as a high school kid.

Glacia became sentimental over the gaudy. "Uncle Waldo gave this to my mother," she said in a small voice. "He was very touched when he learned I had it."

Suddenly I decided that Waldo Loring *had* been her uncle. This decision came as a surprise to me. I'd been under the impression that I had given in to the notion that he was her uncle, but evidently I hadn't until now.

The other object in the metal box was an envelope, and I put a hand in the way of Glacia's hand when she reached for it. "It's still not too late to start using your head," I said.

"Damn you, Mote," she said. And then she asked bitterly, "What would you suggest?" I thought she was going to take a swing at me, and I know she was considering it. "If it's another lecture about going to the police, you can just chew it up and swallow it again. I haven't done anything the police can arrest me for."

The police were out, I could see that. Glacia didn't want any part of them.

"The alternative," I said, "might be to break loose and tell old Mote all. I can't say I'm anxious to be the collection plate for your troubles. But it might help."

"Help what? Your curiosity?"

She had something there. "Help me decide whether I'm heading for jail by associating with you," I said.

Glacia got angry again. She called me an impossible wench, and a damned fine travesty of a friend. It didn't mean too much the way she said it, I decided. She was putting on and taking off her emotions—rage, sentiment, fear, hesitation, decision—the nervous way a man about to be married probably tries different neckties.

"What went wrong with you?" she demanded. "Where did you go right after the body was found? You went somewhere, and something happened to jolt you. What was it?"

All right, you asked for it. I thought.

"I went to ask Doc Savage to investigate the mysterious murder of your Uncle Waldo," I said, and waited for that to sink in and take effect.

She fooled me. She didn't show surprise, or not much of it. She even seemed interested. And she was alert enough to guess what had happened.

"He turned you down," she said.

"That's right, and with trimmings," I agreed. "It wasn't just that I got turned down, either. It was being exposed to their curiosity and then tossed aside that burns me. They opened me like a box, looked in, didn't care for any, and pushed me out."

Glacia's lips were parted a little, as if she was all set to blow out a candle. Her way of showing breathless wonder. "What was he like?" she gasped.

"Eh?"

"Doc Savage… what was he like? Did you really get to talk with him, Mote? He must be a wonderful person."

"That big bronze chew!" I said. "I didn't see anything so wonderful about him."

Glacia began to look as if I was putting verbal toads in the conversation. "Your trouble is, you're not impressed by anything!" she snapped. "Doc Savage has a reputation. Some people are scared stiff when they as much as hear of him. Why by just appearing here, he—"

She bit it off.

She had almost said something, then hadn't. She had nearly said that Doc Savage, by appearing here at the odd hotel, had caused something. Then she had caught herself, and hadn't said what. That was what she'd done. It was as clear as the nose on an anteater. But I did a delayed take on it—delayed about half an hour. At the moment, I didn't even notice that she'd almost said something. All my wheels weren't turning.

I said, "The great Doc Savage is a thin trickle as far as I'm concerned." We were still standing over the safe deposit box and I pointed at it. "That letter is addressed to you. Are you going to open it?"

Glacia opened the envelope that had been in Uncle Waldo's box, and writing on the one sheet of paper that was in it said:

My dear niece:

Feeling that death by violence may possibly come my way, I am penning these few words with the intention that they constitute my last will and testament.

I bequeath to you, Glacia Mae Loring, all my worldly property including Keeper. I ask you to take good care of Keeper. In case Keeper is not in your hands by the time you read this, I direct you to contact my attorney, C.V. McBride, Lathrop Bldg., Phone Cay 3-3101, Los Angeles, California, and have Keeper delivered to you.

(Signed) Waldo D. Loring.
(Witnessed) E.P. Cook.
(Witnessed) Royalton Dvorak.

This was dated two days previously.

"Is that a will?" Glacia asked blankly.

"It says so, and probably is," I told her. "What is this inheritance of yours?"

"Keeper?" Glacia stared at me foolishly. "I don't know what Keeper is. I haven't any idea."

"Oh, all right," I said wearily.

She seemed to think she had been called a liar, and said sharply, "I really don't! It might be—oh, I don't know what. I haven't any idea."

"A profound mystery, eh?"

"Oh, stop acting as if I was pulling the legs off flies! What's got into you, anyway?"

I told her what was wrong. "I'm just getting a little tired of going in here and coming out there. With the same dumb look on my face."

She said that didn't make sense, and she didn't want to hear anymore about it. She handed the strongbox—she kept the piece of jewelry and Waldo's letter—back to the hotel employee.

She was really angry with me. She didn't say where she was going. She just marched off, jamming the document in her purse, then carrying the purse clamped with both hands. I followed. Glacia was going back to our room, apparently, but she passed up the elevator and took the stairs. She did that to torment me, I imagined—I do not like stairsteps, because I go up and down them awkwardly and with a certain fear, having fallen twice and been injured while on a stairway. It isn't a phobia. I just avoid stairs whenever possible, and have done so since childhood. Following Glacia up them now, I wondered if she had chosen the steps deliberately to provoke me. It was not above her to do so.

On the other hand, Glacia, who was wiry and alert and objective, expressed her emotion with action. She was the kind of a person who walked off her troubles. Her answer, when someone else was feeling under the weather, was: "what you need is some exercise!" One of those people. She might be merely climbing the stairs because she was upset.

Possibly it wasn't important. Certainly there were bigger things to do my thinking about. There was murder, my boss hiding things from me, and there was Keeper.

"Race horse," I said.

"What?" Glacia asked.

"Keeper. Maybe Keeper is a race horse. We could get one of those turf annuals or magazines and look in it for a horse with that name."

Glacia didn't say anything.

It seemed to me there was quite a time when she didn't say anything. A long time. I got the idea it might be fifteen minutes or so.

"Well?" I said.

Glacia still didn't say anything.

"Well, could Keeper be a race horse?" I asked.

I didn't see Glacia, and she didn't answer. I looked around for her. I looked hard. All I could see was the ceiling.

"Well, could it?" I said. Then I said, "Well?" a couple more times. After that, I gave the word-making a rest.

Things were very odd. All that was up there was the ceiling. I seemed to be lying on my back on something, evidently a floor.

Chapter V

IT took some time to accept the fact that I was on the stair landing exactly where I had been when I was asking Glacia whether Keeper could be a race horse, maybe. One square look showed that it was the stair landing, but accepting the fact took somewhat longer. But that's where I was. Now, why was I lying down?

I worried about having laid down for a while, then got to my feet. Apparently I was as good as new.

"What did you say?" Glacia's voice asked.

I turned around. She was sitting on the steps where they continued on upward from the landing.

She said, "A race horse? I don't know. Could be." She also got to her feet. She touched her blonde hair absently with a hand. "What happened? Did you fall down?"

"I don't know," I said truthfully.

"I didn't hear you fall," she said. "But you were on the floor."

"Why didn't you pick me up?" I asked.

"But I had barely turned—I didn't even hear you. You were getting up when I saw you."

"Look, honey, I'm getting damned tired of your denials!" I said sharply.

"What denials?"

"You were sitting down when I woke up. What were you doing, sitting there waiting for me to pick myself up?"

She opened her mouth. Denial was there. Then—her lips remained parted—she looked stunned. Shocked.

"I was—sitting down, wasn't I?" She mumbled.

"Glacia!"

She shook her head vacantly. She had trouble with her words, taking them out one at a time as if they were frightened little animals.

"What did—I don't understand—Oh, God, what happened to us, Mote?"

Her frightened small words dived into the silence and were gone.

Jumping forward, I seized her purse and opened it and found the envelope from the strongbox was still there. Uncle Waldo's last will and testament was intact in the envelope. I slid it back into the envelope, dropped that into the purse, and snapped the thing shut.

"Why did you do that?" Glacia asked wildly.

"Because I think we were unconscious. But don't ask me how long or from what cause."

She didn't ask me. I don't think she believed me—for a while. But then she did, and she said again, "I was sitting down, wasn't I?"

We went to our suite, and I told her, "Take a drink. You'll feel better." But she just sat on the edge of a chair, her fingers biting at things, breathing inward and outward deeply.

Later she took up the telephone and put in a call for Los Angeles, for the attorney mentioned in Uncle Waldo's testament, an attorney named C.V. McBride. The call went through, and she told McBride who she was, and that Waldo Loring was dead.

Attorney McBride's voice was deep, but staccato. I couldn't understand his words, but I could hear what his voice sounded like. Like a large drum being thumped.

The lawyer's deep voice began pumping and Glacia only managed to insert words, fragments of sentences. Things like: "Yes, Mr. McBride, I'm staying… But Mr. McBride… What is… This morning… But… What is Keeper… Yes." A "No," and three more "Yesses" finished up the conversation, and Glacia moved the telephone around in the air vaguely until it found the cradle.

There was confusion in her eyes as she told me, "He's coming at once. He's bringing Keeper."

"He had quite a few words, didn't he?"

Glacia folded her hands and said, "Damn him! He out-talked me!" This seemed to be a belated conclusion that she had just reached, and was angry about.

"I take it he didn't tell you what Keeper is."

"That's right. He didn't."

"And you didn't tell him much either," I reminded her dryly. "You left out several things, murder being one of them."

Glacia didn't say anything.

I asked, "Are you going to keep secrets from everybody?"

"You're fired!" Glacia snapped.

I got up and left the room, and as I was closing the door, she called "Mote!" sharply. I didn't look back nor go back. I closed the door behind me, hurried down the hall, took the stairs, and stopped in front of Doc Savage's suite.

The furry and amiable Monk Mayfair opened the door at my knock.

"Ah, the beautiful buffalo hunter," he said.

I pushed past him saying, "You've already demonstrated how funny you can be, so could we skip further proof?"

"Hey, now! There's no call to be—"

"Tell the Great Man I'm here for a retake," I said. "Or do I just walk in?"

"You sound determined," Monk Mayfair scratched his neck with a fingernail. "I guess you *are* determined. Okay. But let me announce you. I was supposed to keep you out of here."

He crossed to a door and opened it, hung his head through and said, "She got in anyway, Doc. She has a look in her eye." He kept his head in the door for a while, then sighed. He told me, "I guess I'm in the doghouse," and held the door wider open.

Doc Savage was wiping his fingers on a towel. He stood beside what could have been a portable chemical laboratory—the table was covered with the odd-shaped glass gadgets that chemists use—and there was an odor of acid fumes in the air.

"Good morning," Doc Savage said.

He was big. I suddenly got all involved with trying to accept just how big he was. It wasn't just his physical size that I was feeling now, although there was plenty of that, without it being out of proportion, and without his being in any sense a physical freak—except that he could probably tie knots in horseshoes.

It was the intangible size of him that was flooring me. Because he was all that they said he was, and more. The way they had looked at him in the lobby yesterday, the awed way the phony Indian named Coming Going had spoken of him. Glacia's idea that I was a dope for not having heard of him—those were the things that had told me what he was. He was all they indicated. He was probably more.

I said, "You're Clark Savage, Jr."

He seemed surprised. "Yes."

"I was pretty slow getting it," I told him. "For some reason or other, the name Doc Savage didn't mean what it should have. I guess I don't know how to meet a legend. Or don't know one when I meet it."

"I don't believe I understand—"

"I have heard of you the way little boys hear there's a pot of gold at the foot of rainbows," I explained. "But I'm not a little boy, nor even a little girl—I'm twenty-four years old. That's too old to believe in anything at the end of rainbows, except maybe rain. But a while ago, Glacia Loring and I went to sleep on a stairway. And then I knew."

He said, "Really?" The word meant two things—that he was suggesting I didn't know what I was talking about, and that he knew I wouldn't believe his suggesting.

"I've heard of that gas."

"Oh."

"I even remember where I heard about it," I said. "It was at one of those lectures the F.B.I. give law enforcement officials. The F.B.I. agent who lectured was named Grillquist, and he said that your anaesthetic gas had been considered for general police use, but that it wouldn't be used. It was too good. Crooks might get it, and use it on people, and the folks they used it on wouldn't know, because most of the time they wouldn't even know they had been gassed."

He didn't say anything. "This is quite interesting. It sounds fantastic."

"Not to me, now that I know you're a fantastic person. You did it to have a look at what Glacia had taken out of the strongbox downstairs, I suppose?"

"You take some mighty long jumps at conclusions."

"Just a hop, that time."

"Does your—ah—employer share your rather unusual hallucination?"

"Glacia? She hasn't said so. She hasn't said anything much, really. But I doubt it."

"I see."

"Glacia," I said, "is in the middle of some kind of a plot, and knows it."

"Indeed."

"She's scared stiff. But she's not giving up. She's going it alone, if necessary. She just fired me."

"You're probably fortunate."

"Lucky that she fired me, you mean? No. No, because I think the silly little blonde is going to need help, and I'm going to stick by her."

He thought deeply. The thing he was thinking about was whether or not he should shake his head negatively. He shook it.

He said, "If I were you, I'd catch the one o'clock bus for Los Angeles."

"No, if you were me you wouldn't do anything of the sort. I've heard about you, remember. If you had a friend who was foolish enough to let greed get her into trouble, you'd stick."

He said nothing to that.

"She telephoned the attorney and he's bringing the inheritance," I said.

It was hard to tell whether he reacted to that. His flake-gold eyes weren't composed. But they were not composed at any time—the gold in them seemed always in motion, alert, wary. Presently I found I was staring at his eyes and they were getting some sort of hypnotic spell on me, or I thought they were. I stopped staring.

"You're in this yourself," I said. "I think you were in it before I was."

"Indeed?"

"That's just an idea that came to me. Would you mind verifying it?"

"You should catch that bus," he said.

I stood up. "All right. Not all right about the bus—just all right, I see I'm not getting anywhere with you. I just thought I'd drop in and let you know I'd figured out that fainting stuff, and to get another look at the great Doc Savage. The first look didn't count. You have to know what you're looking at, to appreciate scenery."

If he thought I meant that as flattery—and I didn't—he did not rise to it. "You've made the morning interesting," he said.

Maybe he was just being cagey. But on the chance that he was being smug, I pointed at the chemistry stuff on the table. "Notice you were doing an iodine vapor check for latent fingerprints. How's it turning out? Find out who killed Waldo Loring?"

For the first time he showed a little emotion. He looked slightly pained. He crossed to the door, opened it, followed me through. Monk Mayfair was in the other room, and Savage told him, "Our visitor has an active imagination."

Monk Mayfair was looking at my legs. His lips phrased but he did not say aloud, that was not all I had. He got to his feet, assisted Doc Savage with the goodbyes—and I got a pretty good idea of what he would presently do, and was not surprised when he did it. He opened the door after I had left and was walking down the hall, and said, "Oh, by the way, Miss Mote."

I stopped. Monk came up. I said, "It's either Mote, or Miss Trunnels, but not Miss Mote, please. Don't tell me I forgot my handkerchief."

"You were probably very careful not to do that," he said amiably. "Look, I didn't follow you just to shine my eyes at you, although that would be interesting, too. I've got a question: are you going to stick with this thing?"

"If you mean stick with my friend Glacia, that's what I plan."

"Okay. Then I got a wee bit of advice. Be careful of new friendships."

"Eh?"

"In new acquaintances can lie danger, whereas old friends are to be trusted, or at least you know which one of them is a stinker."

I looked at him for a moment. "How do you want that interpreted? You sound like a thirty-cent fortune teller."

He grinned. He was so utterly homely that there was something pleasant about his grinning. "It's just a dab of wisdom. Tee it up and take a mental swing at it if you have spare time."

"You mean there's going to be a tall dark man in my life?"

"Search me. The tall and dark ones I wouldn't worry so much about, though."

"How about short ones?"

"If they're short and wide, and run quite a lot to jaw, I'd walk as if I was on eggs."

"Would those that look like that have names?" I asked him.

"Names can be changed. Jaws can't."

"Thanks, pal," I said.

Glacia had a reception ready for me when I got back to our suite. She had the door locked, but the purple carpet of welcome was spread out inside. The door was merely locked because Glacia was scared stiff—she was so frightened that she didn't trust herself to recognize my voice, but made me repeat the name of the kid who had put the civet cat in the teacher's desk when we were going to school in Kansas City. The kid's name was Dan Burton, and I came near not being able to remember it. Then Glacia unlocked the door and threw her arms around me. She made my shoulder wet with tears, told me several different ways that she was glad to see me and then swore at me. "Damn you, Mote, why did you walk out like that? I thought you had deserted me."

"The way I heard it, I was fired."

"Don't be silly," Glacia said. "You just had me upset, is all."

"Upset? Honey, your nerves are vibrating like harp strings."

"Pshaw! I'm all right."

"Uh-huh. Do you know a short, fat man with a jaw?"

She gave me a thoroughly blank look. "What are you talking about?"

"I had another round with Doc Savage," I said. "This time I was properly respectful—or anyway I knew I was before the master. He didn't admit a thing, but he did put out a piece of advice—leave the lodge. But his court jester, that Monk Mayfair, followed me out in the hall and was a little more explicit. He said to beware of a short fat man with a jaw, who would be a new acquaintance."

"All men have jaws," Glacia said woodenly.

"I gather this one is special. Glacia, why are you looking like that?"

The way she was looking was somewhat the same as when she had walked into our room that morning and told me how Waldo Loring was wearing his brains on his face. But she didn't faint this time. Instead, she dived for the telephone. She put in a call for the lawyer in Los Angeles.

Waiting for the phone call to go through, Glacia looked at the floor, the walls, at nothing, and used a voice that was two tones higher to ask me, "Is Doc Savage—did he come here to the lodge because of—of Uncle Waldo?"

"You do the guessing," I said.

When the Los Angeles connection was made, her voice went up another tone, and she demanded to speak to Lawyer McBride. The reply she got was a quick piece of news. She hung up.

"He's left. He's already on his way here."

"With Keeper?"

"I—suppose so."

"Why didn't you ask whoever you talked to what Keeper is?"

"I—" Her eyes went different places, helping her mind hunt for words. "I never thought of it," she said.

"Or you already know what Keeper is."

Glacia shook her head dumbly. "Mote, I really don't know."

She didn't get mad, so probably she didn't know. And after that she wouldn't get ten feet from me. But she wouldn't tell me what she was afraid of, or what she thought might happen. I felt sorry for her. I seemed to be the only person she trusted, and she was too frightened to trust me much.

I spent about an hour with my imagination, picturing different things that could happen when the lawyer got here, different things Keeper could be, and various ways of being a murder victim. By that time, I had scared myself into needing sunlight and fresh air badly, so I suggested a walk, and Glacia agreed. Rather, I said I was going for a walk and Glacia, following her new policy of staying within two jumps of me, reached for her own hat.

It didn't occur to me that things might not wait to happen until the lawyer got here.

Chapter VI

THE portly gentleman was about fifty, gray-haired, with a distinguished face that ran extraordinarily to jaw, and he managed to carry more air of dignity than one would have thought could be gotten away with by a ponderous old boy in a bathing suit.

The dubious redskin, Coming Going, brought him up and introduced him.

"Mr. Montgomery, ladies," said Coming Going. "Heap anxious meet you. Okay?"

We were sitting near the pool trying to look as if we were enjoying a couple of cold drinks, and as far as I was concerned, it wasn't okay. Mr. Montgomery had too much jaw for me to want any part of him.

"Goodbye," Coming Going said suddenly. He must have been watching my face.

"Mr. Going," I said, standing quickly. "Will you show me your tribal totem pole? The one you were talking about." I took his arm and hurried him into the thicket of different kinds of cactus, mostly as large as trees, which bordered the pool and made the lodge grounds a thorny jungle. When we were out of sight on the path, I stopped the puzzled redskin.

"Now," I asked, "where did you get him?"

"Ugh. What tribal totem pole?" he asked.

"Never mind that, Hiawatha. The fat man with the jaw—where did you get him?"

"Didn't. He got me."

"He asked you to introduce him to us? How come?"

"Service to guests." He was uncomfortable, and took off his heap-big-Indian manner and explained, "He asked me did I know you two girls, and I said yes before I thought, and he asked would I introduce him, and I thought of how good soft jobs are hard to find these days, and so I did. Did I do wrong?"

"Is fat jaw—Mr. Montgomery—a guest here at this dopey hotel?"

"Sure."

"How long has he been here?"

"Couple of weeks."

"By any chance did he arrive about the same time as my girlfriend?"

Coming Going shook his head and the feather that was always getting out of order dropped over one eye. "Before her. He got here about two days after her uncle arrived, the way I recall it."

"What else do you know about Mr. Montgomery?"

"He's a mining man—he says. His daughter and a gentleman secretary are with him. Daughter's name is Colleen. Gentleman secretary's name is Roy."

"How come I haven't noticed them, or at least Mr. Montgomery—around?"

He was fiddling with the feather. "They have been staying pretty close to their rooms."

"Do you know anything else I should know, Tecumseh?"

He grinned and shook his head. "It's my turn to ask a question. I hear your friend's uncle met with an accident. This odd curiosity of yours got anything to do with that?"

"Accident—is that what they call it around here when a guest gets his brains bashed in?"

That shocked him. The feather fell over his eye. His jaw sagged. Everything else had gone out of him to make room for the surprise, and genuine surprise it was.

I walked off and left him. I thought I had him measured now. A nice young boy, no more an Indian than I was, who liked the playacting that went with his job. Probably he was a thwarted actor from Hollywood. Murder had floored him, and he was no doubt thinking that I was a hard case. He wasn't fooling with his feather, the last I saw of him.

I went back to the table near the swimming pool. Glacia was worried about me. She jumped to her feet when she saw me, and then sat down again, rather weakly with relief.

"You shouldn't run off like that, Mote," she wailed.

"Relax," I said. "The redmen aren't taking scalps today."

Mr. Montgomery sat at the table. He leaned down, brought Glacia's purse into view, and placed it on the table—conveying the idea, he no doubt hoped, that she had dropped the purse and he had picked it up.

"I don't believe the boy is an Indian at all," he said cheerfully. "Most of them around here aren't. Or am I disillusioning you two young ladies? I'm very sorry."

"Sorry enough to let us stick you for a drink?" I asked, pulling out my chair.

He said he was that sorry, and began waving at a waiter.

He was a well-cared-for old man, all right. He might not be as old as the white hair and the dignity made him seem. He might even be as young as fifty. He was certainly browned by the sun; it had taken a lot of sun to brown him that much; he must have spent years sitting around beaches and swimming pools in a bathing suit with a good drink in his hand. The fingers of his right hand were permanently curled from holding good drinks.

Finally my wondering settled down on one point. What had he taken from Glacia's purse, and where had he hidden it? His tight bathing trunks didn't offer much space for hiding things.

Mr. Montgomery got the attention of a waiter, and began ordering for us. He didn't ask what we wanted. He just said he had something special, and told the waiter what it was, and how the bartender should make it. That took some time.

A young man came around the corner of the hotel. He stood looking at us. He was a rather slender young man with a round baby-like face and soft brown eyes. He was wearing a white linen suit, white shoes, white shirt and a startlingly yellow necktie.

The newcomer did not approach, but gazed at us with puppy-like friendliness. He wanted to approach.

Mr. Montgomery stopped in the middle of telling the waiter how the bartender should pour the creme de menthe over a spoon just so. Presently he smiled rather strangely. He smiled at the young man. The smile would have frozen grain alcohol.

"Yes, sir?" said the waiter hopefully.

Mr. Montgomery gave him the rest of the recipe. He probably slighted the rest of it. Then he arose and went to another table and picked up a chased silver cigar case, a lighter and a heavy knobbed walking stick. He came back with these.

The young man raised his eyebrows. There was a question, and a prayer, in the gesture.

"You'll love the drink I have ordered," said Mr. Montgomery to us. He spoke vaguely. "It's a specialty I picked up—ah—in Cairo."

"Cairo, Illinois?" I asked.

"Eh?"

The young man had taken a tentative step forward. Mr. Montgomery renewed the ice in his smile. He lifted the walking stick and stroked it with his hand.

The young man in white stopped. There was a butterfly almost as yellow as his necktie fooling around a cactus that grew out of an urn nearby.

"Cairo, Egypt, then," I said.

The young man raised and lowered his eyebrows. He turned and went away. Just before he disappeared, he held both hands out at his sides, the palms up, in a gesture of resignation.

"Was it Cairo, Egypt?" I asked.

Mr. Montgomery closed his eyes tightly, and they remained shut for a moment. Then he picked up his cigar case and looked in it and it was empty.

"Will you excuse me a moment, girls?" Mr. Montgomery said. "I must get some cigars. My special brand. Will you forgive my absence briefly?"

He tucked the walking stick under his arm and went away. His jaw did not seem so prominent, oddly enough.

"Glacia," I said. "Let's see what he got out of your purse."

She looked at me, eyes and mouth three round circles in a round face. "What?" she gasped. Then she snatched at her purse, wrenched it open, and dug into the contents. "Oh my God! It's gone!"

"What is gone?"

"The envelope—Uncle Waldo's will." Her face flamed with rage. "That old man—why, damn him! He won't get away with something like that!"

Glacia sprang up and raced off in the direction

Mr. Montgomery had taken. She was angry enough to have forgotten that she considered me a bodyguard.

I didn't follow her. I sat there and chewed over a theory I had. Mr. Montgomery's jaw had seemed prominent as anything when he first arrived at the table, and hadn't later on. There was a reason for that. The jaw, when he first came, had been in motion. Mr. Montgomery had been chewing gum then.

It was a good process of reasoning. Sherlock Holmes and J. Edgar Hoover never had a better basis for deduction. I was proud of it.

I moved to the chair Mr. Montgomery had occupied, put my hands under the table—and didn't feel so puffed up. But I wasn't going to let any fat man with a jaw make a fool out of me. I shed dignity, got down on hands and knees, and looked at the underside of the table as if I was reading hieroglyphics.

It was all right. He had just been cunning, and used his chewing gum to stick the envelope to the bottom of the table in front of my chair. He was cute, all right.

A cute fat man. I looked at the outside of the envelope to make sure it was Uncle Waldo's testament and at the inside to see whether the works were still there. They were. I scraped off Mr. Montgomery's chicle and tucked the thing inside my frock where no one with good manners would find it.

I was getting to my feet, and hurried it up considerably when Glacia began screaming. She was doing her yelling off to the left somewhere in the jungle of cactus and desert plants. I and at least twenty other people ran in the direction of Glacia's shrieking, but a dozen others had arrived ahead of us.

Glacia, suddenly without noise, was pointing at the base of a cactus thicket. Her whole arm shook somewhat.

It was the young man in white. He lay on both shoulders and one hip and one leg was extended, the other leg drawn up and bent at the knee in the position for riding a bicycle. His white suit contrasted, alabaster to absinthe, with the palmetto dagger-like leaves.

His tanned face now had a mongrel coloring; it was marble that had received one coat of inadequate walnut stain. The blood that had left his nostrils was not much, but it had run down—his head was cocked up by the rocks on which it rested—and made a startling woodpecker's head blotch on the gay yellow of his necktie.

I looked hard for death in his face. I couldn't tell. His facial muscles were loose, but there was still some of the puppy-dog friendliness with which he had gazed at Glacia, myself and Mr. Montgomery a bit earlier.

Somebody got down on their knees beside him and began saying, "Hello, there!" in a shrilly voice, as if they were talking to a baby.

If he doesn't answer, I thought, I'm going to exercise feminine rights and scream like hell.

Just in case he didn't answer, I got away from there. It wasn't easy. I didn't know who he was, who had bopped him, why, how— My bump of curiosity about him had grown into moose antlers. But I got away from there. I was worried about Glacia.

A quick pass through the cactus jungle in the vicinity got me nothing but lack of breath. Glacia was not around. Ice began to collect around the roots of my hair.

I went into the hotel, found the fellow who had given Glacia the strongbox to open, and handed him the envelope that Mr. Montgomery had temporarily lifted. "Can you put this back in Miss Loring's box?" I asked.

He shook his head and said, "Not without her key, or a meeting of the board of directors, practically. You see, there are only two keys to each box. The guest gets one, and the other is in escrow as it were—you have to convince about six people you're entitled to use it."

"But I want you to keep this envelope—"

"Why not a box for yourself? It's included in the service. No charge."

The simple solution left me speechless. I watched him arrange the lock box, signed something, put the key in my purse and said, "Will you have Miss Loring paged?"

"Certainly."

In the course of the next five minutes, I wore the upholstery off a lobby chair with my squirming. Glacia wasn't answering to the paging.

I tried the clerk again. "Can you give me Mr. Montgomery's suite number?"

We were old friends now. He gave me the information without an argument. Mr. Montgomery was in the second floor corner suite, northeast exposure.

The second floor hall was cool, almost cold after the desert heat of noontime beside the pool. The air was redolent of sage. They probably had a machine that manufactured the odor and squirted it into the conditioning system.

I listened at what I had been told was Mr. Montgomery's door for a long time, for such a long time that I grew weak as from starvation. Nothing in the rooms on the other side of the door made any more noise than a fly scrubbing his eyes, so I tried the knob. It turned. I pushed on the door. It opened. I gave it a little shove, and it swung wide and hit the wall with a little bump. Later I went in.

It was a wonderful room. Plenty of room for a couple of Russian ambassadors, with huge solid plate glass windows that picture-framed the mountains, and doors to the right and doors to the left. The plurality of doors was bothersome—my mind by now wasn't in a state where it could make a choice readily, even a choice between two doors. Right or left, which should it be? Finally I just started walking. Left, it happened.

That door also opened readily—into a bathroom. The color motif here was pastel blue and green against ivory, and the place was neatly departmentalized. Each department was enclosed in a little glass booth of its own, booths of etched glass and chrome. I tried to imagine how a stuffed buffalo would look in here.

"Good intentions are sometimes like curiosity," said a voice. "Except that I don't know that good intentions kill cats." It was Mr. Montgomery's voice.

I turned around. Mr. Montgomery was backing out of a door across the large room, and he had spoken to someone in the bedroom beyond the door.

He took his time turning to face me, and by then I wasn't there. I was in the shower stall, with the etched glass door closed.

Chapter VII

MR. MONTGOMERY moved over to the table, picked up his walking stick and examined it; with a slight grimace, he picked a brownish hair, complete with root, from the heavy head of the cane, carried it into the bathroom and washed it down the drain. Then he applied soap to the cane, scrubbed it, towelled it dry, and placed it by the window in the sunlight where it would dry.

He did none of this with much urgency, nor was his manner anything but placidly brisk, the air of an elderly gentleman who was self-satisfied.

I saw part of what he was doing—the shower booth door was sprung and wouldn't quite close, leaving enough crack for observation, and to scare me stiff—and there were enough assorted sounds to keep me posted about the rest of his activity.

Meantime, the sound of a typewriter, in the sporadic rushes of creative composition, had started coming from the adjoining room.

Mr. Montgomery tipped a finger of Scotch into a glass, added ice and a jump of soda, then a second hiss of soda after he had tasted the drink. He carried the glass along and went to investigate the typing.

By moving my head half an inch, I could see from the bathroom across the living room into the other room where the typist sat.

She was a smooth, polished svelte number of about twenty-five with dark hair and rather small features. Strictly a custom job. Her slight excess of lipstick was used well, although her large harlequin glasses needed a more exotic face.

Mr. Montgomery was gazing over her shoulder at what she had been typing.

Presently he chuckled. "Very effective, Colleen. I imagine, if I were the young man, I should palpitate. Passionate sentiments, very." He rocked gently on his heels. His smile was contemplative. He added, "Dryden, I think it was, who said: 'Pains of love be sweeter far, than all other pleasures are.'"

His Colleen took two puffs off a cigarette. "If you think I'm in love with the guy, you're nuts."

Her father—he was her father; you could see signs of family resemblance—seemed pleased with that. "That pleases me, my dear. Young Swanberg was an impressionable, callow, easily deluded jackass. His one asset, an overabundance of wealth, hardly entitled him to a passing grade in this life."

The daughter laughed. "Scram, Monty, will you? I can't compose this stuff with you grinning over my shoulder."

"Why compose it at all, my dear? Why bother?"

"Any old port in a storm," she said, shrugging. "If there should be a storm."

Mr. Montgomery's eyes glittered like knife steel. "There won't be."

She swung around slightly to face him. "There could be. After all, you could have hit Roy—"

"The fool! The disobedient oaf!" said Mr. Montgomery bitterly.

"Are you sure you didn't hit him hard enough to crack his head?"

"Bosh! You underestimate both the thickness of Roy's cranium and my experience. As a matter of fact, I also tapped him on the parietal, well back of the coronal suture, which is a substantial area of the skull. When you have occasion to hit a man with a cane, my dear, pick that spot." The old gentleman sipped his drink. "Roy will carry a substantial headache as a reminder. That is all."

"Roy," said his daughter, "didn't mean anything."

"Well, I certainly did when I hit him!" said her father.

"Roy was lonesome. I hadn't been entertaining him according to his ideas of entertainment. His taste runs to blondes, and pretty cheap ones."

"Lonesome, eh? Not as lonesome as he could become in Alcatraz. Even though, as is well within the bounds of reason, he might have us along for company."

Colleen shuddered. "Do you have to put such damned ugly ideas in well-rounded words, pop? Why not just say Roy might get us all in the pokey by showing himself where Doc Savage could see him?"

Mr. Montgomery waved his drink distastefully. "Let's omit Savage from the conversation. I'm allergic to the man's name. It makes me nervous."

The hall door opened. I couldn't see who had come in, but the way the Montgomery family jumped to see the arrival was impressive.

"Ah!" said Mr. Montgomery. He sounded relieved, as if he had nearly fallen into a tank of ice water.

Roy stumbled into view—the boy in white with the yellow necktie. To a nervous man in a business suit who was with him, he expostulated. "I'm all right. I fell, is all. How many times do I have to tell you that?" The man, evidently an assistant hotel manager, said the expected things about the hotel regretting any accidents and then left.

Sheepishly, Roy glanced at Mr. Montgomery. He did not say anything. He went over and lowered himself in a chair and laid his head back gingerly against the chair. His eyebrows went up, down, painfully.

"Colleen," said Mr. Montgomery with bitter sweetness. "Will you be so kind as to place a cold ice compress on Roy's head."

Colleen came into the bathroom for a towel. I could name her perfume. Forty dollars an ounce. I tried to remember whether I had used any perfume myself that morning, and couldn't remember even a little thing like that.

Roy sat in gray-faced shame while Colleen dumped ice in the towel and handed it to him. The glances that came from his brown eyes were injured ones.

Mr. Montgomery kicked the dog while he was down.

"Well, Roy, how did you like your brief look about the hotel?" he asked blandly.

Roy winced. "It was all right."

"Up to a point, you mean?"

"Yes. Up to a point."

"The point should have happened earlier. Prior to the execution of your foolish deed—in other words, before you stepped out of this suite."

"Okay," Roy mumbled.

"Common sense, if not respect for my commands, should have induced you to stay bottled up here."

"Don't rub it in," Roy muttered.

The old man's jaw was quite prominent now. "I shall rub all I damned please, and you shall like it," he said.

"Yes, sir."

"I am—I really am, Roy—irritated with you. Of our group, the only one Doc Savage might recognize is yourself. Should he get one glimpse of you, imagine what might happen."

"But Savage only saw me once, years ago," Roy complained.

"Yes, Roy, but the man's mind is a photographic record. Let us not, at this late stage, start underestimating Savage."

"Yes, sir," said Roy. "Who were the babes I saw you talking with? The pocket-sized blonde... she's old Waldo's niece. Right?"

"Correct."

"Then the other one would be the lady sleuth she brought on from New York as a friend in need."

"Correct again."

"The lady shamus wasn't a bad looker. But should we worry about her the way you've been worrying?"

Mr. Montgomery scowled at Roy for long enough for me to feel surprised that I had given anybody cause for worry. They were afraid of Doc Savage. They were afraid of me, too. That put me in the big league. I felt rather puffed up.

Making a little speech, Mr. Montgomery said, "Roy, you have been using your brain. That is a poisonous thing. We use only one brain around here—mine. I did hope you understood that."

"I understand it," Roy said uneasily.

"You are a stupid incompetent, Roy," said Mr. Montgomery with the heedlessly playful air of a farmer discussing a coming butchering with the hog he is going to butcher. "There is too much involved in this affair—in case you feel I am being overly severe—to take any chances."

"Oh, I know—"

"You know from nothing, Roy! Let me point out the fundamentals to you."

The fat man stuck three fingers of his right hand under Roy's nose and began bending the fingers one at a time as he enumerated points.

"One," he said. "Old Waldo Loring had a secret of fabulous value to sell."

He bent down that finger.

"Two," he continued. "Waldo Loring approached me to serve as broker. He knew I had contacts with people who would pay handsomely for what he possessed. But we could not come to terms—the old sea dog didn't want to pay me a proper commission."

Down went another finger.

"Three. I thereupon began bending my efforts toward acquiring the fabulous item by whatever means feasible."

He had run out of fingers. That bothered him, and he frowned at his hand. He solved the problem by starting over again with three more fingers.

"Four," he said. "Waldo Loring was brained by a prowler he caught searching his room. This was unfortunate, because a dead Waldo could not be induced to tell where he sank that—ahem—where is hidden the item he had for sale."

He paused to shake his head and cluck sadly over that development.

"Five. Waldo Loring was throughout a man frightened by the incredible magnitude and deviltry of the deed he was trying to perpetrate, and in his fear he sought comfort from the presence of his niece, Miss Glacia Loring. He invited her to join him here. I do not know how much of the truth he told her—but he told her some, because she in turn was terrified and had recourse to the only friend she probably has, this lady sleuth from New York."

He was down to the last finger again, and he knocked that one off quickly.

"Six," he said. "Miss Loring has inherited an unknown quantity called Keeper. She apparently doesn't know what Keeper is. But we know—and she must suspect—that Keeper is the answer to where old Waldo Loring's secret now lies."

Through with the fingers, he rubbed his hands together briskly, then picked up his drink again.

Roy grunted. "You left out plenty. How did Doc Savage happen to get wind of it and show up here? That's what I'd like to know."

"That's not a fundamental. I just gave you the fundamentals. And the conclusion you should draw is this: we must lie low and grab Keeper when the latter appears."

"Huh? And not bother about Savage, I suppose?" said Roy skeptically.

"Bother? How do you mean? Concern ourselves over how he got a smell of the affair? That would be pointless. It's easily explained, anyway, if you use a little imagination. Waldo Loring's secret was of such magnitude that its existence has no doubt traveled the grapevines, and it wouldn't surprise me to find that Doc Savage is here representing the interests of the nation. Does that sound too startling, Roy? It shouldn't. The destiny of humanity might well be at stake here, Roy. Savage is a humanitarian, in his rather unorthodox way."

Roy closed his eyes and didn't say anything. He apparently thought the portly old gentleman was using too many words. So did I.

"You mustn't disobey orders, Roy," said Mr. Montgomery. He was a man who liked the sound of his own voice, apparently. He continued, "Actually, Roy, we should both be able to retire after this job. Retirement, you being a young man, may lack appeal. But if you wish, and we are successful, I imagine you could, young as you are, put yourself out to pasture the rest of your days. Now you understand why my feelings were a bit urgent when I tapped you with the cane."

Roy grimaced. "I don't see why you had to knock me cold. It made a rumpus."

"My temper got the best of me," said the fat man blandly. "I'll tell you why. I haven't mentioned it. While I was sitting at the table near the pool with the two young ladies, I filched from Glacia's purse an envelope containing Waldo Loring's testament."

Roy brightened and sat up straight. "You think it'll tell where—"

"We shall never know, I'm afraid," said Mr. Montgomery bitterly.

"Huh?"

"Listen carefully, Roy. I stuck that envelope to the underside of the table with a bit of chicle. Then you appeared and upset me so that I went to hunt you and urge you to return to our rooms. I did not find you at first, and then I chanced to observe Glacia's friend in the act of recovering the envelope from beneath the table. She had found it. I was naturally enraged with you, and when soon afterward I found you, I expressed my feelings."

"Good God!" Roy blurted. "They're wise to you?"

"Thanks to you, I'm sorry to say," agreed Mr. Montgomery.

Whereupon Mr. Montgomery slapped Roy. The fat hand was a broad poisonous serpent's head; it darted out and there was a pop of flesh on flesh. It must have been a harder slap than seemed logical, because Roy fell back in the chair again, and his eyes turned in their sockets like white mice investigating their own tails.

"My dear boy," said the fat man. "I'm very irritated, I assure you."

I wasn't exactly irritated, but neither was my mind going tra-la. I hadn't dreamed that Mr. Montgomery had observed me finding the envelope—and it followed naturally that he knew what I had done with it after finding it. If he still wanted it, I might be in for some trouble. Because Mr. Montgomery was a lot worse article than I had anticipated.

Where was Glacia? I still didn't know that, and the fact that the fat man hadn't mentioned doing Glacia any harm within the last half hour didn't mean a thing. There were probably many things in Mr. Montgomery's life that he wasn't mentioning. The things he didn't mention were the ones to worry about.

I began to have a vague idea that I'd underestimated almost everyone and everything. I'd underrated the fat man. I'd missed the boat on Doc Savage—because I hadn't really believed he was involved. Oh, I'd told him he was. I'd told Glacia he was. But I'd been telling something I didn't quite believe. As for mysteries and fabulous secrets—well, I hadn't even been playing in that league.

I'd supposed the thing, even if it was pretty complicated, would be a matter of Uncle Waldo having done someone a dark deed, and the donee getting even with the donor for it. It seemed there was slightly more to it than that.

Apparently I now knew everything but a couple of salient facts. Uncle Waldo'd gotten hold of something terrific, and he'd tried to sell it, and the selling had gotten a trifle complex and now Uncle Waldo was dead and nobody knew the whereabouts of the merchandise Waldo'd had on the market. That was what the scuffling was about. Where was the button?

Mr. Montgomery had just gone over all this with Roy, but I went over it again just to be sure. It sounded farfetched, even though I had stood in a shower bath booth and heard it. But I was sure it was true. Mr. Montgomery had left out just enough to make it sound like truth—he had left out what Uncle Waldo's secret was, and he'd omitted the matter of who murdered Waldo. He knew the details. Or he'd guessed at them. It followed that he might know who killed Waldo, or might be the one who had done it.

Probably I wasn't gaining a thing by standing here restating facts to myself. But it made me feel better, so I did it. Far better, it was not long developing, that I should have looked to business closer at hand—was there, for instance, a bathroom window through which I could make a flying exit?

There was no window, but maybe it would have done no good anyway. Because Mr. Montgomery's voice, not quite calmly, said, "I don't know what bard said familiarity placed a blindness on one. Maybe one didn't say it. He should have."

He had the shower booth door open by then. He was fast for a fat man, which was no surprise. Not nearly as much a surprise as seeing such a large gun in his hand. Somehow I'd imagined him as a deft old gentleman who disdained firearms.

"It was a long time dawning on me that a shower curtain doesn't have quite your silhouette, young lady," he said.

He must not have liked the way my head went back.

"Don't!" he said. "Don't scream. I shouldn't like it."

It was a good thing he said that. I didn't want to do anything he shouldn't like. Not when he had that look on his chubby face, lips loose like a kid's collapsed toy balloon, eyes big and all whites like boiled eggs.

"Colleen," he called over his shoulder. "Colleen, will you step in here and bolster me in misfortune?"

Colleen came forward walking with lithe strides. She looked about as scared as a cat at its cream saucer. "It's Nell-the-girl-detective," she said. "Well, snatch my girdle and call me unrestrained!"

"Search her," said Mr. Montgomery.

Colleen did an experienced job with her hands, and I was invited into the living room. Roy still sat in the chair and did not look any different, except that he had probably forgotten his headache.

"What I want somebody to tell me is how the hell she got in here?" remarked Colleen.

"That really should concern you, since she entered while you were here alone, obviously." Mr. Montgomery didn't sound too kindly toward his daughter. "Your search was also inadequate. Take her into the bedroom. Find that envelope containing Waldo Loring's final testament."

"I'm afraid of her," Colleen said with disapproval. "Me alone in there with her? She'll probably wring my neck."

Mr. Montgomery said coldly, "I am in a frame of mind to enjoy the act by proxy if she does. Get going. Find that will."

Colleen got me into the bedroom. There were two of the latter connecting with the suite, I noticed. "Pops is in a bad mood, honey," Colleen told me. "I'd be very meek, if I were you."

I didn't argue the point about her father's mood. If she said it was bad, I would take her word for it. I was convinced he had brained Waldo Loring while feeling a bit irritated, the way he was now.

One search didn't satisfy Colleen. She did it over, then inventoried my purse, sneering at the brand of my lipstick, and counting my few dollars before she folded them neatly and tucked them in her stocking. She wasn't happy about settling for the receipt for the lock box they'd given me downstairs, but she settled for it. She carried it in and tossed it down before fat papa.

"She probably locked it up," she said. Then, not liking the boiled egg look her father's eyes got again, she added hastily. "That's right. They stamp the time on those receipts. That one is stamped not more than forty minutes ago."

Mr. Montgomery scooped up the receipt, eyed it, threw it on the floor.

He swept up the gun. "Step over here, dear," he said.

I stood exactly where he wanted me to stand. The look in his eye told me where. I stopped there, and registered as much cooperation as I could.

I wasn't scared. I was paralyzed.

He asked, "You have a good memory? You will recite the exact contents of that document. Beginning in five seconds."

"I don't remember," I said.

That was the wrong thing. I should have waggled my mouth around and let nothing but squeaks of terror come out. I should have been too scared to speak. That wouldn't have been hard to do, if I had thought of it.

Mr. Montgomery drew in a deep breath, a deep one. And he smiled. A little smile.

Roy came up out of the chair. He didn't stand up. He just seemed to rise somewhat on the cushions, as if he were being hauled up by the hair. His face looked that way, too.

"Father!" Colleen screamed.

They knew him, so they must know what his expressions meant. I didn't know him, but I thought I understood his grimace, too. Because it wasn't really a smile.

He was going to kill me. Shoot me. He was a suave, egotistical, show-offish old gentleman with too much soft flesh and too many words. But he was blowing his cork.

The only reason he didn't shoot me—quite a good reason it was, too—was the loud noise knuckles made on the door.

Someone at the door didn't change Mr. Montgomery's glazed madness. But it electrified his daughter and Roy.

Roy pushed Mr. Montgomery down into an overstuffed chair. He tried to take the gun away from the old man, but Mr. Montgomery wouldn't give it up, so Roy compromised by shoving the old fellow's hand down beside him, between the cushion and the side of the chair—the hand and the gun.

Colleen grabbed me and hustled me into the bedroom. The last I saw of Roy for the nonce, he was walking toward the door with his eyes wide and tragic. The fist was banging the door again.

I heard who the visitor was. I was in the bedroom, but I recognized the voice.

"Heap sorry," it said. "Got short circuit in wiring."

Coming Going. My redskin pal.

"There's no trouble with the wiring in here," Roy told him. Roy sounded all right. A little shaky with the last couple of words.

"In switchbox," Coming Going argued. "Got to take a look. Electricity in other rooms won't work. Fuse box in here. Take a minute. Okay."

"There's no switchbox in here, you crazy Indian."

"Look anyway. Okay?"

At this point, I woke up to the fact that there was a man outside the bedroom window. He was standing there, apparently on thin air, but probably on a ladder. I knew him. Another pal. Monk Mayfair.

Now that I had finally discovered him, Monk Mayfair shrugged—the shrug meant I'd certainly taken my time about noticing him—and then he made little circles in the air with a finger. Indicating I should persuade Colleen to turn around. He illustrated my next move for me—he popped himself on the jaw with a fist.

"Colleen," I said. "There's a man behind you."

She had a little gun. Where she'd gotten it from I didn't know. She sneered over the gun and said, "Nuts, darling."

"There really is."

"Keep your voice down," she breathed viciously.

"Oh, but there really—"

Monk Mayfair helped out by tapping on the window. Whereupon Colleen went off as if she had exploded. Her arms flew out from her sides much as if she was spreading them preparatory to flying. Her mouth opened, but whether she would have screamed I never knew, because I closed the mouth again, hard. It wasn't a very orthodox punch. I think I used both hands. Both at once, the way you lift a heavy weight.

Chapter VIII

COLLEEN took plenty of time deciding to drop. The small gun fell. She showed lots of eye whites, let her arms down to her sides, managed two steps backward and one to the right, before deciding on the floor.

I was already passing her. The window was locked. I unfastened it. Monk Mayfair started to climb inside, which complicated matters, because I was endeavoring to climb out.

"Take it easy," he said.

"Get out of my way," I said.

A gun went off in the living room. If there had been any preliminaries in the way of words, they had been softly spoken. But the gun was definitely loud, almost as noisy as the second one that answered it.

I passed Monk Mayfair. Probably I crawled over him. I went down the ladder, and halfway I passed Doc Savage. I had never imagined two people could pass on a ladder with so few formalities.

"Is it safe to go into the hotel room?" he asked.

"Certainly not," I said.

He looked up and shouted, "Monk! Stay out of there!"

Monk Mayfair was already through the window. He didn't answer.

The shooting continued inside the hotel for a few moments, then came to a spotty end. I was trying to reach the bottom of the ladder as if it was everything on Earth that I wanted, and it was. Then I got down there on solid earth—and didn't know what to do.

It hadn't occurred to me that there would be any question about what to do next once I reached terrafirma and liberty. There were many courses open. Run was the first one. Then there were the assorted organizations I could hurriedly notify that a fat man had been about to kill me, these including the police, the sheriff, the F.B.I., the hotel house sleuth if it had one, and the U.S. Marines. Now, though, that I was on the ground and comparatively safe, unless hit by a ricochetting bullet, or someone leaned out of the hotel window and took a shot at me, I somehow did none of the obvious things. I waited to see what Doc Savage would do about all this. I tried to tell myself that I was curious about how the great man worked. Actually I probably thought his neighborhood was about the safest available spot.

Whatever went on in Mr. Montgomery's suite happened in comparative peace. There were no more shots. Doc Savage, having demonstrated that he had no control over Monk Mayfair when the latter was excited, went the rest of the way up the ladder himself and disappeared in the window. That was my cue to start reclimbing the ladder. Whether Savage wanted to be a protector or not, I was going to elect him.

Not too happily, I crawled back into a hotel suite I had quitted not so long ago. Mr. Montgomery, Colleen, Roy, were gone, as was Monk Mayfair, while Coming Going was walking around yelling and ruining an expensive rug with the blood that was coming from at least two holes in him. The theme of his yelling was that he was calling on hell to open wide and receive the United States State Department.

"Where did they go?" I asked.

Coming Going looked at me and yelled, "Out! Where did you suppose they went?" And he had been so cute and kindly with his heap-big-Injun ways.

Doc Savage was hauling a chair across the room. I watched him. He got on the chair, and unscrewed a light bulb from the ceiling chandelier, selecting one particular bulb.

"The fat man's party left hurriedly, as Mr. Going intimates," Savage told me. "Monk presumably followed them. They were all gone when I got into the suite."

"Aren't you going to—won't Monk need help?"

"He won't get it, if he does. But he won't need it. Monk never does."

I thought that was a pretty dirty trick. The notion must have shown on my face, something like the look the baby rabbit gives the alligator that is going to swallow him. Because Savage looked patiently pained himself.

"We've been watching Mr. Montgomery's party for days," Savage told me. "We didn't want him alarmed. Monk will alarm him—which, incidentally, is my understatement for today."

I admitted that being alarmed by Monk Mayfair would probably be rather special. "But suppose he needs help? That Montgomery isn't exactly a lamb."

"If Monk needs help, he'll call for it," Savage said briefly.

He wrapped the light bulb he had removed in a handkerchief and pocketed it carefully.

Pointing at the pocket, I said, "Don't tell me that's a microphone?"

He nodded. "Yes. Only one we have in the fifty-watt size, too. It's a special job—practically indetectible even on inspection. It lights like an ordinary bulb, as well."

Coming Going asked Hell to also keep its gates open for all meddling human females. He was looking at me.

"Oh!" I said. "Oh, I see now. You were eavesdropping on what went on in here, and you had to change your plans and save my life."

"Something like that," Savage admitted.

"I don't see why it should gripe your redskin friend so," I said.

"He happens to understand how disastrous this setback may be."

"I see. Pardon me for having a neck that needed saving."

Nobody had anymore to say until we had carried our bad tempers out of there—curious guests were just beginning to collect and ask what had happened—and adjourned to Doc Savage's suite. Savage began dressing Coming Going's injuries—bullet paths in, respectively, an arm and a neck muscle. Savage was deft, knew his business. Coming Going had stopped importuning hell to take care of me and the United States State Department, and sat on a straightbacked chair. The back of his neck, the backs of his hands, became wet with perspiration that pain made.

"Mr. Going," Doc Savage told me, "is with the organization he has just been condemning with such sincerity—the State Department. He was the man first assigned to investigate this matter. It was at his suggestion that I was involved."

"Oh," I said, in a small way.

I dragged out and inspected my previous idea that Coming Going was a dopey ham actor from Hollywood whose speed was playing phony Indians. Just a nice, harmless boy, I'd thought him, who had been floored by the news that Waldo Loring had been murdered. The idea was like some others I'd had in my time. Rather sour.

"Then you're all secret agents," I said.

Savage snorted slightly. Quite a display of emotion for him. "Mr. Going might be remotely so classified. But I haven't been able to do anything secretly for years."

He might be right. Come to think of it, his here at the lodge had been as unobtrusive as the arrival of a circus in town.

"I don't get it," I said.

Coming Going looked up at me. "Neither have we. And now we may never get it." His feather was over his eye again.

"It's partly your own fault," I snapped. "God knows, I came running to you both for information.

And what did I get? Big-eyed innocence." I was pretty upset about it. "What was I to do? My friend, Glacia, was in trouble, and it was up to me to help her."

"Some girlfriends you pick," said Coming Going.

"There's nothing wrong with Glacia except that she's money-hungry!" I yelled. "She wouldn't harm anyone intentionally."

Doc Savage patted the air vaguely with his hand that was holding a bottle of antiseptic and told me, "We know more about Glacia Loring than you do, and probably know things about you that you've forgotten. We should—there have been nearly a hundred agents sifting you both the past few days."

I asked a question that I had been afraid to ask.

"Where is Glacia?"

Savage caught Going's eye, hesitated, finally said, "We don't know."

Both of them watched me for a time. Going finally muttered, "For God's sake, either faint or stop looking as if you're going to."

"You mean—she's not at the lodge?" It was my voice, coming from a spot several feet distant, the voice of someone who had been swallowed.

"We don't know," Savage said again.

"But surel… Glacia left me at the pool, ran off in a rage to hunt Mr. Montgomery because he'd rifled her purse… Oh my God! She didn't find him and he—"

Savage's hand was up, his voice sharply urgent. "No, no, she didn't find Montgomery. We kept track of her for a while—or Coming Going did, but—"

"I wish you'd stop calling me Coming Going, or Mr. Going," the phony Indian snapped peevishly. "My name is Lybeck. Joseph Lybeck… No, Mote, I lost track of your friend. She didn't lose me consciously. I just zigged when I should have zagged, and lost her."

"There is no reason to think she isn't perfectly safe," Doc Savage told me.

"No reason! When there's been one murder? And that fat Montgomery was going to kill me in cold blood if you hadn't—" I took hold of myself with both hands, my knees anyway. I could feel them shaking. "I'm sorry," I said. "Glacia may seem a little screwy to you fellows. But she has done a few things for me, enough nice things to outweigh the other kind."

"You think a lot of her," Savage said. It was more statement than question.

"Yes. A lot is right. Call it the attraction of opposites or whatever you want to. But the fact is that I swing my last punch for her if necessary."

Savage nodded. "She knows that. It's why she sent for you."

"Probably."

Savage's expression and manner now showed that he had a problem to solve. The result of what I'd said, evidently. I didn't know what it was.

I didn't know, either, why we were staying in the room making small talk. Action seemed called for. Glacia was missing. Monk Mayfair was missing. Mr. Montgomery and party had flown. Yet we were here, doing what never solves problems—talking.

When he had finished patching Coming Going—I couldn't think of him as anyone named Joseph Lybeck, although I had no trouble accepting him as a federal agent—Doc Savage stepped back. He told Coming Going, "I think she should know the whole story."

Coming Going said, "Ugh!" He added, "Oh, all right. Everybody else seems to know everything anyway."

Savage went into another room to fetch a small radio that was not a conventional table model, but more resembled the communication apparatus that amateurs use. He switched it on. After it warmed up, the speaker did not emit the usual static cracklings, but a slight high-pitched hissing. I knew what it was. A V.H.F outfit. Very High Frequency radio.

Without explaining why he had turned on the radio, Savage told me, "Your guess about Waldo Loring's previous profession was accurate. Exact. He was a ship captain. Master of freight steamers."

My nod was probably just a gesture I should have made. I was thinking of Glacia.

"I won't bore you with a lengthy summary of Waldo Loring's life," Doc Savage continued. "It was a rough life, and there was some sharpshooting in it, but probably no more than the average tough sailor does. We'll skip down to the year before the war ended, the month of September. That was when—"

He jumped, bit off his words, eyed the radio. It had emitted a deep sound like a long steady breath. Savage watched the radio. Coming Going watched it. The radio stopped making the breathing sound without making any other.

"September. A freighter. The *Victory Tumble.* Captain Waldo Loring commanding." Savage still had his eye on the radio. "The *Victory Tumble* loaded a cargo at a Canadian port. Destination of the cargo: England. There was the greatest secrecy—even Captain Loring didn't know the destination. Only a Lieutenant Commander Roger Peelman knew that. Peelman was U.S. Navy. He went aboard with orders that made him Captain Waldo Loring's senior in command."

The radio for a moment proved more of a magnet for his interest than the story he was telling. After about a minute, he pulled away from it enough to continue:

"Perhaps if the Navy man had been more diplomatic, none of this would have happened. Waldo Loring was an egotistical, hardheaded old sea dog, and his opinion of the Navy was considerably lower than the Navy's opinion of him. Captain Loring and Lieutenant Commander Peelman did not get along well. Peelman complained to Washington about it before sailing, but nothing was done about it—a bad bit of neglect, probably."

"Something happened to the ship?" I asked, jumping at a conclusion.

"It sank. Some three weeks later, a destroyer picked up a lifeboat containing the survivors. They consisted of Captain Loring and some of his crew. Peelman had drowned. The story they told—the ship damaged by an enemy torpedo, then a storm, and the ship going down—was corroborated by all survivors. The logs checked. Apparently the ship had sunk in deep water, three hundred miles at sea." He hesitated, then added, "Apparently."

"Apparently?" I said.

"Well, yes. You see, after the war, the Navy took pains to check enemy submarine reports and they found that the *Victory Tumble* had been torpedoed, all right—but a couple of hundred miles from the spot Captain Waldo Loring named."

"What about the log books; aren't they reliable records?"

Savage shrugged. "Easily altered. Captain Loring kept the master's log, which was a digest of the day log. He could have made false entries and no one else would have known."

"What about the crew members who were picked up with him?"

"Seamen. No officers. They wouldn't have known. Every pain was taken to keep the *Victory Tumble*'s cargo, course and destination secret.

"Oh."

"Because of the nature of the cargo," Savage continued, "the Navy kept Captain Loring under surveillance. They checked enemy sub reports after the war, as I told you. And then they really watched Captain Loring. They watched him and they watched people he contacted—and they found out, a few weeks ago, that Captain Loring was trying to sell the cargo of the ship that had sunk."

"You mean his vessel didn't sink?" I gasped.

"Oh, it went down all right. But not where Loring claimed—the Navy had sounded the whole area, and made Geiger counter tests—"

"Wait a minute!" I yelled. "Geiger counter? I've heard such a gadget mentioned, or read of—"

"Naturally. A device for indicting the presence of radioactivity."

I thought I had it now. "This cargo wouldn't have been atom bombs?" I demanded.

"No. On an unguarded ship? Certainly not."

"Then what—"

Savage glanced questionably at Coming Going, who shrugged, said, "Might as well tell her. The State Department has the delusion that only three people in the world know what that cargo was. They won't mind this lady being a fourth. Much."

"Want to bet I can't name at least two nations with aggressive notions who don't know by now?" Savage demanded. "Particularly since Waldo Loring has been trying to sell the stuff to them?"

"I was just being funny in my odd way," Coming Going said bitterly.

"Uranium," Savage told me. "Not freshly mined ore. Processed. That is, it had gone through the two preliminary processing stages. Intended for atom bombs, of course."

"But why on a steamer going to—"

"Let's not go any deeper into top secret stuff," Savage said. "You know that England and Canada were working with us on the bomb."

"But why is it so valuable? The war is over—"

"Over? There is some doubt about that in a few quarters. Let's just say that all uranium sources are closely guarded and every speck of ore accounted for since the war ended. There's enough ore on that ship to furnish the makings of quite a few bombs. Enough to be worth—well, the destiny of a few nations, perhaps."

Coming Going, with grating vehemence, said, "Don't underestimate the value of that cargo, honey."

I decided that I wouldn't. I had read those conjectures about what a dozen or so bombs planted in American cities, perhaps months ahead of zero hour and timed to let loose all together, would do to our defense plants. Pearl Harbor would be like nothing.

Glacia… Glacia was involved in something like that… my silly, self-centered, dollar-hungry little friend….

Doc Savage came over and placed a hand on my arm. "Don't get the wrong idea, Mote. Glacia doesn't know it's uranium. Waldo Loring told her it was gold, and I think she believed him."

My face felt dry and like bone and it must have looked like bone because Savage looked concerned and went to a writing desk, hauled open the drawer, and took out the Indian warclub that had been in Glacia's room.

He said, "You were worried about this club, I believe. You needn't be. Monk got it from your room—to run a few tests to see if it could be the murder instrument. It wasn't."

"I knew Glacia didn't kill him," I said tightly. "I never let that quite get into my mind."

He tossed the club on a chair. "Well, it's not comfortable having such things around trying to get into one's mind. You can forget it."

The radio did what they had been waiting for it to do. It made the husky breathing sound again, added words, remarkably clear words—Monk Mayfair's voice—and said, "Doc, I ran into something too rough—"

There was urgency in Mayfair's voice. Not fear, but sick urgency. A quality that made my hair feel as if it was being combed the wrong way.

"—no out for me," Monk was saying. "Get this quick, Doc! It's not Montgomery! It's another one who knows where the ship lies. It's nobody we suspected. Watch out for her—"

That was all. I don't know what a radio transmitter sounds like over the air when it is being smashed. Probably like the sound that came from our receiver.

Chapter IX

IT was quiet in the lodge bar now, and cool and semi-dark, rather like a sepulchre, for the day was done and a couple of hours of the night had gone, and they were having a party in another part of the lodge, which accounted for the bar being empty. A party. On the house. Everyone was there. The dead are dead, and the living must live. The bar was dank and still, a repository for me and my fears.

I moved my glass back and forth and it made wet smears on the table and they were symbolic of something or other, the mess things were in, probably. The waiter went past silently, like a ghost walking on eggs. There was only one waiter, and he would look at me each time he passed. He didn't seem to see me.

I knew what was wrong with the waiter. He didn't like what we were doing. We were even. Neither did I.

The waiter didn't have a friend who had vanished into thin air, and I didn't imagine anyone had tried to kill him today. He hadn't spent an afternoon locked in his room with little cold-footed fear-things stampeding over his skin every time someone walked down the hall. He'd probably spent the afternoon shooting pool. And he was getting twenty dollars for what he was doing. Twenty, and the privilege of assisting the great Doc Savage.

Not that I'd decided Doc Savage was less than the reports said. He was good. He was marvelous. He had functioned all day with the acumen and skill of the F.B.I., Sherlock Holmes and all the fictional sleuths ever created with words. The trouble was, he hadn't been good enough to find Monk Mayfair. Nor Glacia.

My sitting here was Doc Savage's idea. I didn't necessarily need to be in the bar, but my room had gotten too much for me. I had stayed in that room until I began seeing things walking on the walls. I felt as if I could walk on them myself. So I was in the bar. Being at the party wouldn't do—I was supposed to be in mourning. I had lost an uncle. My uncle Waldo Loring. I was Glacia Loring.

The waiter would say I was Glacia Loring. Or he would if he earned his twenty dollars. The desk clerk would say so, too. That had been arranged.

"Miss Loring?"

It was the waiter. He had walked straight to me and I had watched him and hadn't quite seen him. I jumped. "Yes, waiter," I said.

"A gentleman inquiring for you. A gentleman named McBride."

"Show the gentleman where I am."

"Very well, Miss."

"Wait—what does the gentleman look like?"

"He's about forty-five, Miss."

"Show him to me."

Attorney McBride didn't look forty-five, or wouldn't with the worried look scrubbed off his face. He was about thirty, but he did appear very tired. He was a large bushy young man in slacks, Hollywood shirt, sunburn and a deposit of desert dust.

"Miss Loring?" he asked. "Miss Glacia Loring?"

"Yes," I said, and wondered how well he remembered Glacia's voice from having heard it over the telephone.

"This is certainly a relief." Apparently he didn't remember it so well. "I'm Attorney McBride."

"Oh, yes, indeed. I spoke to you on the telephone."

"That's right." He dropped on the seat opposite. "Oh, man! Whoeee!" He looked at the waiter. "Can a man get coffee laced with whiskey in here?"

"Certainly, sir."

"Then produce it," said Attorney McBride. He turned to me and said, "If I seem dithered, you can rest assured that I am."

"Has something happened?"

He nodded. "Your uncle was the damnedest client."

"How do you mean?"

He blew out his breath. "How? Whoosh! I never heard of a client, much less had one, who left the sort of a legacy he left you, Miss Loring."

"Keeper, you mean?"

"Oh, my Lord, yes," he said.

The McBride voice was not as yapping as it had sounded over the telephone—from what I had managed to overhear of Glacia's conversation with him—but it was not exactly dull.

"Did you bring my inheritance?" I asked.

"My Lord, yes," he said.

"Could I see it?"

"It?... Oh, I see. Uh—you apply a very good word to the inheritance. Calling it *it,* I mean. Very appropriate. I had thought of some words for it myself, but they wouldn't bear repeating in polite company."

"Mr. McBride, I have no idea what Keeper is," I said.

He sat back. His jaw dropped. His eyes were as round as shotgun barrels.

After wincing and hesitating, he asked, "Have you had dinner, Glacia? I may call you, Glacia, mayn't I? If you haven't had dinner, you'd better. You'll need your strength."

"Look here," I said sharply. "I don't know why you are so excited, but I'm beginning to wonder. What are you trying to do, upset me?"

"Upset? Oh, no. Forbid and preserve," cried Mr. McBride. "I only want your courage at full tide, bright and sparkling, so you'll have the nerve to take it off my hands."

"It?"

"Whew! I mustn't frighten you. Oh, no! I mustn't!" gasped the attorney.

I tried to pin him down with a frown. "Just what is wrong with this inheritance?"

"I don't believe I'd better start answering that, because I want to start back to Los Angeles tonight. But if you want a fault, here is one of the milder ones: it eats a hell of a lot."

That settles it, I thought. A race horse. "How many races has it won?"

"Races? Eh? Can it run?" He couldn't have been more confused if I had stood him on his head and put a carrot in his mouth.

"Isn't it a race horse?"

"Oh, no. Well—no!" said McBride. "Race horse? Good Lord, what a description for—well, never mind." He mopped his forehead, although the desert nights weren't hot and the hotel air conditioner was still going. "What a characterization—race horse. Whoee! Whoee! Whatever gave you such a wrong idea? Oh, I see… Uh, what *did* give you the idea anyway?"

"You," I said, "seem to be twittery. Keep it up, and we'll both be that way."

"McBride is twittering, all right," the attorney-at-law said. "Oh, thank God!" The last because the waiter had finally come with his coffee and a side of bourbon.

I decided to wait him out. This might be an act. I didn't know what it was.

Doc Savage might be able to make a head or a tail of it. I took a chance and moved my purse a little on the table, edging it to a spot where it would better pick up our conversation. I supposed that moving it would make a terrific rumpus in the little microphone. Because there was a microwave transmitter—that was what Doc Savage had called it, whatever that was—in the purse. The theory was that I was a traveling broadcast station, and I was supposed to pretend to be Glacia, and that was supposed to lead to something. We hoped.

Lawyer McBride finished his laced coffee. He looked at me as if he was very sorry for me. He blew out a considerable breath. "Miss Loring," he said, "you might as well see the bad news."

Whereupon he led the way outdoors and toward the parking lot. The desert night was clear. They were probably always clear, the sky cloudless, because the adjacent country didn't look as if a drop of moisture had ever fallen on it.

Attorney McBride approached a trailer. With misgivings. "I usually announce myself by throwing a rock," he told me nervously. "But this time, we'll take a chance."

The trailer was an unlighted, beat-up affair, and he knocked timidly on the door. No response. Without more preliminaries, McBride snarled, "Why the hell should I worry? I'm getting shut of him!" and he hauled off and kicked the trailer door. That got action.

"Oaf," stated a deep-throated male voice inside the trailer, "derives from the Iceland *alfr*, meaning originally an elf's child, a changeling left by goblins, therefore a foolish or deformed child, an idiot, a simpleton. Hence it may refer to one person who disturbs another. Will you go away?"

"Harold!" said McBride. "Harold, your new owner is here."

There was a prolonged silence from inside.

"Harold!" said Mr. McBride.

"Yes, sir."

"Come out. Miss Loring, who inherited you, is here."

"I don't want to come out," the voice said. It sounded as if it was being manufactured in a barrel.

"Harold," said Mr. McBride patiently. "You wish to be fed, don't you? And guided, and managed, and cared for?"

"Yes, sir."

The lawyer yelled, "Then get the hell out here and meet the nice lady who has inherited you."

Oh, Lord, I thought—I was beginning to react like Attorney McBride. I had, or Glacia had, inherited something that talked with a man's voice.

Presently it opened the trailer door. Older than I had thought. Too old to be very interesting; at least more than forty. And fat. Not short, but tremendously fat, egg-shaped.

"This is Harold," said Attorney McBride.

Harold's head was quite large, like a melon placed crosswise, and his mouth was large out of proportion, as were his eyes. In front of the latter, he wore shell-rimmed glasses that, regardless of what they did for his vision, certainly made his eyes startling. None of his clothing fit well, all either too large or too small.

"Harold, this is Miss Loring," added McBride.

"Girl!" exploded Harold. "Girl was originally the name of the Goddess Vesta, or the human young of either sex, but the term is now applied to the female child, a maiden, a mare or filly, a maidservant, a sweetheart, or a roebuck in its second year."

He slammed the trailer door in our faces.

There was a silence.

"The last one fits me," I said.

"Eh?" said McBride.

"The roebuck in its second year."

"Oh." McBride cleared his throat. "You—ah—I have a paper for you to sign. A receipt for your inheritance. If you will sign same, I will be going."

"Wait a minute, brother," I said. I gripped his arm. I led him a few yards from the trailer, and I held my purse so the gadget in it would be sure to pick up and relay what we had to say. "What's the matter with Harold? Is he nuts?"

"Nuttier than a fruitcake," said McBride.

"Who is he?"

"Harold Keeper. You've inherited him. Now, if you will sign this paper—"

"How come, inherited?" I said, gripping the attorney's arm. "Give. What is this, anyway? Waldo Loring never told me what Keeper was. Who is he?"

McBride sighed elaborately. "Harold was the old man's—your deceased uncle's—friend. Sort of a flunky, I surmise. A sailor. Harold was a sailor on your uncle's ships."

"Oh, Harold is some crazy sailor whom Uncle Waldo was taking care of?"

"Well—yes. Only your uncle did say that Harold had not always been—shall we say—cracked. It seems that during the war uncle's ship was torpedoed, and your uncle and Harold were in the boatload of survivors. They suffered great hardships in the open sea in the small boat. The experience affected Harold's mind. Your uncle feels, or felt, duty bound to care for Harold."

"I don't think I like this," I said.

"I was afraid you wouldn't," McBride said wearily. "Are you going to sign—"

"Not," I said, "until I think it over."

"You can't do that to me!" yelled McBride. "My God, unless you accept Harold, I'm stuck with him!"

I walked back to the lodge. McBride hopped along beside me, complaining that I was cold-blooded and arguing that Harold had good points. He tried to enumerate Harold's points, and couldn't think of any.

"Listen, I'll talk this over with you in the morning," I said.

"But—"

"You've done enough to me for one evening. Goodnight, Mr. McBride. In the morning. Say about eight."

He stamped into the lodge. I could hear him screaming at the registrations clerk about the price they were going to charge him for a room. A very excitable nature, Mr. McBride.

I moved a few paces and stepped into the shadow of the lodge, waited. Presently, without noticeable sound, there was a large form beside me. Doc Savage.

"Did the gadget work? Did you pick all that up?" I asked.

Doc Savage said he had.

"Were you surprised?" I inquired. "I was. Keeper a man, a screwball. That's the last thing—"

But Doc Savage had something more urgent on his mind than a discussion. His hand touched my arm. Not a hard grip. But as solid as a stone building.

"Let's watch the trailer," he said. And that was all he said until we had reached another wedge of darkness beside a parked car thirty yards or so from the trailer, which was still dark.

"Why doesn't Harold turn on the lights?" I said uneasily. "He—he gives me cold chills. I never did like psychos, and—"

All of a sudden, I wondered if I was going to lose my balance wheel. This whole thing of Harold Keeper, the way it seemed to bear no relation to Waldo Loring's murder, or Glacia's disappearance, or a shipload of uranium ore, was unnerving. It was like starting to a funeral, and finding you were in a circus instead.

"I'm coming loose," I mumbled. "I didn't expect anything like this. My stomach feels funny."

He tried the door of the parked car. It was unlocked, and he opened it. "Sit down here," he said. "Not in the seat, where you will be seen. In the door. Now, just what is upsetting you?"

"It's Glacia!" I blurted. "No word from her. And I thought this Keeper would be a document or a map or something that would solve everything. It hasn't. I feel so damn thwarted."

Savage said, "You've made a lot of progress."

His voice was wonderful. It built confidence underfoot as solid as a concrete sidewalk.

"Waldo Loring never had a friend named Harold Keeper," he said.

"How do you—"

"Waldo Loring's past has been investigated every way possible. We can almost tell you what he ate in every meal for the past five years. We would know if Waldo Loring had Harold Keeper. Rest assured, we would know that."

"He was supposed to be in the lifeboatful of survivors—"

"No. He was not. I know where every man in that lifeboat can be found. And not one of them will be found in that trailer."

I felt better. Chilly. Nerve chills, but they were better than the awful feeling that I wasn't helping Glacia. I just sat there. The big bronze man had seated himself on the ground beside me, between this car and another. He was silent. Somewhere far off there was a giggling and yapping, and it sounded like several girls noisy from too much to drink. But it was coyotes. We were in the desert. Close to wild nature. But nature wasn't as wild as some of the humans around here.

"What is the rig?" I asked. "What are they trying to pull?"

"No rig anymore, lady," said a voice.

It wasn't Doc Savage's voice. But it was close enough to have been. I looked up. I didn't make it out at first, except that it was big and hung with gross flesh. Why I didn't seem to understand that it was Harold was a mystery.

"Not anymore," Harold said. "The rig is off. We have left just what is in my hand. So don't move."

We didn't move. Harold's gun was a big thing. Anybody but Harold would have needed a wheelbarrow to cart it around.

The night was still around us for a moment. Except for the coyotes far away, about as far away as my mind seemed from my body. I think my mind had fled that far because it couldn't stand staying in a place as scared as my body was.

"Lady, if you faint, do so quietly," Harold said.

Chapter X

ONE of those impatient men, Harold. He waited for me to swoon, and I didn't, but I probably tried. Savage had not moved, which showed good judgment.

"Lie down on the ground. Spreadeagle," Harold told Savage.

"Face up or face down?" Doc Savage asked.

"Down, of course."

"Whatever you say. But a man can get going from a face down position a lot quicker."

"You can give a demonstration of it if you want to," Harold said grimly. "It's about as wide as long with me."

There was a little silence, then Savage lay down on his face. Even lying on his face, obeying the order of a grossly fat devil with a gun, he did not surrender any of the competence that was always with him. Even in the darkness, where there was barely enough light to distinguish more than the presence of a hand on the end of an arm, he kept that feeling of ability. Harold got the same idea, evidently. Because he made a hissing sound through his teeth, ugly and serpentine.

"Mr. McBride!" Harold called softly.

The darkness stirred nearby, then the figure of Attorney McBride shaped up in it. He lingered a few yards distant. He seemed to be wishing he was a dried leaf and could blow away.

"Come here, Mr. McBride," said Harold.

The lawyer ventured closer. As if he was pushing his way through steel.

"This is Doc Savage, Mr. McBride," said Harold.

If Mr. McBride was breathing, he didn't show it.

Harold said, "You have heard of the sun that makes the tides, the U.S. Marines that make whatever marines make. Well, Mr. McBride, that gives you some idea. Because this is no less than Doc Savage."

McBride had no words.

"We didn't fool the great one, it seems," Harold said.

McBride replied with a deep breath. It shook coming in, and shook going out.

"We wasted our time," Harold said. "We went to a lot of trouble fixing a deal. And did we fix us a deal. Brother!"

Harold grew tired of McBride's answers.

He asked me, "Mote, isn't that what they call you? Mote. Well, Mote, didn't you think it was a nice deal?"

"It took me in," I said.

"That didn't make it good enough." Harold sighed, and in that pile of body, it was like steam going through a heating system. "You know what the deal was, don't you?"

"No," I said.

"Baby, you should see it by now. I was going to be your puppydog, see."

"Why?"

"Just to be around. Eyes open, you know. There were some flies in my ointment, and I was going to do a little fly-catching. Specifically was Doc Savage on this case? How much did he know—enough that we would have to knock him off? The answer to the last is yes. Yup. Maybe we didn't waste all that finagling."

He seemed to have plenty of words. I didn't know what he was doing, trying to button up his own courage perhaps. And I didn't know how much of what he had said was lying, beyond the part of wanting to know where Doc Savage was involved in the case. He had known that all right, if he knew anything at all about what was going on, and he did.

Pretend to be Keeper so that he could find out just who was suspected of doing what and how much? That was more logical. It must be quite a mental strain to have someone like Doc Savage on

CARTIER
47

your trail, and have him pretending that he wasn't. The temptation to do something about finding out just where the firm of Savage was going to do business—the temptation would be great. It would, when it ate on you long enough, be irresistible.

Yes, I could see where Harold would want to learn what Doc Savage was doing. It was even logical that Harold would go to the length of doing something slightly foolish in order to learn where the axe was going to fall.

And now I knew what was eating Harold. He was thinking along the same lines—he was reflecting what a damned fool he had been to pull Harold Keeper on us. The ruminations weren't doing his temper any good.

Evidence of how accurate my notion was, Harold now kicked Doc Savage in the side. He did it twice, grunting both times with the effort.

If this did Harold's ego good, it wasn't noticeable in the deep-in-a-barrel voice when he spoke. The barrel was pretty tinny. "Search him, Mr. McBride," Harold said.

McBride didn't move, didn't speak, probably didn't breathe.

"McBride," Harold said. "Do you wish him to pull some gadget on us? The man isn't lying there letting me kick him in the ribs because he is afraid of me."

"Shoot him!" McBride blurted, finding his voice.

"I wish to God that I dared," Harold said. "On proper provocation, I probably would. But my brother wishes to consult him. Damn you, McBride, search him! You're as useful as lipstick on an old maid."

McBride, operating as if he was driven by gears, got along with searching Doc Savage. While the hunt was in progress, Harold said, "I know about that anaesthetic gas you use, Savage. I'm holding my breath." I thought he was, too, part of the time.

"Feels like he's got a bulletproof vest on," McBride gasped.

Harold wasn't impressed. "I've been aiming at the back of his neck, anyway. We will retire to the trailer and do this more thoroughly." He cocked his gun impressively, and the sound was like a well-thrown horseshoe ringing the stake. "Let the retiring be of good judgment."

We entered the trailer, and I could see why Harold would feel disgusted. He had gone to a bit of trouble to decorate the trailer interior with the personality of Harold Keeper. He had filled it with dictionaries, nearly a hundred of them, all shapes, sizes and colors. I remembered how he had started off impressing his character on me by orating cock-eyed definitions. Girl, the roebuck in its second year. He had evidently intended that to be his theme.

McBride began searching Savage again.

"Strip him," Harold said.

They did that, let me turn my back, and supplied Savage with what Harold said was his bathing trunks, and they gave Savage the appearance of a bronze statue standing in a sack.

"Throw his stuff in the back of your car," Harold told McBride. "We'll dump it somewhere. I imagine it's full of bombs, or something. Oh yes, then hook your car to the trailer."

McBride went out, and Harold took my purse and spent five minutes stealing glances into it and cracking open the little portable U.H.F. radio transmitter. He seemed to know what the latter was. "Ingenious," he said. "But no more than I expected."

I had been watching Doc Savage. I couldn't help it. The man's physical development was astounding, so much so that it was a little unnatural. Harold was impressed, too. He said, "You bat an eye at me, Savage, and I'm going to shoot you. Because looking at you scares the hell out of me. I don't know how I had the nerve to bring you this far. I must be crazy."

There was the sound of an automobile engine, followed by a slight jolt from the trailer, and metallic clanking. McBride showed us a face the color of an unbaked biscuit and said, "I'm hooked on."

"You know where to go," Harold told him. "Go there."

"But—" McBride swallowed quite audibly. He was having trouble with the simplest sentences.

"But what?"

"The trailer—the people at the hotel know it was here—won't they—it being gone—"

"I don't know what you're talking about," Harold told him. "But if you're saying we should be cunning some more, it's ridiculous. I'm winding this up with a bang."

"But we'll be suspected!" McBride wailed.

"Suspecting and catching are two different birds," Harold suggested. "We'll solve that problem in a broad-minded way. We just won't be there."

McBride didn't think much of that. "You mean flee? Leave my law business?"

Harold sneered at him with his melon face. "Leave what law business? I thought you did a deal with us because you didn't have any law business."

"Oh, my God!" McBride wailed. "Where will we go?"

"I know a little place in Patagonia, right next to where Adolph Hitler lives," Harold told him bitterly. "You can go along with me if you wish."

"I'm not joking," gasped the lawyer.

"Neither am I, brother. What about getting this caravan in motion? Are you giving that some thought?"

McBride ducked out of sight and Harold told us, "We had all better sit down. I have a hunch he is going to tow this trailer like a nervous bull dragging the chain in his nose."

He was right.

Later, when we seemed to be on a highway, I asked Harold a question. He appeared to like conversation anyway, because he had been doing plenty of it.

"McBride had the location of the *Victory Tumble,* the ship loaded with the processed uranium?" I asked.

"So you know about that, too." Harold said. "I guess it was a good thing I didn't leave you behind."

"I'm surprised Waldo Loring would give a lawyer information like that," I said.

Harold commented on this. "He didn't. Not exactly. He left an envelope with Attorney McBride. You should have seen the envelope—more wax seals on it than a high school diploma. We were even scared to open it. Thought it might be booby-trapped."

"Oh, you've opened it?"

"Uh-huh. You want to know how that came about, honey? We were very clever—yeah, very. Just like sticks of stovewood are clever. But we finally ferreted out that Waldo Loring had a lawyer, and the lawyer was just about as shady as he was unprosperous, and so we presented the lawyer with a business deal. Sure we got a look at the envelope."

"Was the location of the *Victory Tumble* given?"

"Sure."

"Then you feel pretty good about everything, don't you?" I said.

"Shouldn't we?"

"I suppose so. You managed to kill Waldo Loring without anybody suspecting you."

"Thanks," Harold said. "I'm glad to hear it. I was having some doubts."

I had caught Doc Savage's eye. He had given me the slightest nod of approval. Not that he probably hadn't guessed all this far ahead of me, but he liked the way I was checking it.

"Was the envelope named Keeper?" I asked Harold.

"That's right, dear."

I thought Doc Savage had shaken his head slightly.

"So you killed Waldo Loring, Harold?" I asked.

The melon face looked at me. It became different.

"Baby, if I said yes to that, what would then have to happen to you?" Harold asked.

I knew why Savage had been shaking his head. He had known that I would talk myself into something. I had. Harold was still watching me and the melon face was now something that even the devil wouldn't like.

Chapter XI

IT was a ranch. It had to be a ranch, because they couldn't just camp out on the desert, for that would be a little conspicuous. But what surprised me was that Mr. Montgomery had owned the ranch for quite a while. Long enough for his name to be painted on the mailbox and for the weather to peel away most of some of the letters. The mailbox was one of those capacious ones, big as an elephant's stomach, which you see along the roads out in the open spaces where the mail order houses do most of the business.

There was also a LAZY-M RANCH printed on the mailbox, and from that there was two miles of dusty road, then a squat adobe ranch house and bunkhouse and corrals made in the Mexican fashion of living devil's-walking-stick cactus.

A reception committee of three rifles and Mr. Montgomery, his daughter Colleen, and his flunky, Roy, was on hand.

Harold peered out of a window. He could read Mr. Montgomery's moods readily, it seemed.

"My brother is angry," Harold said.

I really believed then that Harold and Mr. Montgomery were brothers. And I was sure of it when I saw them together, for there was a sameness to their fatness, and they had identical ways of overusing words.

Mr. Montgomery used plenty of words when he saw Harold. All profane words—they came from the gutters of many parts of the world and some of them from the best dictionaries, and the last ones were even worse. The total of it was that Mr. Montgomery felt Harold had wrecked everything. Not in those words. Not in words that anybody would want to say the way they were being said by one brother to another.

"All done?" Harold asked.

"No."

"Okay—this is just to fill in while you get your breath, brother. You make me laugh. Me ruin the pitch by grabbing Savage and the lady sleuth? Why, you fat jackass, you shot that phony Indian twice. Shot a federal gent—that's who that Coming Going was. You're wanted for that. You're hiding out here. How could you be in any worse fix?"

"But you—you weren't suspected." Mr. Montgomery yelled at him. "Savage didn't even know you existed. You could have played Harold Keeper, the half-wit the girl had inherited, and strung along and kept tail on Savage for us."

Harold went yok-yok bitterly. "That was your stinking idea, brother, and I'll tell you what I think of it sometime when I have half a day," he said. "It didn't work. Savage caught on before I even got the chair warm."

He went on to tell Mr. Montgomery exactly what had happened. Half the words he used were brotherly opinions that came to him as he went along.

"We've got old Waldo Loring's chart of where the ship lies on a bank in water shallow enough for any fourteen-year-old kid in a bathing suit to reach," Harold finished. "Waldo is dead. Nobody knows for sure what was what—even if Waldo had the ship spotted and for sale. Savage, the lady sleuth, Savage's big monkey, are all here. We can dead them, too. Then we can take a nice trip until the skies clear. Now tell me more that's wrong?"

The recital had sobered Mr. Montgomery.

"Why didn't you shoot Savage on the spot?" he yelled.

"And make the world a present of his body?" Harold yelled back at him. "That would make some stink, that would."

Mr. Montgomery said, "Oh!"

Harold continued bellowing. "But if you want the plain truth, I was afraid to kill him. I'd rather assassinate a President."

Mr. Montgomery started to sneer. Harold stopped that.

Harold said, "Now you tell me why you didn't knock off Monk Mayfair? Or even the Loring girl? I want to hear it."

Mr. Montgomery was slow with his answer. "Come in the house," he said.

"You were afraid yourself, that's why?" bellowed Harold.

"Come in the house."

I said, "Glacia is here!" I think I said it, because nobody else looked as if they had made the funny little wailing.

Glacia was dead. That was what I thought. Mr. Montgomery had killed her, and killed Monk Mayfair, and that was why he wanted his brother to come into the house. He wanted to display the handiwork.

We all went into the ranch house. It was still night, and the lights were on. Kerosene lanterns, two of them smoking from poorly trimmed wicks. The stuff in the house had been used hard a long time ago, and then not used for a few years. Nobody had taken the trouble to brush away dust, and Glacia's face and clothing had collected quite a bit of it.

Glacia was a mess. A thoroughly scared mess, but she looked wonderful because she was alive. She had only to be breathing to be gorgeous. She looked at me, and she bleated, "Oh, Mote, they've got you, too!" And she turned—or turned as much as she could, tied to a table—and called Mr. Montgomery words I didn't know she knew. She didn't equal Mr. Montgomery's recent performance on his brother, but she did make herself clear.

It wasn't about herself that Glacia was angry. It was for me, because they were bothering me. I wanted to fold my knees, just fold everything, and sob. Because Glacia, although half of the time she might be mean and self-centered, would come through when someone else was in real trouble. Not that I'd been afraid she wouldn't pay off in blue chips. Or had I? Maybe that was why I wanted to cry.

Monk Mayfair was tied to a table. Under a table, really. So was Glacia. There were two heavy tables, evidently from the days when the place had a heavy complement of hungry cowhands, and the prisoners had been placed under these, roped to the four legs. The whole effect was ridiculous, but I could see that it was efficient. Mr. Montgomery's imagination had been at play, probably.

Monk Mayfair had first word. "How's Joe Lybeck?"

"As fine as anyone can be in the hospital," Doc Savage said.

Who was Joe Lybeck? For a minute I didn't get that one. Coming Going. Joe Lybeck was Coming Going.

Monk pointed at Harold with chin and glare. "That one was my downfall," he said. "I hadn't placed him as in this. Him and the lawyer. I tried to tell you to watch out for her inheritance—meaning Glacia's inheritance, which would be so-fat here—just as they got to me."

"How did they trap you?" Doc asked.

Monk said, "I am ashamed to say it, but they didn't. They just walked up and pointed a gun at me. I tried to talk to you and he smashed the radio, and brought me here."

That seemed to settle that, so I asked Glacia, "How are you, dear?"

"I'm great," she wailed.

"They scare you much?"

They had scared her enough that she didn't want to try to tell me how much. Instead, she howled, "There's something so damned undignified about being tied under a table. You feel like a dog." And she burst into tears.

Mr. Montgomery liked to make little speeches so well that he made us one now. He said, "Yes, indeed, there are few less dignified places than under a table. If you want to undermine an individual's morale, just tie him under a table—"

"Oh, shut up," Harold told his brother.

"All right, brother," said Mr. Montgomery.

"Words all over you all the time like fleas," Harold complained.

They looked at each other. They weren't angry. They just looked at one another, and the question being argued visually didn't have a thing to do with words. It was: who is going to do murder wholesale? Kill the prisoners. You? Me? Roy? Lawyer McBride?

They both looked at Roy.

Roy said, "Huh-uh. Not Roy." He got it out in little gulps, as if someone was trying to give him poison.

They looked at Attorney McBride. But not for long. He was more than pale; he was beginning to turn a cyanosed blue. He wouldn't be slaying anyone. He might even die himself, unaided.

Finally they glanced at Colleen, and she didn't say or do anything, did not even smile.

Doc Savage spoke. His voice doubtless wasn't as quiet, even, unfrightened as it seemed. It couldn't have been. But compared to the other voices that had been making words, it was deep peace. It made me realize how terrified everyone else was—the brothers of the job of killing us, and us of being killed.

Savage said, "This is a logical time for our side to be grasping at straws. Will you take that into account, listen to me a moment, and accept the fact that what I say isn't straw-snatching?"

"Shut up!" Harold said.

"It won't take long. Two sentences," Savage said.

"Let him say two sentences," Mr. Montgomery growled. There were beads of perspiration on his forehead, neck, the rim of his jaw, the places where nerves were close to the surface.

Savage said: "You carry a cane habitually, Mr. Montgomery. Don't you know that portable radio gadgets can be made small enough to fit in a hollowed-out cane of the size of yours?"

Nobody said anything for longer than I was able to hold my breath. Then Harold asked, "You got that stick here, brother?"

Mr. Montgomery said something that had no sound. It did not seem to be the word yes, but it was assent anyway.

"The girl sleuth had one in her purse," Harold advised. "It was smaller than a hearing aid."

His brother wheeled and went into another room and came back carrying the large walking stick. He brought it close to one of the kerosene lamps. The sweat on his palms had made shiny spots on the nodular surface of the wood. He put his eyes much closer to the stick than the stick was close to the lamp, and for something like two minutes the loudest noise in the room was made by a fly walking across a window pane.

When Mr. Montgomery lifted his face, it had come apart. His jaw had sagged far down in his chins and only the rubbery lips were visible.

"It may be just a scratch," he whimpered.

Harold screamed, "Has that stick been tampered with?"

"A scratch. It may only be a scratch," Mr. Montgomery said, using stark horror instead of breath to make the speech.

"Break it!" Harold yelled. "Goddam it, break the thing open. Let's see what they've done to us. How the hell could they have gotten that stick?"

Savage said, "We've been watching you for days. Mr. Montgomery was very careful with that walking stick. He stood it in the left rear corner of the clothes closet each night."

Mr. Montgomery bought that.

"The left rear corner—oh my God," he wailed. "They did! They—"

"Break it open!" screamed Harold.

Savage said, "The purpose of a tiny radio transmitter, of course, would be to keep accurate tabs on your whereabouts. The other agents working with me will naturally have located you here and—"

Somewhere somehow I had gotten the idea that Doc Savage never told a lie. Where the notion came from, I don't know. But it was a lie. There was no radio in the walking stick. Or maybe, the way he had told it, he had merely stated a hypothetical possibility so convincingly that it seemed truth.

Because, when Mr. Montgomery brought the cane up—high over his head—to slam it down on the table and smash it into bits, every eye was on it. Every eye, all of everybody's attention.

It was buildup. That was all. Done wonderfully. Everyone thought there was a gadget in the cane, and nobody was thinking about anything else.

Savage stepped to Harold and sank hand, wrist and some forearm into Harold's midsection. The effect was somewhat as if a partly inflated inner tube had been squeezed, causing the rest of the inner tube to suddenly fill out. Both Harold's arms flew out from his sides, stiffly; he looked like something in a Macy parade.

A bright object flashed past me. Harold's gun.

Going about his business, Savage brushed against Colleen, knocking her into my arms. I went to work on her. Her hair first, with both hands.

Roy tried to run backward and use his gun at the same time, but it wasn't a success. His feet merely beat up and down on the floor, and his hand raked the rifle hammer twice, trying to cock it, but couldn't get the hammer far enough back to stay on cock. He was trying vainly to fire the uncocked gun when Savage hit him.

Mr. Montgomery appeared to be frozen in an attitude of high sacrifice, holding the walking stick aloft. Probably that was an illusion, the result of things happening rather rapidly.

Monk Mayfair was having convulsions under the table. Trying to take the legs off the table. He seemed quite disappointed with the results—as if he'd never entertained a doubt but that he could jerk all four legs from the table with ease. But he wasn't doing it. He began to yell.

Most of this impressed itself on me in a detached fashion, because Colleen was doing enough to me that I could hardly be classed as a spectator. Colleen knew some sort of judo. Anyway, I was very busy trying to keep her from taking off one of my arms.

The lawyer, McBride got a running start and left his feet head-first for a window. His window-diving technique was correct. He hauled his coat up over his arms and head to protect his face as he hit. But there was a detail he hadn't noticed. The window was covered on the outside with heavy planks spiked in place. He knocked himself out neatly.

The ranch house shook a little, possibly from Mr. Montgomery falling, and I think I yelled for fifteen minutes for someone to detach Colleen from me. Somebody finally did.

Chapter XII

IT was exactly 8:10 a.m. and the sun had finally managed to climb over the tops of the mountains in the east. It was throwing a great deal of angry light, and already some heat, over two blanketed and feathered phony Indians who were stuffing the luggage of a departing guest in the back seat of a sedan. The automobile departed, and the redskins began an argument concerning the tip they had received. It was a dime, and the argument was about exactly what word they should use to describe the guest if they wished to refer to him during the day, which they probably would.

Coming Going said, "Let me look at that map again." Later he said, "Now this is what I like. A regular honest-to-God treasure map."

Monk Mayfair suggested, "The old guy didn't show much imagination."

"Who wants imagination? If old Waldo Loring had any imagination, he'd have known anybody who would buy a shipload of uranium these days would knock his brains out. You say Mr. Montgomery had this on him?"

"Right in his hip pocket."

"Tell me more," Coming Going urged. "What was really in the walking stick?"

"Nothing," Monk said. "We hadn't touched it. Doc just remembered that you had searched the room, and said the cane was standing in the closet while they were asleep."

Coming Going grinned happily. "I wish I had been there."

"I would have sold you my part of it cheap," I said.

"Mote, you were wonderful!" Glacia said delightedly.

I nodded. "That's right. I gave the star performance. I was the only one on our side who got licked."

They had converted a second-floor room with an eastern exposure into a hospital room for Coming Going, alias federal agent Joe Lybeck. Presently Doc Savage came in with the news that the fat brothers and Colleen and Roy were locked up, and that attorney McBride had nothing more serious than a fractured skull.

Then Savage asked Glacia and me if we would care to have breakfast with him. He got an acceptance halfway through the invitation.

"We certainly played hard to get that time," I told Glacia when we were in our room trying to make ourselves look as if we hadn't been up all night letting people frighten us.

"He's a gorgeous hunk of man," Glacia said. She hung stars on the statement.

I was starting to put on a shoe, and I just sat there with it in both hands. It was all right, probably. Glacia was Glacia, and a little thing like last night wasn't likely to change her. But she was so damned objective. She knew what she wanted, and went after it. It was pretty obvious that right now she had Doc Savage in mind. And was I upset about that? I'll tell the world I was.

I put the shoe on carefully. I straightened the seam of a nylon. I hoped I looked cool and collected, because I wasn't. It had just dawned on me how interesting life could be. It probably wouldn't be. But possible? Who knows?

They don't shoot you for hoping.

THE END

BILL BARNES FLIES AGAIN!

by Will Murray

When Street & Smith saw the success of *The Shadow Magazine* exploding in 1932, they resolved to launch companion hero titles in the other major pulp genres. *Doc Savage* and *Nick Carter* were the adventure and detective entries, respectively. *Pete Rice* corralled the Western readers. Early in 1934, their aviation hero first took flight.

Bill Barnes, Air Adventurer centered on the exploits of a young former U.S. Air Mail pilot who organizes a private air force at Barnes Field on Long Island, all of whom fly planes of Barnes' own invention, for the blond aviator was also a budding aeronautical engineer. Among his futuristic aircraft were the jet-assisted autogryo called the Bumblebee, and the Porpoise, which could navigate the sea as well as the air.

Major Malcolm Wheeler-Nicholson was the first writer to pen Bill Barnes novels under the house name of George L. Eaton. He soon moved on to found what later became DC Comics, where he recycled Bill's debut story, *Hawks of the Golden Crater,* as a comic strip serial, featuring pilot Barry Noble. Wheeler-Nicholson was replaced by Charles Spain Verral, a Canadian artist turned writer who had followed *Bill Barnes* editor F. Orlin Tremaine from the defunct Clayton pulp chain to Street & Smith. Verral ran the club page, "The Flying Falcons," which was soon renamed "The Air Adventurers." Under the pen name of "Ace Tracy," he had a short story in the first issue of *Bill Barnes Air Adventurer*.

When Wheeler-Nicholson departed, Tremaine tapped an astounded Verral to take over. Verral had never penned a novel before this, only short stories. His first effort, *Wings of the Snow Country,* was well received, and Verral kept going, working with cover and interior artist Frank Tinsley—brother to *The Shadow*'s Ted Tinsley——to develop increasingly sophisticated but realistic combat aircraft for Bill and his crew to fly into battle, which included the *Scarlet Stormer* and the *Silver Lancer*.

In 1935, the magazine was reformatted as *Bill Barnes, Air Trails.* Two years later, it became simply *Air Trails*. Bill was phased out in 1939, but a few months later, he returned as a back-of-the book feature in *Doc Savage.* Verral had previously left the series to freelance and script the *Mandrake the Magician* radio series (starring Raymond Edward

Photo courtesy of the Wheeler-Nicholson family

The lead novel in *Bill Barnes Air Adventurer* #1 was written by Major Malcolm Wheeler-Nicholson, founder and original owner of DC Comics.

Bill Barnes wordsmith Charles Spain Verral and editor John L. Nanovic

Johnson with Francesca Lenni and Jessica Tandy as Narda), but was called back to pilot the new series.

By this time, Bill was flying the *Charger*, introduced by interim writer Harold P. Montanye and Frank Tinsley. Verral retained that amphibious plane for the duration of the series. Over an additional twenty short stories and novelettes Bill, his teenage sidekick, Sandy Sanders, and the surviving members of his flying circus, among them Shorty Hassfurther and Red Gleason, battled numerous sky threats ranging from the Hawk, who appeared in several tales, and the Crimson Front.

The series had been on hiatus during much of 1941 when Verral was asked to restart it. His return story was entitled "The Eye of the Cobra," and for a villain Verral revived a Japanese spy ring he called the Yako. He had introduced them in his second Bill Barnes novel, *The Blood Flower*, back in 1934.

"The Eye of the Cobra" was slotted for the January, 1942 issue of *Doc Savage*, which went on sale December 19th, 1941. The issue was in production when the Japanese Navy struck at Pearl Harbor on December 7, 1941, and hit the newsstands just two weeks after the destruction of the U.S. Pacific Fleet. The parallels between real life and the fictitious plot Bill Barnes attempts to thwart are uncanny.

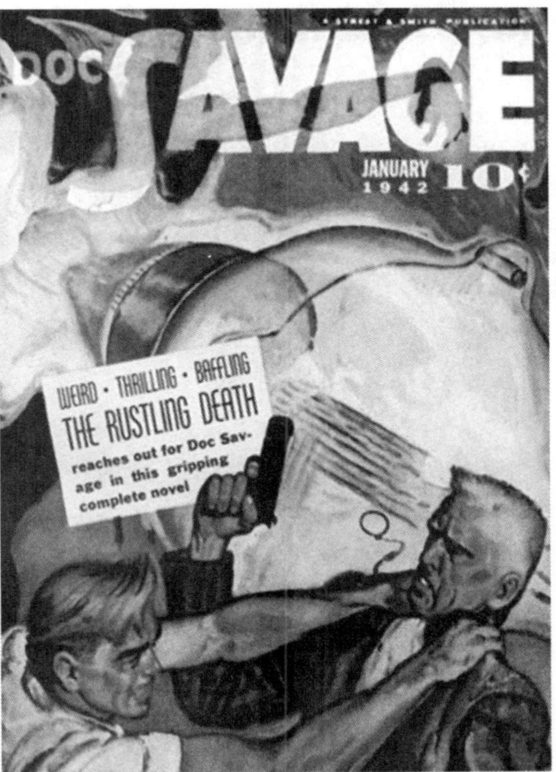

"The Eye of the Cobra" appeared in the Jan. 1942 issue of *Doc Savage*.

In later years, Verral recalled that editor John L. Nanovic praised "The Eye of the Cobra" as the perfect pulp story. Perhaps it was that, too. But Nanovic might have been celebrating the fact that he had published a story that could not be more timely.

For the duration of this final phase of Bill Barnes' career, he flew secret missions for the U.S. Army's Counter Intelligence Corps, code-named G-2. This story marks the final time acclaimed aviation artist Frank Tinsley illustrated a Bill Barnes exploit.

So turn the page and read one of Bill Barnes' most celebrated missions. If you like it, we may reprint more. •

THE EYE OF THE COBRA

by George L. Eaton

The Yako—the Oriental spy ring—had found a way to destroy U.S. warships. So Bill Barnes, air ace, had to find a way to destroy the Yako!

FATE weaves strange webs and men know not the hour in which their lives will be caught in the pattern.

It was so with Peter Edwards, star reporter of the San Francisco *Banner*, on that fog-filled night on September 30th. If he hadn't seen the lights of Sam's Corner Diner glowing through the mist, he would never have gone inside for a warming cup of coffee—and never heard the eerie cry of the racing ambulance. He would never have met the strange woman or listened to her terrifying story of wholesale murder and flaming destruction to come.

But Pete Edwards went into the white-walled diner and, by his simple act, Fate claimed him for her own—and on her loom began carefully spinning a web of death.

He was a tall, sparse man in his middle thirties—Pete Edwards—with deep-set blue eyes and a fighter's chin. Days of little sleep and endless worry had penciled lines in his gaunt face so that he appeared older and broken.

"Coffee, Sam," he said to the fat owner as he climbed up on a stool. "Black."

"Black as sin and hot as hell," Sam said cheerfully. He dried his big hands on his apron and eyed Pete appraisingly. "You look done up, Mr. Edwards. Is there anything wrong?"

Pete reached down and pulled the folded special edition of the *Banner* from his pocket. Without a word he spread it flat on the counter.

Headlines screamed across the front page:

THIRD U.S. CRUISER DESTROYED!

The four-column hanger said:

THE ROCHELLE SINKS
WITH ALL HANDS AFTER
NEW MYSTERY BLAST

Sam stared at the paper. "Glory be!" he gasped. "Another one!"

"Yes, another one," Peter echoed grimly. It had been less than a week since the country had been stunned by the sinking of the two heavy cruisers, *Winchester* and *Weston*, by unexplained explosions—and now the *Rochelle* had been wrecked in the same way.

"Can't they find out who's doing it?" Same demanded.

Pete's lips tightened. "They know who's doing it," he said savagely. "That yellow-faced gang from the Pacific—the Yako. But they can't dope out what's causing those blasts, let alone get a shred of proof."

Sam's beefy face paled. "But there must be some way to stop 'em!"

"I just came from Naval Intelligence," Peter said. "Commander Riddell's got Steve Drake, the ace G-man, working with him. Even Bill Barnes and his men have flown out here to help. They're all doing everything possible but—"

"Glory, Mr. Edwards!" Sam exclaimed. "Three of our ships gone! Maybe a lot more will follow."

That was it, Peter thought desperately. If this thing wasn't broken wide open fast, the entire Pacific fleet was menaced. And with it the new thirty-five-thousand-ton battleship, *Alabama*, on which his kid brother was a gunner.

A SURGE of cold rage swept through him. If he could only do something to help, instead of idly standing by while the pride of the U.S. fleet was being destroyed.

"Let's have that coffee, Sam. I need it," Pete said.

It was then, as Sam picked up a cup and saucer, that the distant wail of an ambulance siren sounded. Pete listened, his head cocked, as the scream came nearer. It finally ended with a snarled awwwwwww somewhere nearby.

A siren to the man on the street indicates either trouble or distress. But to a newspaperman it means possible news. And despite his fatigue, Pete forced himself off the stool and headed for the door.

"I'll be back, Sam," he said over his shoulder.

The fog had thickened to a swirling gray curtain and it took Pete fifteen exasperating minutes before he found the ambulance parked in front of a shabby apartment house. A crowd had already gathered.

Pete shouldered his way to the uniformed policeman at the street door. "What's up?" he asked, showing his press card.

The moonfaced cop shrugged. "A dame took a shot of poison," he said indifferently. "Go in, if you want to. First floor apartment, front."

The ambulance attendants were lifting the woman onto a stretcher when Pete walked into the cheaply furnished apartment. She was about thirty-five and had once been good-looking. But now her face was contorted in pain, and so pasty-white that the rouge on her cheeks stood out in ugly patches.

"We'll pull her through at the hospital, O.K.," the blond young intern told Pete. "Her name? Paula Miller. Yeah, she's married, but her husband's away."

"Oh, let me die!" the woman whispered as the attendants carried her from the room. "Let me die!"

Pete walked beside the stretcher. "Why did you do it?" he asked gently.

She opened a clenched hand, and Pete saw she was grasping a crumpled letter and a gold signet ring. "My man… wrote for the… last time… and sent me his ring." She said faintly. "He's killing himself tonight. And… I want to die."

"Killing himself?" Pete let out. "What do you mean?"

The stretcher was now being carried down the front steps to the street and Pete bent closer to catch the woman's words.

"It's those yellow devils," she sent on. "They forced him to work with them. And now they're making him kill himself. Those terrible Yakos."

The Yako! The Oriental spy ring!

Excitement surged through Pete like a high fever. "Is your husband a member of the Yako?" he blurted out.

"Yes," she gasped. "I wasn't supposed to know… and when I found out they said they'd—Oh, I can't talk! They'll torture me!"

"Quick!" Pete said. "Who's your husband? Where is he? Maybe we can save him!"

The crowd on the sidewalk was pressing closer, forming a ring of curious faces.

"His name's Ernest Miller," the woman said. "But it's too late. He and all the others will be dead before dawn."

"Where is he?" Pete demanded. His voice was low, but his words drove at the woman. "Tell me. Hurry!"

Her eyes flickered shut, and for one awful minute Pete thought she had died. Then the whisper came, so faint that he had to bend his head even closer. "He's a sailor," she said. "A sailor on the battleship *Alabama*. It's being blown up tonight!"

PERHAPS it was numbing shock that sent Pete staggering erect. Perhaps it was intuition or a sixth sense of danger. He took a step back from the stretcher, half turned—and the blood in his veins turned to ice.

A thickset Oriental was standing in the outer fringe of the crowd. Pete saw the man's arm rise and fall in a lightning gesture. Something slim and shining catapulted from his hand, slashed through the air.

Scarcely before Pete knew what was happening, the knife had hissed past him and, with a sickening thud, buried itself to the hilt in the sick woman's throat.

A bloodcurdling scream shuddered from her gaping mouth. Her body wretched backward as if pulled by a giant spring; rose twisting in convulsion. Her cry of anguish was abruptly cut off, and she dropped limply down on the stretcher and was still.

Shouts of terror broke from the crowd. Pete caught a blurred glimpse of the Oriental diving away into the fog; of the policeman jerking his service revolver from his holster and plunging after him.

For one brief second, Pete stood transfixed, his

mind paralyzed. Then, he spun around and dropped down beside the dead woman. He opened her hand, snatched the crumpled letter and ring from it.

The intern saw him. "Hey!" he blurted. "You can't do that!"

But Pete scarcely heard him as he pushed his way frantically through the panicky onlookers. The terrible warning was still dinning in his ears that the fate that had sent the *Winchester*, the *Weston*, and the *Rochelle* to the bottom was now swooping down on his kid brother's ship—the superbattleship, *Alabama*.

There seemed to be only one hope—one slim chance of saving the dreadnought. And that was to get the letter, the ring and the vital information to Naval Intelligence as fast as possible.

PRECISELY three hours later, the famous pilot, Bill Barnes, was crouched in the forward cabin of his Charger monoplane, gunning the sleek ship dead into the northwest. The sky was blue-black and studded with stars, but to the east the first touches of dawn were timidly creeping above the horizon.

"What's the time, Steve?" Bill said.

"Five o'clock… Pacific," Steve Drake said. The veteran F.B.I. agent was strapped into the bucket seat next to Bill. "Hold her wide open!"

Bill nodded grimly and his hand went again to the throttles. Through the soundproofing of the cabin, the thunder of the twin diesels in their wing nacelles sounded shrill and far away. The Charger was trembling under the excessive speed like a thoroughbred horse straining to get out the last ounce of power.

Bill's fingers tightened around the control column as excitement flared through him. Ever since Peter Edwards had rushed with his incredible story to the office of Naval Intelligence, where Bill had been in conference with Drake and Commander Riddell, not a second had been wasted. A coded radio message had been dispatched to the U.S.S. *Alabama*, far out in the Pacific, warning her of danger and ordering the arrest of Ernest Miller, crew member. The moment confirmation had zipped back from the battleship, Bill and Drake had hurried to the Charger at the San Francisco airport and taken off—Sandy Sanders, the kid ace of the Barnes flying organization, going with them as radio operator and gunner.

And now they were on their way, tearing high across the night-shrouded sky of the Pacific, racing for the *Alabama* to pick up the prisoner, Miller, and bring him back to San Francisco for questioning.

A burning intensity glinted in Bill's blue eyes. No one had yet figured out exactly what had caused the deadly explosions that had sunk three cruisers and killed every man aboard. Naval authorities had assumed the weapon used had been either floating mines, submarine torpedoes or, perhaps, even aerial bombs—although the odds against scoring three perfect bull's-eye hits from the air had virtually dismissed that method. But now the list included treachery—foul treachery—aboard.

Bill felt his heart hammering faster in his side as the Charger hurtled on. After days of futile searching, of praying for some clue that would lead to the murderous Yako spy ring, the break had come at last. Once they got this Ernest Miller back to land, he'd be made to talk—and talk fast; to tell everything he knew about the sabotage plot and how the Yako had planned to destroy the *Alabama*. The mystery would soon be solved.

Suddenly Bill stiffened as a clammy thought crossed his brain. True enough, Miller was now a prisoner incapable of doing any damage, and the *Alabama* had taken every precaution against enemy attack—the ship had been thoroughly searched for time bombs; the ocean ahead of her was being swept for mines; her destroyer escort was spread out, alert for the first sound of approaching submarine or plane. But suppose, in spite of everything, the Yako struck! Suppose a blast of destruction erupted and the mighty battleship was sent plunging to the bottom, taking Ernest Miller with her!

The thought grew and turned into flaming alarm. Not only would the loss of the *Alabama* be a terrific blow to America, but Miller was their *sole* lead to the Yako! And if death sealed his lips, as it had his wife's, the situation would be more hopeless than ever. They'd be left with nothing to go on except the letter Miller had written and his ring—and both seemed sterile of clues.

BILL twisted around and looked back to where Sandy Sanders was squatted down in the radio operator's seat at the rear of the cabin. The kid was hunched forward, intently examining Ernest Miller's ring in the small light from the radio board. He'd been at it since the takeoff.

"Have you found anything yet?" Bill shouted.

Sandy turned his freckled face. "Naw," he said disgustedly. "And I thought I was gonna pick up a nice juicy clue."

"Let me look at the ring again, Sandy," Drake said.

Sandy got to his feet and started across the darkness of the cabin. He'd taken no more than two strides when he let out a yip. "Jumpin' jelly beans!" he exclaimed.

"What's wrong?" Bill asked sharply.

"Golly!" Sandy said. "When I looked at the inside of the ring back there in the light, there was nothing on it. But now, in the dark, I can see something glowing. Jeepers! It looks like a drawing of a snake!"

"Let's see it!" Bill said.

The ring was a large bloodstone set in a heavy gold mounting. Bill held it under the instrument lights and peered at the back of the stone. It was, as Sandy had said, perfectly smooth and clear of any markings. But when Bill moved the ring away from the light and into the darkness, a thrill coursed through him. There *was* something drawn on the inside of the bloodstone, drawn in glowing, luminous paint.

Drake was looking over his shoulder. Bill heard his quick intake of breath. "I see it," he said tensely. "Jupiter, it does look like a snake—a hooded cobra. Even the eye's marked!"

"Yes," Bill muttered. The lines were finely drawn, making a design that was not unlike a cobra with its broad hood and curled body. And more prominent than anything else was one dot of phosphorescence representing the snake's eye.

"Golly!" Sandy whispered. "Do you suppose it's the Yako's secret sign?"

"It's not their insignia," Drake said. "But it must be something important, else why would it be put on the inside of a ring with stuff that can be seen only in the dark?"

Bill's forehead was knitted. Obviously, the ring with its queer sign *was* important—but what could it mean? And what help would it be unless they could find out? His thought train was abruptly chopped off as he saw the red square on the radio panel blink into life.

"Sandy!" he shouted. "A call's coming through. Get it!"

The kid dived back across the cabin, snatched up headphones and mike and bent over the set. The Charger swayed drunkenly as an up draft hit her, fell off on one wing.

By the time Bill had yanked her back into line and sung around, Sandy was leaping to his feet. "It was Commander Riddell!" he yelled breathlessly. "They've discovered Ernest Miller's been using a phony name. His real moniker's Ernst Mueller. He isn't even a citizen. Used forged papers to get in the Navy."

"Blazes!" Drake let out. "That's how come he's tied up with the Yako."

"And that's not the half of it," Sandy hurried on. "Mueller told them the ship's gonna be blown up no matter what they do!"

BILL'S heart shot into his throat. The *Alabama* destroyed! But how? Wouldn't the rigid precautions that had been taken against aerial bombs, torpedoes, mines and time charges be enough? Was something else going to be used—a secret weapon? Or was it just a bluff on Mueller's part?

"Hurry, Bill!" Drake said. "We've got to get there—fast. How much longer will it take us?"

Frantically, Bill's gaze whipped from the instrument panel to the chart case at his side. He made a lightning calculation.

"Twenty minutes," he said. "Maybe fifteen."

There were no more words spoken as the Charger pelted on through the sky. Sandy had come forward and was kneeling beside Drake, staring out through the front glass.

Bill eased the control column forward and took the big plane surging down. The darkness of night was fading very rapidly and far below Bill caught a glimpse of the flat surface of the Pacific, an ominous dull-gray.

At two thousand feet he leveled and again pressed the throttles home. "Keep your eyes open!" he whipped out. At any minute, they should sight the mighty *Alabama* and her screen of destroyers.

He crouched lower over the controls, peering across the bosom of the ocean while a nerve at the base of his throat began hammering. He strained his eyes, but nothing broke the flat surface of the Pacific ahead, and for one awful moment he had the terrible feeling that perhaps he'd failed in his calculations. If he had—if they missed the one chance of getting vital information on the Yako—the result might well mean terrible defeat to the United States, itself.

Sandy's voice broke across the cabin. "Straight ahead, Bill!" he shouted. He was pressed close to the glass, pointing. "See?"

Bill eagerly followed the direction of the kid's pointing finger. At first he saw nothing. Then—there *was* something there. One large shape on the surface of the ocean and smaller ones around it. He waited, holding his breath, waited while the terrific speed of the Charger had whirled them closer. Then he was sure, and the pent-up breath gushed from his mouth.

The superbattleship *Alabama* and her screen of pirouetting destroyers was dead ahead. Nothing had happened to the dreadnought. They'd arrived in time.

"We've made it!" Drake sang out jubilantly. "Now land, Bill. And make it fast! I can't wait to get my hands on that rat, Mueller!"

Bill reached to close the throttles and send the amphibian gear down into position. And even as his fingers clasped the knobs, instinct born of making a thousand and one landings made his eyes sweep upward to see if the sky was clear. He started in utter surprise.

Another plane had just come diving out of the overcast thousands of feet above! A biplane with negative stagger to her clipped wings and a sharp bullet-shaped nose. She was ultramodern and speedy. And even though she was four thousand feet away, Bill's trained brain instantly indentified her. She was a Kammato attack bomber—a military plane of the Oriental power across the pacific!

What such a machine was doing away out here in the middle of the ocean in the vicinity of the threatened *Alabama*, he didn't know. But he was going to find out—and find out fast. With one tug of the controls, Bill yanked the Charger out of her downward glide.

At the moment, the foreign biplane passed directly over the *Alabama*—and it happened!

Bill was positive no bomb dropped from the enemy machine. Yet, on the calm waters of the Pacific, all hell broke loose.

One minute the thirty-five-thousand-ton battleship was there, steaming ahead, white water churning back from her sleek prow, her mighty shape dwarfing the destroyer greyhounds that circled her on all sides. In the next minute, a terrific blast of scarlet flame burst from amidships. The *Alabama* was split in two as if cleaved by a giant knife. Her mammoth bow rose into the air. Her stern was torn asunder. Fire and black, oily smoke spewed up from her vitals in a horrible continuous fountain.

The detonation from the terrific explosion caught the Charger broadside. The heavy monoplane was lifted and literally hurled across the flame-dyed heavens. Debris pelted through the air, whistling like a million pieces of shrapnel, crashing and tearing into the Charger's wings and fuselage.

Half stunned by shock and the fury of the blast, Bill held to the controls with a grip of steel, his body straining against the safety belt. His mind was dazed, incapable of thinking or reacting. Across his consciousness zigzagged the one appalling fact. The *Alabama* had been wrecked, destroyed!

It was the abrupt crash of a heavy piece of debris against the side of the cabin that brought Bill to his senses. A jagged hole gaped in the cabin wall, and the radio apparatus was demolished. Sandy was lying on the floor, holding tight to one of the wall supports. Blood was streaming down the kid's cheek, and his face was white.

The Charger was careening like a maddened horse, was out of control. Bill shouted, "Hold on, Sandy," and rammed his feet hard against the rudder pedals. He fought savagely to bring the staggering machine into level flight. Out of the corner of his eye, he caught a glimpse of Steve Drake clutching to his safety belt.

Of the next few minutes, Bill remembered little except that he knew he was struggling not only for his own life but the lives of his two companions. Perhaps the battle lasted five minutes, perhaps only a handful of seconds, he was never sure. But with one last mighty effort, even as the Charger pelted downward for the ocean in a howling power dive, Bill horsed back on the stick.

Bill yanked the Charger out of her downward glide.

The elevators reacted, biting into the air—and with a bellow from her twin power plants, the Charger roared out of her dive and into level flight.

Perspiration gushed down Bill's face. "Are you O.K., Sandy?" he managed to get out. "You, Steve?"

"Yes," Steve Drake said. "I'm... all right."

Sandy was climbing uncertainly to his feet. "O.K., Bill!" he said in a faint, shaky voice. "Something hit me on the side of the head, but—Look! Look at the *Alabama!*"

Bill's gaze stabbed down through the now-cracked cabin glass and utter horror seized him. Far below, almost directly beneath them, was a scene of unspeakable chaos. A patch of ocean was being whipped to a bubbling, frenzied caldron of white water. And in the center, alive with cracking red flames, the stern of the once-proud battleship, *Alabama*, was sliding beneath the Pacific. For a moment, she seemed to hesitate, then with a ghastly eruption of foam and steam, the man-o'-war vanished from sight.

A gasp was wrung from Drake's lips. "They all must've died!" he said. "All of them! No one could've lived through that! But now ... how did it happen—"

Bill cut him short. "There goes that biplane!" he shouted. His right hand jabbed toward the northwest. "She must've had some connection with that blast!"

Suddenly he knew what he had to do. The destroyers were at the moment racing for the scene of the disaster to pick up any survivors who might have escaped the holocaust. There was no need to land the Charger. They could offer little help. But there was one thing that could be done!

With a lighting movement of his hands and feet, Bill yanked the Charger around on a wing tip until her nose was aimed straight at the far away biplane. "We're going after her!" he said. "And we're going to catch her!"

LIKE a great silver bullet shimmering in the early morning light, the monoplane hurtled across the sky. Except for the hole in the cabin wall, she had seemingly come through without damage.

"Get the first aid kit, Steve!" Bill shouted. "Fix Sandy's head." The wind was whistling through the damaged wall in a piercing scream.

Drake groped his way to his feet. "I'll attend to him, Bill," he said. He stood holding to the back of his seat, ducking down to look ahead through the window at the distant silhouette of the biplane. "Look! It's going into the clouds."

Bill cursed under his breath as he saw the biplane abruptly zoom and vanish into the overcast. Without a moment's hesitation, he swung the fog camera into position. The infrared-ray telescope mounted in the nose of the Charger enabled one to see through rain and mists and the blackness of night. *It's my ace in the hole*, Bill thought grimly. *If I can once spot the biplane up there in the overcast, I'll never lose him!*

Three minutes later, the Charger rocketed upward into the overcast at the approximate place where the biplane had vanished. A blanket of gray mist instantly engulfed the ship, swirling around the cabin glass and burying the wings. Bill quickly put his face against the eyepiece of the telescope, his gaze drilling down its barrel. The effect was like looking along the path of a searchlight cutting through the night.

He saw no sign of the biplane, and immediately swerved the Charger to the left and then to the right to widen his vision. He depressed the nose and elevated it. But it wasn't until five minutes had passed that he admitted to himself that he'd been beaten. The biplane had vanished—as suddenly as it had appeared.

Bitter disappointment ate into him. And rage followed. It was vital that the biplane be trailed and its pilot seized. The man, Bill was convinced, was somehow responsible for that murderous explosion. How it had been done, he hadn't the faintest idea. Not by a dropped bomb and not by a lurking submarine, for the *Alabama*'s destroyers would have detected an undersea craft. Yet the terrible secret had to be learned without delay. Four of Uncle Sam's warships had already perished. If more went, the ocean defense of the West Coast would be wiped out—and armed invasion might easily follow.

The thought sent a shudder down his spine. He *had* to do something! If he only had a clue to where the biplane might be headed—where its base was!

His cheek muscles hardened. The enemy ship had been holding to a northwest course when last seen. And the Kammato type of attack bomber hadn't any extraordinary flying range. That would seem to indicate that the plane would have to reach its base fairly soon. But where could such a base be in the vast expanse of the Pacific?

He reached out to the chart case, quickly rifled through the maps and selected a detailed chart of the northern Pacific. Then, switching on the automatic pilot, Bill spread the map out, his eyes glancing along an imaginary line running northwest from the scene of the disaster.

Right away he saw that the only islands within the Kammato's flying range would be up near the Aleutians, close to Alaska. There were hundreds of land dottings shown on the map in that general vicinity. Anyone of them might serve as a base.

Suddenly his breath caught in his throat. One particular group of islands was arranged in a strange formation—a formation he'd seen before!

His shout brought Sandy and Drake rushing from the passage leading to the gunner's cockpit aft. Sandy's head wound had been dressed and a wide bandage circled his forehead.

Bill held up the map and drew a circle around the island group with a pencil.

"Great guns!" Drake exclaimed as he looked down. "Those islands make a design. Why, they're in the shape of a snake—a cobra! The same as the drawing on Mueller's ring!"

"Exactly!" Bill said. His heart was pounding wildly. "And the biplane was heading dead on for those islands when last seen. It all ties together. The biplane's base may be up there!"

"Golly!" Sandy broke in excitedly. "The Yako probably handed out secretly marked rings to their agents so they could find their way there if they had to!" His freckled face clouded. "But, jeepers, Bill, the base might be on any of those islands! It'd take a week to look 'em all over."

Bill silently took the signet ring from his pocket and held it shielded from the light so that the luminous paint glowed. "What part of the design is the most prominent?" he asked Sandy.

"Why—the eye of the cobra," the kid said quickly.

Bill nodded, his face a grim mask of determination. "And the eye is where we're heading—right now!"

AT 11:30 a.m. the Charger was floating gently on the surface of the ocean at Latitude 55,

Longitude 180. A fog, thick and green, eddied around the ship, cutting off almost all visibility.

"Got the anchor down, Sandy?" Bill whispered.

"Yeah." The cabin lights had been extinguished and Sandy's figure was just a vague shape in the gloom. "I'll get the rubber boat out now."

"Good," Bill said. "Be careful. Don't make any noise."

"O.K.," Sandy said, and disappeared along the passage to the rear of the cabin.

Bill felt the touch of Steve Drake's hand on his arm. "You're sure we've landed in the right place?" he asked, his voice hushed.

Bill was busily removing the fog camera from its fixed position. "As sure as I can be, Steve," he said. "But it's pretty much a gamble in this soup."

A gamble! Why, the whole thing had been a gamble, Bill reflected, ever since he'd sent the Charger screaming through the sky in the direction of those northern islands. All during the flight with the endless drumming of the engines in his ears, his doubts over his decision had multiplied. With the radio out of commission, they were cut off from all communication—and all help. And there was no telling what they might run up against if his guess about the island proved right.

And then, when they had almost reached their destination, they'd run into a blinding blanket of fog. It had been a menace, and at the same time a godsend. Under cover of its murky curtain, Bill had shut off his engines and glided silently down, knowing that he was invisible to anyone below. He had used the night telescope to inspect what lay beneath and had seen shapes of land sticking out of the ocean—land that he had recognized with a hill as the very islands he was seeking.

It had taken delicate flying after that to set the big plane down on the calm waters of the Pacific. But he'd made it, his eyes locked to the telescope. And now the Charger was riding easily at anchor within four hundred yards of the "eye" island.

Bill removed the night telescope from its track and held it in his hands. No sound had come from the island. There had been no indication that anyone inhabited the place. But every precaution had to be taken.

The Charger rocked gently, and Bill realized that Sandy was undoubtedly placing the inflated rubber boat in the water alongside the floats. The wind made a shrill, hissing sound around the wings of the plane and there was a faint steady lapping of the water against the amphibian undercarriage.

Bill lifted the telescope and aiming it in the direction of the fog-obscured island, looked through the eyepiece.

"Do you see anything?" Drake asked tensely.

"Just rocks," Bill said. "I can't make out any sign of a house or a hangar." He moved the telescope until he'd covered the entire shoreline of the island. It was rugged with bits of stunted undergrowth growing in clumps between the masses of rocky terrain. But there was nothing to suggest that man had ever stepped on the place.

He heard Drake's sudden whisper. "Listen, Bill. That sounds like an airplane engine!"

Bill had already heard it. "An airplane engine, all right," he muttered. "It's heading this way, Steve."

The drumming came from the south, and was growing louder by the second until it finally swelled into a deep-throated roar. Then, abruptly, the noise was cut off and Bill caught the sound of spluttering muffled explosions.

"The throttle's been closed," Bill whispered. "Maybe... it's the Kammato biplane! We could easily have beaten her here. The Charger's much faster."

Bill lifted the telescope and held it trained on the island. Tension gripped him. The spluttering sound had died away, and now there was nothing but the whimpering of the wind and the waves. He waited, scarcely breathing. If his guess about the island had been right and the strange plane was the Kammato, the ship would probably make a landing. His fingers tightened around the barrel of the telescope.

"Steve!" he rapped out. "I see her. It's the Kammato. And she's gliding down for the island."

He held the magic lens of the night telescope on the ghostly shape of the biplane that had suddenly come swooping down into his range of vision. The ship was heading in a steep glide for the island, streaked lower and lower, and then vanished from sight behind the rocky shoreline. An instant later, the silence of the fog was sharply broken by the sudden burst of a gunned engine. Then, silence again.

Bill lowered the telescope. "She's down on the island!" he said. "Likely landed blind in the fog on a special radio beam." A dryness was in his throat and his mouth felt stiff. "This is it, Steve. Come on. We're going ashore."

Bill's thought raced. His gamble was working out. It seemed obvious now that not more than four hundred yards away lay the secret of the terrible disasters that had scourged the U.S. Navy—the secret that could bring his valiant country to her knees unless exposed and smashed.

A numbed excitement gripped him as he followed Drake into the rubber boat where Sandy waited. The telescope had been left in the Charger as too cumbersome to handle. And now, with oars muffled, the inflated boat moved stealthily toward the shore, Sandy sculling. Bill sat crouched, his blunt-nosed automatic held firmly in his muscular right hand, his eyes straining to see through the pea-green soup.

There was not even a whisper of talk. Each man knew that his very life depended upon silence. It seemed to take forever before the rubber side of the boat touched the rocky shoreline. Carefully, Bill stepped out and motioned the others to follow.

It was only after the boat had been pulled up on a ledge that Bill said: "O.K., you guys. We'll scout across the island. Keep close together, and if you see anything give the word instantly." He paused, glancing through the mist first at Steve Drake and then at Sandy. Had he any right to take these two on this mission? It was likely that if they ran into any trouble, the odds against them would be overwhelming. And if this was a Yako base—as he was now positive—none of them could expect any mercy if captured. The diabolical spy ring had proved beyond any possible doubt that its members were ruthless murderers.

"Listen, Steve," Bill whispered. "And you, Sandy. Wait here for me. I'll give the situation a look-see, then—"

A muffled growl came from Drake. "I'm going with you," he said.

"An' if you think I'm gonna be left behind," Sandy said, his shrill voice hushed, "you're nuts. Anyway, who found that secret design on the ring, anyway?"

For a fleeting moment, a smile twisted Bill's lips. Then he said: "O.K. Let's go. Keep your guns ready. There's no telling what we'll find."

Five minutes later, after a cautious advance over the sharp, rocky surface, the three of them were crouched behind a large boulder on the far side of the island. Excitement throbbed through Bill. For not more than fifty yards away, discernible through rifts in the fog, was the Kammato biplane!

THE machine was poised on a long smooth runway, her sharp nose pointed out to sea in the direction from whence she'd come. Obviously set for a takeoff. And two slant-eyed mechanics were at the moment pumping gasoline into her fuel tanks from a portable reserve drum.

Beyond the biplane, the shoreline of the island swung in, making a natural small harbor. A low building, dim and indistinct in the fog, nestled the rock along its side. A square of orange light glowed warmly from a window and, in its reflection, Bill made out the ghostly form of a speedboat tied up to a makeshift wharf.

He reached out and touched Sandy and Drake. "Make for that house," he muttered. "But watch your step. If those mechanics hear us—we'll be through."

The advance to the low building was nerve-racking and slow. They skirted the area where the mechanics were chattering as they refueled the biplane. Innumerable times Bill flattened himself on his belly, expecting a harsh challenge to ring through the air. But luck was with them, and finally he felt the wet side of the house in front of him. Steve Drake and Sandy crowded in.

"Stay here," Bill whispered. "I'm going to risk a look through the window."

"Be careful!" Drake said. His voice showed his tension.

Bill nodded and moved stealthily away, hugging the wooden side of the building. Tendrils of fog, cold and damp, licked against his face like dead fingers, and he shuddered. Civilization seemed suddenly very far away, and he experienced a throb of fear—not for himself, but fear that he should fail on this vital mission when so much depended upon it.

When he reached the window frame, he hesitated, gathering his courage. What lay inside that room? Would he find the answer to the terrible secret weapon that had ripped and smashed Uncle Sam's powerful warships like toys and sent them, a mass of wreckage, to watery destruction? The questions dug into his mind, steeling him.

Slowly, he edged closer to the orange glow that was pouring from the window, took one quick look inside and drew back, startled.

Three men were seated in the room. One was a thickset, stalky Oriental with a saffron face and a cruel mouth. He wore heavy flying clothes and had pushed amber-tinted goggles up over his helmet. The other two were large blond men, Teutonic in appearance, and garbed in warm nautical reefers.

Bill made a quick guess. The Oriental obviously was the pilot of the Kammato biplane. The other two—had they come in the speedboat?

The mummer of voices reached his ears through the badly fitting window and once again he drew nearer. He was just in time to see the Oriental nod his head toward the larger of the two blond men.

"You could not have come at a more auspicious time, Captain Bruckner," the Oriental said in still English. "But it would have pleased you had you been with me when that Yankee battleship went down. *Puff!* And it was all over."

Bill clenched his fists and forced himself to listen.

The man addressed as Captain Bruckner spoke impatiently. "Let's not beat around the bush, Muziko," he said in a guttural snarl. "You know why Lieutenant Hess and I have come to this God-forsaken place in that damn little boat. I don't intend waiting around to hear your idle boasts."

Muziko raised his eyebrows. "You, Captain Bruckner, and you, Lieutenant Hess, forgive, please." His singsong voice was taunting. "It is because I feel especially flattered that your great country should send two of its brave officers to learn how my simple weapon works."

Bill caught the faint scrape behind him and,

turning, saw Sandy creeping up to him. Drake was behind.

"What goes on?" Sandy whispered.

"Shhhhhh!" Bill said. "For Pete's sake, keep still! They're talking in there and—"

Captain Bruckner's harsh voice suddenly cut him off. "Don't be a fool, Muziko!" he said. "This isn't a personal matter. Our countries are partners. They've made a deal to share this… secret weapon of yours. So let's have it."

Bill saw the Oriental bow again and smile sardonically. "It is quite simple, my comrades in arms. It is astonishing that your great scientists should have overlooked such a means of destruction." The saffron face went back into its mask. "You have heard of the klystron beam discovered by the Americans?"

Lieutenant Hess said, "Of course."

"I have gone beyond that," Muziko said. "I discovered long ago a beam which I have called the balistron ray. When it is directed at a tri-metal combination, eddy currents are set up in the tri-metal, heating it to flash point very, very quickly."

Bill's fingers gripped the window ledge in his anxiety.

"The balistron beam mechanism I have had installed in my biplane," Muziko went on. "I receive word as to where the American warships I wish to destroy are cruising. I fly in that direction under cover of night. One of our brave agents is stationed on the victim ship, prepared to die in our great cause. He manages to throw delayed flares overboard that do not show until the battleship has gone on. The flares enable me to generally find my objective with little trouble. I fly over the ship. I turn on balistron beam. And the ship blows up!"

Muziko paused, picked up a cigarette and lit it. Then when no one spoke he went on. "This morning I ran into difficulties. Our agent, Mueller, had been arrested by suspicious Americans. He was unable to drop the flares. So I had to wait until daylight until I could see for myself, the *Alabama*. The gods of fortune were with me. For not only was the battleship destroyed—but a strange airplane what might have given me trouble was caught in the explosion." He blew twin jets of smoke from his nostrils. "It was simple, Captain Bruckner and Lieutenant Hess."

Bruckner was scowling. "Now look here, Muziko," he said. "You say the balistron beam will heat a tri-metal combination to flash point. But how does that blow up a battleship?"

Muziko's eyes half closed. "You are very, very stupid, captain," he said insolently. "Long ago we made plans for these victories. A piece of tri-metal combination need not be very large. It is easy to conceal. In fact, our agents have seen to it that a small piece of such metal is concealed aboard almost every one of the U.S. warships where it would do the most good." He paused again. "In the powder magazine, Captain Bruckner."

BILL took a step back, horrified. There it was—the full secret of the terrible weapon! A piece of tri-metal dropped in a powder magazine where it would likely go undetected even from a search party. The ray striking it from far above in the sky. The metal being heated to the flash point of the powder. Then—the terrible devastating explosion!

Instinctively, Bill jerked his gun up, his finger tense on the trigger. The criminal, Muziko, was sitting right there before him, a smug gloating expression on his yellow face—while thousands of American sailors were lying dead and mutilated at the bottom of the ocean.

Bill's mouth twisted. Three mean were inside. Two Yako mechanics were at the biplane. Five against Drake and Sandy and himself. A fight was looming. A desperate final fight with no quarter given and none asked. The payoff would have to come on this island. Those killers could never be allowed to escape—to use their murder weapon again.

Hastily, Bill motioned Drake and Sandy to him. In tense whispers, he told them what he'd learned. "Keep on your toes," he said. "When the moment comes, I'll give the sign. Then shoot—and shoot to kill!"

With an effort, he forced himself to listen again. Whatever Bruckner and Hess had said, he'd missed. For now Muziko was again speaking.

"A demonstration will give you the best idea," the Oriental said in his slurred English. "My biplane is being refueled. And to the south, the main battle squadron of the U.S. fleet is in maneuvers near Midway Island. I shall shortly take off to destroy that entire concentration of ships—and you shall go with me, Captain Bruckner and Lieutenant Hess. You shall see with your own eyes the final destruction of American Naval might. When those ships are gone, the United States of America will be defenseless on the Pacific. Then, our joint high command will be able to act."

Hate boiled through Bill's veins as the devilish details of the plan hit him. What Muziko said was true. If that large array of U.S. Navy ships was destroyed, the country would be laid wide open for invasion. Muziko and his murder observers could never be allowed to leave the island. The time to act was—right now.

Bill swung around and then his heart shot into his mouth as a snarling voice said, "You put your hands up quick! All of you!"

A SURGE of wind parted the fog long enough for Bill to see the two Yako mechanics rushing at them, revolvers gripped in their yellow hands. Something had undoubtedly aroused their suspicions. They'd come to investigate.

"Give it to them!" Bill ripped out. As he spoke, he whipped his automatic up and pulled the trigger. There was no time for anything but flaming action.

The weapon bucked in his hand as it belched scarlet fire. One of the mechanics reeled drunkenly from a bullet in the leg, stumbled and fell flat. But the other one was shooting—shooting fast.

Bill heard the sharp screech of a lethal slug whip past his head and bury itself in the side of the house. Sandy and Drake had their guns out now and were firing. The crashing of explosions blasted against Bill's eardrums in a deafening fusillade.

A scream cut thorough the noise, horrible and bloodcurdling. The second Yako mechanic went down and lay writing in pain on the rocks.

Bill spun around. That took care of the two—but they weren't important. It was the men inside who mattered. One flashing glance through the window showed him Captain Bruckner and Lieutenant Hess charging out the door of the house after Muziko.

"Come on!" Bill shouted and flung himself wildly along the side of the building. As he rounded the corner, he saw three indistinct shapes in the fog.

"Put your hands up!" he bellowed.

In answer came the sharp blast of a fired gun. Something red-hot seared across his left shoulder. He reeled back. He'd been hit.

But those men couldn't be allowed to get away. "Get 'em!" he shouted to Drake and Sandy.

Drake's breath was coming in heaving gasps. Bill saw him lift his heavy revolver. The G-man fired once, twice, three times. One of the shadows in the fog dropped out of sight. But another tongue of flame jabbed out from the murky mist.

Bill lined up his sights, waited until the enemy's gun flashed again—then he pulled the trigger.

His aim was deadly. A rasping, choked cry shuddered through the air and his assailant fell headlong.

Bill broke into a run, stifling the pain that knifed through him. Had they got all of them? Had any escaped?

In a moment he stumbled over the prone body of Captain Bruckner. Lieutenant Hess was cursing in a foreign tongue nearby and trying to reach his fallen gun with a blood-soaked hand. There was no sign of the oriental, Muziko, anywhere.

Suddenly, from the distance, Bill caught the sharp whine of an airplane engine starter. It was instantly followed by the roar of an engine bursting into life.

Muziko, the killer, was getting away in the plane! Escaping! And if he ever got free, he would be certain to put his murderous plan into operation.

Bill didn't wait. One glance told him that Sandy and Drake were looking after the wounded foreigner. Then, Bill was racing across the rocks in the direction of the biplane. Ahead he saw flame stab from exhaust stacks. He put more speed into his now-aching legs. If he failed to stop Muziko—

He made out the shape of the biplane, a furry blur in the mist. The ship was moving!

With one last desperate lunge, Bill threw himself forward. The fuselage was now visible and the helmeted head of Muziko showed in the cockpit.

Bill leveled his automatic as the biplane spurted for a takeoff. He scarcely waited to take aim. He pulled the trigger again and again until the explosions blended into one continuous roar.

The biplane raced on and for one awful minute Bill thought he'd missed. Then, abruptly, the Kammato plane suddenly veered. With a sickening lurch the machine careened off the runway, bounced into the air. Its nose came up, and for one long second the biplane seemed to stay motionless in the fog. Then, with a scream of thunder from its engine, the powerful ship dipped—and fell.

It landed with a deafening crash against a pile of jagged rocks. There was a spurt of flame—another explosion. The biplane seemed to split open as had the *Alabama* before it. A crackling surge of flame and smoke gushed out.

Bill stood frozen in his tracks. There was no earthly chance of saving Muziko's life now—even if he still lived. In a flood of dancing fury, the flames raced back over the fuselage, over the cockpit, covering the murderer and his murder machine.

IT was late in the afternoon when Bill sighted the U.S. fleet just north of Midway Island. "There she is, fellas!" he yelled. "Now to land and talk to the admiral."

"And turn our friends over to the gentle confines of the brig," Drake said.

Bill nodded and looked back. At the rear of the cabin, securely trussed up, lay Captain Bruckner, Lieutenant Hess and the two wounded Yako mechanics. Bill's eyes hardened. If these men had had their way, those fine battleships down below would by this time have been wrecked and sunk.

But now the deadly Yako sabotage plot was through forever. Once the magazines of all American ships were searched and the pieces of deadly tri-metal found, those mighty vessels would again be safe to continue their proud patrol of the seas.

Wearily he closed the throttles and shoved the stick forward. The day had been filled with excitement and terrific tension and more than anything he craved his bed and sleep.

THE END

BILL BARNES IN FOUR COLORS by Anthony Tollin

Just as "The Eye of the Cobra" had suggested elements of the Japanese attack on Pearl Harbor, another *Bill Barnes* story would correctly predict that World War II would be brought to an end by an atomic bomb attack on Japan!

Just months after Pearl Harbor's "Day of Infamy," Walter Gibson foreshadowed America's future use of an atomic bomb in its war against Japan in a groundbreaking 34-page comic book story illustrated by Jack Binder's comic art shop. In the July 1942 issue of *Bill Barnes America's Air Ace Comics*, Gibson suggested that a U-235 bomb could be detonated within the Marianas Trench to topple the island nation into the ocean.

"The way it came about was John Campbell, the editor of *Astounding Stories*, said to me, 'Look, I've got this idea for a comic story. These fellows take a plane from a hidden island and it looks like they're bombing Tokyo, dropping all these bombs in the harbor. One is a dud bomb, and the dud bomb just sinks. But it's inside a case, and the casing will melt in the water. When that's melted, the bomb's going to go off. So these fellows know they have 24 hours to get away, because that's the one that's going to do the damage.'"

Recalling that Japan had earlier been hit with devastating earthquakes, Gibson enhanced John Campbell's plot suggestion with elements from Asian mythology: "I dug into some Japanese lore, and I found out that there was a tradition that someday the whole of Japan would tilt up and flop in the Pacific deep. So that's what our bomb did in the double spread—it showed the whole island going over! That was written up by Justin Phillips, who was a reporter with the New York *Mirror*. And he ran a story in the *Mirror* when the comic came out. Immediately the government wanted to know what the hell is this? Where had Campbell gotten the stuff? Well, Campbell showed where he'd picked it up. So much writing appeared in scientific magazines, mentioning the possibilities of this thing, that he fit it all together!"

The original *Bill Barnes Air Adventurer* pulp had evolved into *Bill Barnes Air Trails* in October 1935 and became *Air Trails* in February 1937, with new Bill Barnes novelettes continuing to appear in the increasingly non-fiction publication. Following the demise of *Air Trails* in 1939, Bill Barnes moved into the back pages of *Doc Savage* until the pulp was downsized to digest format late in 1943.

However, by that time, the Air Ace had already moved on to the greener pastures of the exploding comic book phenomenon. On January 21ST, 1940, Bill Barnes made his four-color debut in *Shadow Comics* #1, along with such Street & Smith stalwarts as The Shadow, Doc Savage, Nick Carter, Frank Merriwell, Iron Munro and Carrie Cashin.

While many of the features in the earliest issues of *Shadow Comics* suffered from less-than-inspired scripts and artwork packaged by the Harry Chesler

***Bill Barnes America's Air Ace Comics* #7 featured a prophetic story by Walter B. Gibson (left) and Jack Binder (right) in which the American pilot ended World War II by dropping a U-235 bomb on Japan.**

The 1940 Walter Gibson-Jack Binder story in *Bill Barnes America's Air Ace Comics* #7 explained and foresaw the devastating power of a U-235 bomb and visualized its destructive might!

AND THIS IS BUT THE FIRST EFFECT!!!

VISIBLE AT MORE THAN 1500 MILES, EVEN AROUND THE CURVE OF THE EARTH, IS THE BURST OF THE "DUD" CONTAINING THE U-235..... SURPASSING BY FAR THE FULL EXPECTATIONS OF SCIENTIFIC MINDS, THAT BOMB HAS PRODUCED THE GREATEST UPHEAVAL THAT THE WORLD HAS EVER SEEN!!

comic art studio, Bill Barnes' comic book debut benefited from being illustrated by the longtime cover and interior illustrator of the Air Ace's pulp magazines, renowned aviation artist Frank Tinsley.

The younger brother of backup Shadow novelist Theodore Tinsley, Francis Xavier Theban Tinsley (1899-1965) was born in Manhattan and apprenticed in the research department of the Metropolitan Museum of Art. Beginning in 1928, after serving in the War Department's design section and as a scenic artist for silent films, Tinsley sold pulp cover art and interior illustrations to a variety of pulp magazines including *Western Story Magazine*, *Action Stories* and *North West Stories*, but soon began focusing on such aviation pulps as *Bill Barnes*, *Sky Birds*, *Air Stories* and *War Birds*.

Obviously reformatted from unsold *Bill Barnes* newspaper strip samples, Frank Tinsley's artwork on "Bill Barnes vs. the Yellow-Jackets" is superior to most 1940 comic book art. Though the proposed *Bill Barnes* newspaper strip failed to sell, Tinsley fared better with his next attempt. The same year the Street & Smith comic book line was launched, Tinsley's *Yankee Doodle* (soon retitled *Captain Yank*) comic strip debuted, distributed by the McNaught Syndicate. The strip featured the exploits of a Marine pilot and ran in newspapers from 1940-1946, until peacetime brought an end to the war-themed strip.

Sanctum Books is pleased to present this rare story from *Shadow Comics* #1 to commemorate the 75TH anniversary of the four-color debuts of Bill Barnes and other Street & Smith pulp superstars! •

***Bill Barnes* artist Frank Tinsley moved on from pulps to illustrate the *Captain Yank* newspaper strip.**

BILL BARNES, AMERICA'S ACE—Bill Barnes is truly America's ace. He is the famous aviator whose stories have long been the favorite of DOC SAVAGE Magazine and AIR TRAILS. They are illustrated by a prominent aviator and all of the incidents are accurate.

A 75th anniversary illustrated classic from Volume 1, Number 1 of *Shadow Comics*

as illustrated by Frank Tinsley

I'M DYING, BOY— SMASH THE YELLOW-JACKETS BEFORE THEY GET YOU ——
I'M AFRAID HE'S GONE, BILL.

THEY HAVE MURDERED MY FATHER'S OLDEST FRIEND. —THE YELLOW-JACKETS SHALL PAY FOR THIS!

BEARING THE BODY OF HIS FATHER'S MURDERED FRIEND, BILL BARNES' PLANE RETURNS TO ITS HOME PORT.
BB-1

I'LL HAVE TO NOTIFY PAT MICHAELS— THE OLD MAN'S DAUGHTER.
IT'S GONNA BE TOUGH ON THE POOR KID.

THIS MUST BE THE YELLOW-JACKET'S' BASE —THIS TINY ISLAND CALLED MANTIGO
YOU'RE RIGHT, BILL. THE BEARINGS CHECK.

I JUST CALLED WASHINGTON, SHORTY. THEY SAY "GO AHEAD"— BLAST THE YELLOW-JACKETS OUT OF THE WATER!

as illustrated by Frank Tinsley

WE'LL TAKE HER ALL THE WAY UP TO THE CEILING—THEN CUT THE GUN AND COAST IN.

32,000 FEET—WE MUST BE NEAR OUR CEILING. THE CONTROLS ARE GETTING SLOPPY — GIVE ME THE COURSE...
TWO POINTS NORTH OF WEST, SIR LIEUTENANT.

MEANWHILE, DARK FIGURES ARE SLINKING THROUGH THE UNDERBRUSH.... THEY CLOSE IN ON THE SIDE GATE OF BARNES FIELD....

QUIET! WE ARE ALMOST THERE... CAUTION THE TROOPERS TO HOLD THEIR GRENADES UNTIL THEY HEAR MY PISTOL.
IT WILL BE DONE AS YOU ORDER, SIR.

UNCONSCIOUS OF DANGER, ONE OF BILL BARNES' EX-MARINE GUARDS STEALS A QUICK SMOKE AS HE STANDS IDLY IN THE OPEN PORTAL...

AS THE "YELLOW-JACKETS" CLOSE IN ON BARNES FIELD, SANDY SANDERS SITS IN THE RADIO TOWER, IDLY TRYING TO DECODE A QUEER WIRELESS MESSAGE THAT TONY LAMPORT HAS ACCIDENTALLY PICKED UP.

MAYBE WE'RE BEING SILLY, KID, BUT IF YOUR SOLUTION OF THIS MESSAGE IS ANYWHERE NEAR RIGHT—WE'D BETTER CALL BILL QUICK!

as illustrated by Frank Tinsley

THE BOMBER PEERS THROUGH HIS SIGHTS...

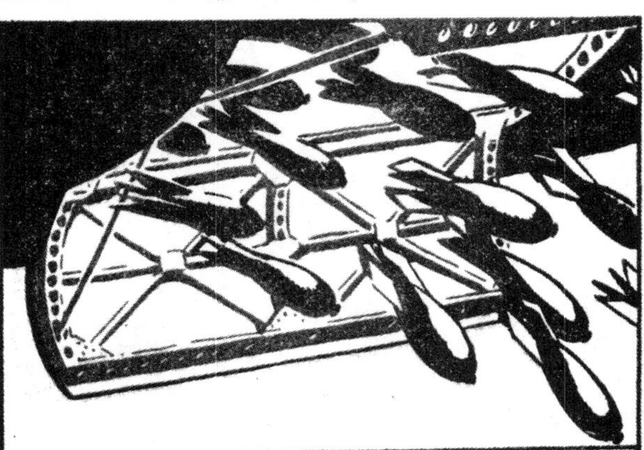

A SHOWER OF TINY THERMITE BOMBS POURS FROM THE OPEN BELLY OF THE SEAPLANE.

FIERCE CHEMICAL FIRES SPRING UP IN A HUNDRED PLACES AS THE THERMITE BOMBS EXPLODE AROUND THE HANGARS!

BILL BARNES IS UP AGAINST ONE OF THE WORLD'S MOST RUTHLESS GANGS. HOW HE RETALIATES FOR THE DESTRUCTION OF HIS AIRPORT AND PLANES IS TOLD IN THE NEXT ISSUE OF SHADOW COMICS

A 75th anniversary illustrated classic from Volume 1, Number 1 of *Shadow Comics*

THE MEN BEHIND DOC SAVAGE

Lester Dent (1904-1959) could be called the father of the superhero. Writing under the house name "Kenneth Robeson," Dent was the principal writer of Doc Savage, producing more than 150 of the Man of Bronze's thrilling pulp adventures.

A lonely childhood as a rancher's son paved the way for his future success as a professional storyteller. "I had no playmates," Dent recalled. "I lived a completely distorted youth. My only playmate was my imagination, and that period of intense imaginative creation which kids generally get over at the age of five or six, I carried till I was twelve or thirteen. My imaginary voyages and accomplishments were extremely real."

Dent began his professional writing career while working as an Associated Press telegrapher in Tulsa, Oklahoma. Learning that one of his coworkers had sold a story to the pulps, Dent decided to try his hand at similarly lucrative moonlighting. He pounded out thirteen unsold stories during the slow night shift before making his first sale to Street & Smith's *Top-Notch* in 1929. The following year, he received a telegram from the Dell Publishing Company offering him moving expenses and a $500-a-month drawing account if he'd relocate to New York and write exclusively for the publishing house.

Dent soon left Dell to pursue a freelance career, and in 1932 won the contract to write the lead novels in Street & Smith's new *Doc Savage Magazine.* From 1933-1949, Dent produced Doc Savage thrillers while continuing his busy freelance writing career and eventually adding Airviews, an aerial photography business.

Dent was also a significant contributor to the legendary *Black Mask* during its golden age, for which he created Miami waterfront detective Oscar Sail. A real-life adventurer, world traveler and member of the Explorers Club, Dent wrote in a variety of genres for magazines ranging from pulps like *Argosy, Adventure* and *Ten Detective Aces* to prestigious slick magazines including *The Saturday Evening Post* and *Collier's*. His mystery novels include *Dead at the Take-off* and *Lady Afraid.* In the pioneering days of radio drama, Dent scripted *Scotland Yard* and the 1934 *Doc Savage* series.

William G. Bogart (1903-1977) forsook college and the prospect of being an engineer, and by a circuitous route that included managing a Child's Restaurant, became a prolific pulp writer.

His first sale was a short story to Woolworth's *Tower Mystery Magazine,* but he found filling the back pages of *The Shadow* and *Doc Savage* his steadiest market. He moved to Yonkers in July, 1936, freelanced, and operated a small literary agency for pulp writers. Soon after, he joined Street & Smith, becoming one of editor John L. Nanovic's many sub-editors.

Quitting his Street & Smith staff job in December 1938, Bogart began contributing to periodicals ranging from *Detective Story Magazine* to *Unknown.* His 1940 hardcover novel, *Hell on Friday,* was the start of a series featuring Johnny Saxon, a pulp writer turned private eye.

Bogart committed some of his sub-literary sins under other bylines. Taking the maiden names of his mother and wife respectively, he became "Russell [sometimes Russ] Hale" for the Spicy pulp chain and "Will Gibson" for the low-rent detective pulps. When Steve Fisher went off to Hollywood, Bogart continued his Danny Garrett shoeshine boy detective series as "Grant Lane" in *The Shadow.* Writing as "Kenneth Robeson," Bogart ghosted a total of fourteen Doc Savage novels. He also wrote a single Skipper short, "Quest of Death, published in the January 1938 issue of *Doc Savage* and reprinted for the first time in this volume. When Street & Smith's pulp line shrank in 1943, Bogart moved to Chicago, where he worked as a copywriter for N. W. Ayer, an advertising agency. He continued to moonlight as a pulp writer. Lester Dent called him back to ghost Doc Savage in 1946, but after a handful of novels, the series went bimonthly and Bogart hooked up with the Chicago-based Ziff-Davis chain, where he recycled some of his old Doc plots and penned a faux Doc novel called *The Crazy Indian* for *Mammoth Adventure.*

Bogart faded out as a writer in 1947, the year his novelization of the film *Singapore* was published as a Centaur Mystery. His career after that time is unknown. He died in Burlington, Vermont on July 20, 1977, just as the Bantam Books reprint of his 1940 Doc Savage novel *The Flying Goblin* was rolling off the presses.

–Will Murray